D1028217

Fifth Born II
THE HUNDREDTH TURTLE

A NOVEL BY
Zelda Lockhart

LaVenson Press
HILLSBOROUGH, NORTH CAROLINA

ALSO BY ZELDA LOCKHART
Fifth Born
Cold Running Creek

Excerpts appear in *Chautauqua Literary Journal.*
Reprinted by permission of *Chautauqua Literary Journal,*
Copyright © 2010 by Zelda Lockhart.
Excerpts appear in *Fifth Born*, published by
Simon and Schuster © 2002 by Zelda Lockhart
Excerpts from "When My Brother Fell" by Essex Hemphill
© 1992 Essex Hemphill from *Ceremonies: Prose and Poetry*,
reprinted with permission of the Frances Goldin Literary Agency.

For information address LaVenson Press,
Post Office Box 1432, Hillsborough, North Carolina 27278

Library of Congress Control Number: 2010927194
HARDCOVER
ISBN 13: 978-0-9789102-3-5
ISBN 10: 0-9789102-3-0

SOFTCOVER
ISBN 13: 978-0-9789102-4-2
ISBN 10: 0-9789102-4-9

First LaVenson Press hardcover edition June 2010
First LaVenson Press trade paperback edition June 2010

10 9 8 7 6 5 4 3 2 1

Manufactured in the United States of America on recycled paper
(50% pcw).

Book design by Angela L. Williams, Villanelle Productions.

For information regarding special discounts for bulk purchases,
please contact LaVenson Press at 919-819-4910,
www.LaVensonPress.com, or LaVensonPress@aol.com

Fifth Born II

LAVENSON PRESS

Author's Note

I would like to thank the talented and smart people who worked on this project: designer Angela L. Williams, copy editor Brent Winter, and photographer Brooke Collins. Thanks to the folks who read through drafts of the novel and gave powerful feedback: Jamie Lamkin, Polly Beere, Oliver Collier, and Krista Bremer.

Thank you to UNC Wilmington librarian Tonia McKoy for pointing me in the direction of so many resources, and to the librarians at The Schomburg Center for Research in Black Culture.

My deepest gratitude to my brothers LaVenson Lockhart and Kerry Lockhart; the one who taught me to live my dreams and the one who taught me to fight for the right to live my dreams. Thank you to my sister Francheska Lamb for telling me that what I do is brave not crazy.

For inspiring my "southerness," thank you to fellow writers Dorothy Allison and Randall Kenan.

Thank you to Essex Hemphill's estate for allowing the use of lines from his poem, "When my brother fell."

I am always and forever grateful to my children Travis and Alex who inspire me, then watch what I do so closely.

Dedication

This novel is dedicated to those family members we have found through the clarity of consistent love, to those we have lost to the disease that our own fears have kept us from defeating, and to those we have lost to the velocity of family abuse.

Sea Turtle Hatchlings

Though there are approximately one hundred hatchlings from each laying of eggs, though all of those eggs hatch under cover of night and the hatchlings follow the light of the moon toward the breaker waves and the safety of open sea, only one in one hundred hatchlings will survive. The hundredth turtle will swim past the breaker waves and spend the next twenty years eluding countless predators and beating the odds on survival. Led only by her instincts, she will manage to mature, and return to the beach to lay eggs and insure the continuation of her species.

Part 1

Chapter 1

ELIZABETH MAE LACEY, Ella Mae, is my biological mother. I had no memory of ever meeting her, but she gave birth to me in my grandmother's bathtub the summer of 1964 in Starkville, Mississippi. Until I was thirteen years old, her name brought crimson memories of the mirror game us kids used to play. "Ella Mae, Ella Mae," we'd whisper before we turned out the lights, to lure the mythical wild woman out of the mirror. But, all myth is based on truth. Ella Mae was considered the crazy heathen in our family because she was born out of her Indian grandfather's rape of her mother. Rape and incest weave themselves around the pains of my life tighter than the weave in Ella Mae's rag rugs. What looks like a confusion of discarded, discolored old clothes up close is really a landscape once you get some distance.

THE NIGHT I WAS BORN, they lied to Ella Mae and told her I was stillborn. After all, I was the offspring of *my* father's rape, and something had to be done to keep Ella Mae's sister Bernice from looking like a fool when somebody else's baby turned up looking just like Bernice's husband. Some Starkville neighbor in some unknown wood hid me for days until I was placed in the hands of Bernice—the aunt I called Mama. Mama was an expert at covering family pain with family myth. So I was raised, Odessa Blackburn, the fifth born of Bernice and Loni Blackburn's children, born on summer vacation. Mama told folks she carried me so light, couldn't nobody hardly tell she was pregnant. Said she'd been fishing in the creek on the day her water broke. In the myth of my birth, off to the hospital she went and came home with a summer baby. For my homecoming to St. Louis, I was swaddled in a cloak of lies that hid the blood-tinged truth and provided false safety for me and all the St. Louis kin.

Back and forth from St. Louis down to Mississippi we went each summer to visit Granmama and Grandeddy, Bernice's parents, and Ella Mae's. The summer of my third year, Granmama committed suicide, which is the truth, but in the family myth she had a heart attack. Either way, like the other women of my ancestry, she took with her some bottomless well of truths that shimmer like sediment on the bottoms of Mississippi creeks.

SOME IRONIC PROPHECY would have it that my eyes followed the line of Deddy's hands, and I would see the things none of the other kids would see. He murdered his own brother. Uncle Leland got too close and opened a door through which we could have all crawled out, but before we could escape, Deddy slammed it shut like a guillotine. And I remembered the things none of the girls remembered: Deddy's face in the dark over my body, and the ripping of my virgin flesh. When I last saw Deddy, he reminded me that Mama conspired to keep his secrets, and that the light that played a ring of truth around my iris would equal abandonment.

There was something about the way Mama was round, and wanting for Deddy's touch; the way she took care of us kids with one hand and blocked Deddy's punches with the other; the way she turned truth into lies, like Moses turning water to blood; and I wanted her the way children want mothers, with open mouths waiting to be fed. I stood within the radius of her swing, and when no one was looking, she slapped me around to keep me from telling that my Deddy was my rapist; that her husband had murdered his own brother. The more she hurt me, the more I craved "mother." The way that, when we are hurt, we cry "Mama" even if we've never known her, even if we don't like her, we cry our first word, "Mama," and with that word we mean our first color, red, we mean love, we mean comfort.

In front of the other kids, Mama lied and said I did awful things in order to deserve her beatings. And in my siblings' eyes, I watched the desert that we all groveled in swell into a sea of estrangement as wide and deep as the tunnel through the palm of the hand.

By the time I was twelve years old, I didn't feel human any more; just felt like a raw thing bobbing around in that sea, hoping for touch. Then, on the thirteenth summer vacation to Grandeddy's, some combination of my hurt, my need for "Mama," and my need to survive sent me wandering off Grandeddy's land, into one field, then another, until there was no way to go back without being beaten, and no way to stay where the open land could not hide me. In that space between the lie told thirteen years before and the land that had borne witness to four generations of my family's pain, I bent down to hold my ashy ankles and cry, and I found myself coiled up in my real mother's yard, all the while thinking she was just a long lost aunt.

ELLA MAE AND I had a hard time of it all that day and the next, crying and telling each other stories of our upbringing. She said, "I tell you 'bout my folks, and you tell me 'bout yours, and sho nuf we talkin 'bout the same people." Still, we thought we were new-found niece and aunt sharing our pains.

Just before dusk on my second night away, just as the window was closing on my ever being able to go back, Ella Mae said she was fed up. She said, "That's enough runnin' away for the both of us," and she marched me right back to Grandeddy's house. She was ready to confront Mama and Deddy, and I needed to keep Mama and Deddy from separating me from my siblings the way they had separated Ella Mae from hers. But I learned two things that night: you can't reason with evil, and the truth can't stay hidden forever.

Ella Mae and I moved up the steps of Grandeddy's porch, silent like storm clouds. When we got to the top step, Deddy stopped rocking, and I stepped down to put distance between us. The porch light showed the thinness of the hairs on the crown of his head—specks of gray in his short Afro. He stood up; his white shirt tucked in, his stomach slightly hanging over the waist of his slacks. He walked to the edge of the porch, his heels knocking on the weathered boards. Like a young man, he leaned with one arm high on the beam, and smirked, then let loose a laugh, amused at the sight of me and Ella Mae.

He struggled to get himself together. "Ain't this some shit. You call yourself runnin away from here, and you run to one fucked-up motha-fucka. I guess you had one night of her and found out she was 'funny,' and here you come back. I figured you be back. Your ass ain't too crazy. You know the difference between when you got it good, and livin in some old bug-infested, raggedy-ass log cabin with somebody who's fuckin crazy."

He was still smirking and grinning. Ella Mae and I stood solid. I looked up at him and asked with my teeth tight together, "Where is Mama and them?" He laughed again.

"You done missed your callin. Ain't nobody waited around here for two days for your ass to decide to come back. Hell, don't nobody give a damn about you runnin off into the woods. Me and Bernice figured you was up there to her house anyway. Your mama ain't had enough backbone to carry her ass up there and get you, but just like I told her, you'd come right back here."

While he worked on unbuckling his belt, he talked to me and Ella Mae like we were both his children. "Now you, 'Dessa, is gonna get your ass whipped, then we getting on the road. And you, Miss Jim Dandy, gonna carry your hermit ass back up in the woods, and think about stayin the hell out of my business."

The two of us still hadn't moved. It was like Deddy was onstage. I didn't know what else to say but the truth. "No, thank you. I think I'll stay here with the hermit." His head moved back in exaggerated surprise. I concentrated on not shrinking back from my own words.

"You think that shit is funny?" His belt bridged the space between us. Without warning, the leather strap came whipping through the darkness and slashed across my face breaking my unyielding stare.

In the time that it took me to reach up to calm the sting on my cheek, Ella Mae lunged from where she stood. She came down on Deddy with her whole body. Their weight boomed on the decaying porch, a hollow slamming to the floor in the sitting space. Air escaped from my lungs.

Ella Mae's voice was deep like thunder. "Don't you ever touch her again. I ain't gonna never let it happen that you gonna ever touch nobody again."

She slammed his head to the floor of the porch, and the images of Uncle Leland's murder washed over me, and my body stiffened with a premonition of black dresses, and chrome handles on dark wood, satin lining. I reached for my ears, but their bodies were still slamming against the porch floor. I didn't want him dead, I didn't think I wanted him dead.

DEDDY ROLLED OVER and got his handgun out of the back of his pants.

Time slowed, the air thickened, Ella Mae rolled over to get up. She moved way too slow to catch up with Deddy's palm around the gun handle, his finger working with his perfect vision to pinpoint his hunt.

It was hard to stay, not stiffen to a hard plank and stand silent and dead until the confusion steadied itself into my next grieving. And out of the darkness, leaning against the porch, Granmama's rifle, the one she used to put the goat out of its misery, the day Grandeddy carelessly backed over it with his truck. My body was moving fast now. I counted my movements faster than I counted Deddy's. I cocked the rifle the way I saw Granmama do it. I pulled the trigger.

In the explosion everything—Deddy, Ella Mae, Grandeddy's house—disappeared, leaving only white light for a second, then smoke, then a dark calm. The porch light was gone, the crickets were silent, then a voice entered, it was Deddy's, "You stupid bitch!" Blood was pouring from between his fingers where he held his shoulder. He stood up to see where I was, where Ella Mae was, where his gun was. The rifle was still in my hands, and I cocked it again and held on tight even though my arms were trembling and numb. I knew I would never be able to fire a second shot. My eyes darted back and forth from Deddy to where I thought Ella Mae should be. Though he was bleeding, Deddy smirked at my trembling and took a step closer grimacing before smiling again.

"I see that bitch done taught you a thing or two about actin like you crazy, but you a fool, 'cause I think she done run off like a wounded animal and left you here to fend for yourself."

He reached down to pick up his belt, keeping his eyes on the quivering barrel of the rifle, my eyes at the other end meaning to aim again if it would save me.

He pulled a handkerchief from his pocket and used his teeth to help him strap the belt over the nicked shoulder. He looked satisfied to free up both hands and before I could think, he snatched the rifle by the barrel end.

The moon rose up like a second sun in the darkness to the left of Grandeddy's porch. And, there Ella Mae stood behind him, the light picking up the shiny sleekness of her hair. She held Deddy's gun to his head.

Her voice came shaky but strong. "Odessa, move on away now." I still could not see her eyes, but scurried to get up on the porch behind her. Her big hand was around the back of Deddy's neck now, and my heart beat in my throat.

Deddy was grimacing in pain but laughing, high-pitched like he did when he was drunk.

"I ain't got time to stand here and listen to your crazy ass. What the hell you supposed to be, a super fucking hero? I don't give a damn what you do with Odessa. She right where she belongs, down here in the fuckin country. I ain't never wanted

Bernice taking your bastard child back to St. Louis no way. Your half-Indian mama was crazy as you. Bernice should've let her bury 'Dessa out in the woods somewhere like her crazy ass was fixin to do."

Her hand went limp from Deddy's neck, but the gun was shaking now, the trigger loose against metal as it tapped Deddy's head—metal and skull bone, my teeth grinding against teeth.

Your bastard child—bury 'Dessa out in the woods somewhere— bury 'Dessa in the woods somewhere—your bastard child.

My gritty hands made mud on my damp face, and I struggled to hold in the cry that escaped from my mouth, past my palms. It pealed out in the bare space around the house.

The sound of my cry was silenced by the shots; they rang out again and again and again, until his gun was empty. I had never stopped screaming. I opened my eyes.

Ella Mae held the gun over her head—wood chips and pieces of wasp nest fell from where she had mangled the porch ceiling. Her breath was so heavy, angry grunts, she screamed, "Leave! Leave! Leave!"

Deddy hurried to the van, trying to maintain some amount of cool in his step. When he stood safe in the door of the van, he had the last word, and I was glad that I could not see his eyes for what he said to me.

"You ain't been nothin but a fuckin pain in the ass, 'Dessa, I don't give a damn what you been told, you ain't my damn kid." Then he turned to Ella Mae, who was still holding the gun above her head. "Who Jim Dandy let fuck her up in them woods didn't have shit to do with me. Me and Bernice just tried to save your ass and give you something different than livin down here like a heathen. But I guess ain't a damn thing I can do to keep the truth a the matter from comin full circle.

"If either one of you ever round here when I come back down to bring my *real* kids to visit they grandeddy, I'm gonna try to shoot another hole in your ass."

My eyes receded into the place before there were glasses,

before I watched Granmama's last walk up her porch steps, before I was born, and I was numb. He sped out using one arm to steer. The van careened in the path of its own light.

I remember Granmama rocking me on the last night singing.

I'm gonna fly away
I'm gonna fly away

Kissing my sweaty cheeks that night.

To a land where
To a land where
Sickness will be no more.

And the next day, I strained to see her through the dirty glass of the back window of the station wagon. I saw her climb the stairs, and she was gone, she was gone. Everything that was familiar fled with her. Rocks pinged on the bumper of the wagon. My mother, my father, my sisters and brothers— sticky hands, spankings on Sunday mornings, whispered secrets of things that were now mute.

I slumped down on the musty porch. I was lost. Everything had been cut loose from me.

I floated away in the path of the moonlight. Rain began to fall from the sky in big drops. Ella Mae sat on the steps like the morning after we first met. The space between us was massive. I could feel the rhythm of her breathing, and I closed my eyes.

Her hand passed the ridge of my neck in an uncertain, almost touch, until finally her embrace surrounded my perishing body. The rain fell heavier now, but the revelations kept us still in that moment.

From her chest came a trapped breath. Her cry rose up from Granmama's porch in long guttural sighs. No words, but pain, love, loss, rising up loud and coming down quiet, moving like thunder over the terrain of her tongue and lips, a familiar comfort from someplace lost.

I let go of what held my limbs taut, and let her hold me. Her tears came like a warm stream salty into my mouth.

The two of us held each other tight, making a bridge over streams of our family's blood.

She muttered, "My baby . . . my baby."

Chapter 2

THAT NIGHT we walked back to Ella Mae's, my real mother's house, and I made my bed on Ella Mae's porch. I lay there with my glasses on and listened through the darkness until Ella Mae was quiet in the house, and then I could sleep, where I could hear and see if anyone was coming.

After I fell asleep, I dreamed Deddy's journey home:

He had been grazed by a bullet before, and he knew that once he stopped the bleeding he had roughly twenty-four hours before infection set in. He stopped at the filling station. After gassing up the van, he stood under the swarm of bugs in the fluorescent light and examined the shoulder rag with dried blood. He adjusted the tightness of the belt before going inside

"Just a little graze from coon huntin," Deddy said to the clerk. "Got any Excedrin? I'll take a pack of Kools and a six-pack of Michelob. Lemme have a stick of that beef jerky too."

The young white man did not respond, just held his face in a squint of disapproval at a nigger smelling up his store more than it already smelled of dirty hands, mud-caked boots, chewing tobacco disrespectfully spit into corners. The odors all mixed with the smell of the sweet saltiness of pasty fishing bait and damp wood from behind the leaking cooler case. The store clerk's buzz-cut blonde hair stood on end like porcupine quills that glowed white under the humming tubes overhead.

Deddy kept talking. "You a Marine? Been to 'Nam?" *'Nam*, said in a grimace of pain as he hoisted the six-pack onto the counter with the injured arm. The young man's expression did not change, thin lips pressed together, jaw tight and angular, teeth clenched. The clerk snatched open the paper bag, a sound that caused Deddy to harness a flinch, but he stayed still; only his eyelids flickered. The young man waited for Deddy to remove his hand from the six-pack, then lowered the beer into the erect bag, grabbed the Excedrin from behind him, a piece of jerky, and scooted the change across the counter. Then he grabbed his cigarette from the smoldering metal ashtray of butts and turned back to adjust the antenna on the fuzzy TV set.

My dream ended with the image of the van pulling away from the gas station, Deddy steering with one hand and turning not north, toward St. Louis, but south, to return and finish off me and Ella Mae.

IN THE MORNING I sat on the porch. I was skin and bone and blood, but I could not feel my body there; I just felt myself floating outside my flesh. The spiders in their sticky webs in the rafters above my head, the busy wasps in and out of their nests, seemed more tangible than my own skin. I did not want to hear human voices. The chill of a fear I could not understand went up my spine each time Ella Mae called out, "You okay out there?"

Behind me, she busied herself like a bird preparing a nest. She took the old cushioned chair off the porch and made me a bed in the house, and my heart raced at the thought of my body stretched out within the confines of walls and ceiling. What if she was crazy? What if there were rats in the house? What if Deddy came after both of us in the night, the walls muffling the sound of the van coming up the driveway?

She tilted her head in my peripheral vision; her step tentative on stopping, on comforting as she passed me with the two peach crates that became my dresser. I peeped through the sceen to see her cordoned off the cubicle that was my new room with a shower curtain, and she hung two shower curtains from wall to wall where her bed lay beyond the loom.

"Woo," Ella Mae hollered as she came out onto the porch. "It's hot. What you want to do? Want to go to the creek?"

"No, thank you," was all that I could say as I sat on the porch, trying to understand why I could not feel myself breathing.

"We got to get you somethin to keep you busy," she said. Twice that day she rolled off to Walgreens in her rusty red truck; she came back with crossword puzzles the first time, Archie Comics the second. I smiled, and thanked her, and she did not know not to come back to coax me over and over. Neither of us knew that I sat on the edge of a high cliff above the horrors that I had not fully realized until escaping them. She came back onto the porch with a cool Mason jar filled with cold well water.

I felt something inside my mind tip me away from the sun, through the Mason jar, and I tried to hold on to something in the present, the color blue on the bluebird who flew back and forth, the blue dome of sky above my head, the pinched-closed morning glory that crept up the post of the stairs, but I could not feel my breath in my own body, and I was gone.

I looked at the cool Mason jar and heard Mama say, "It's just a cold." She forced my mouth to the jar: homemade whisky cough syrup. My pulse throbbed against the ceiling of my skull, and pain shot up my leg. My arms, heavy as lead, dropped away from the glass, and I heard it hit the floor boards. Then felt the weight of Deddy's body on mine. Brine and grit burned in my throat as I screamed while my soul rose up and sat on the girl's room windowsill, frightened that he might see me there, and then a strange voice came:

"Dessa."

I opened my eyes and did not recognize the woman with light brown face, hair straight, Mama's almond eyes on someone else looking at me. *Get away, get away*, my mind said as I gathered my strangely heavy body to scoop away from her, then my hands up to keep her from reaching me; the wall of the porch not flat enough to swallow me away from the sight of hands much too big for what I thought was my five-year-old body. Above my head I could hear my own funeral dirge, the congregation moaning in harmonic swells, "Oh Death." My kindergarten hands turned huge, then my own dizzy head, then death—but my soul could not leave my body. The arms of the strange woman held me still, her hot tears rolling down through the matting of my cottony hair.

Then there was my own green tennis shoe at the edge of the stairs, the slither of a sleek green lizard out of the sun and into the shade of the porch, the blue-bird again, and Ella Mae's glassed-over eyes, and I remembered my brother Lamont first; the first sibling who held me, the smell of his body, and I cried for them all. Ella Mae's voice brought me back.

"I'm so sorry," she said, rocking me, "I'm so sorry. Loni ain't gonna hurt you no more, and one day you gonna see yo sisters and brothers again."

The sun came full onto the porch, and Ella Mae brought back the cushions and let me lie there in the heat until I could smell the mildew in the fabric, feel the vinyl cut into my skin, and know that I was not dead. When dusk moved the sun below the horizon, I carried the cushions into the house myself.

Chapter 3

M Y WINDOW FACED WEST. In the evenings I felt displaced without the comforting disharmony of sibling voices clambering inside the brick-and-wood structure of the St. Louis house. From my quiet window, I watched the sun shine through the thickness of clouds and set with a combination of summer crimson and peach. In the solitude of only-child peace, I listened beyond the fading scent of honeysuckle, the sweet smell of wet hay. And I imagined the lazy slide of thumb and bass and sweaty tenor fingers over guitar strings coming from way out toward Grandeddy's. The sound of cows like fog horns in the waning light took me into the past, and I remembered a night earlier that summer, when I was still fifth born of eight Blackburns.

One of the older cousins had stood with one booted foot on the bottom step, his guitar on his knee. Some mismatched coupling of aunts and uncles with a little too much Johnnie Walker in their blood shuffled in the dry, gravelly dirt, trying not to end up in what my sister LaVern called "copulation pose"; sweat and too few clothes between them, their children wide-eyed before a storm. We watched from the porch with scuffed, sleepy knees, the smell of the night; cigarettes and whisky hung in the air dangerously, warning us teenagers to be quiet so the adults would forget we were there while we witnessed the mystery of how slide fingers on guitar, whisky, and heat could lead to divorce.

The memory faded, and I slipped away from my loneliness, and for the first of many times, my fingers slid beneath the covers and into the humid place where a rough, new tangle of hair snagged on fingers that sought smooth clitoral flesh, and I comforted myself into sleep.

IN ELLA MAE'S GARDEN, my mind did not race with wondering about home, with replaying things Mama and Deddy had done or said. In the garden I heard the warm, thick breeze whisper, heard the occasional slither of a lizard or a copperhead through the dry grass around the garden, felt the sun on my skin. I sank past the brown in my muscle, felt my bones warm and my body release the sweat that would keep the ticks away. I was there under the sky without the noise of voices, and the silence was intoxicating. The grief had slipped away to a manageable place, even though only two months before, the grief of losing my siblings had been tangled around new home and new mother like the choking honeysuckle vine.

ON LABOR DAY, Ella Mae came to where I kept myself busy in the garden. "Come on," she said, handing me a sun hat. "I gotta show you somethin."

We walked to the creek that morning, down through a path in the woods to where the ground began to give beneath my army-green sneakers. I could hear the water hushing like wind through the trees. I looked up and a hawk took flight, thick feathering around its talons.

The sun is brighter here, hotter than in St. Louis, I thought. And it was; the way it stored inside my skin and made my brown merge with the clay earth, which I could taste on the back of my tongue now.

"Here we are," Ella Mae said, and she cut off through a thicket of vines to the bank of the creek. "Here we are," she exhaled, and breathed deep before stomping down the muddy incline, and I held on to trees and followed behind her, unsure of my footing, cakes of mud collecting on the crescent white moon of the toes of my Keds.

The sun shone on the water and made shimmery spotlights on Ella Mae's red-brown skin. In the place where there were no rocks or fallen branches for the flow of the creek to contend with, it was smooth, brown coffee; but just upstream, where a big, gray boulder humped up out of the water like a tortoise-shell, the foam and force of the current were visible.

"That's where we're goin." Ella Mae said. She rolled up her pant legs, and I widened my eyes into a frown that surveyed the blackberry vines, with their thorns anxious for my bare ankles and arms. I surveyed the orange mud turned brown clay around my sneakers; the swarm of mosquitoes above the black silk of Ella Mae's hair as she descended to the water.

The crows cawed above, and I looked around to see who might be watching us—me in tattered overalls with no shirt beneath, my new breast buds itching, Ella Mae in blue work shirt cut off at the sleeves, jeans rolled up to her thick calves.

The water was cold and welcome on this hundred-degree day. I took my shoes off, tied the laces together, and dangled them around my neck the way Ella Mae carried her boots. Then I steadied myself and walked into the water next to her. The cold current around my ankles took rhythm with the flow of my blood.

We stood next to the gray boulder. "Be still," she said, and she did not have to tell me why. I felt the slow leaching of pain flowing away with the tumbling current, and I stuck my hands down in it; the sun and movement of water over them transformed hands into shimmering fish. Then I lay down, the whole sky above me, the current below me. I closed my eyes and heard the lapping water laugh, *hallelujah*, and felt the current leach the pain away from my head, my heart. I opened my eyes to see Ella Mae—the solid bone trunk of her silhouette over me smiling.

THE PATH HOME from the creek took us out of our way, up a hill with tall, heat-hardened grass where things slithered near the roots. The sun came full and seared my back, and a cloud of steam lifted from my wet overalls. By the time we returned to Ella Mae's house, I was dry and new and safe. The overalls went into the bag of rags for her rugs. The treasure of new clothes came out of a separate bag of rags, and she handed me a sack with a raffia handle.

"I don't know if this stuff'll fit," she said, "but some things it ain't right to buy from the thrift store or fetch from the dump."

The paper shopping bag was filled with a pair of Buster Brown loafers, white socks, white underpants, and three bras that were different from the lacy things with cups that Mama used to wear. These were cotton-white, like Ace bandages to hold my untamed breasts in place. That night, the frogs croaked and chirped, having eluded the snakes all day, and the owls called to each other in a woeful, mating hoot.

The next morning I sat on the porch and watched three *v*'s of geese cackle their fall homecoming. School would start tomorrow, and I would no longer be Odessa Blackburn: I would enroll as Odessa Lacey. School would take me out of the still life of Mississippi visits and wrap me in the patchwork quilt of dialect, loyalty, and primal survival of a Mississippi I was born in, and would have to grow and thrive in.

Chapter 4

ON THE FIRST DAY of school, I walked quickly to the bend in the drive that would hide Ella Mae's house behind pine brush.

The bus brakes squealed farther up the road, where my cousins lived. Dafreeta was the only one of them who hadn't dropped out yet to work in the chicken factory. My heart thumped in my ears, and I took deep breaths so I would appear calm before stepping up on the bus. I did not look at the other children, but I bit my lip to stop the involuntary quiver of nerves. I sat in the first seat and looked occasionally into the driver's mirror at Dafreeta's eyes, so much like mine. She chanted, "We's gonna be woods people. We's gonna be free. Me, my crazy-ass Ella Mae and me." The girls with her giggled, but I slipped away from them as I studied the pattern of fields, watched them as they turned into streets. In case the bus broke down, I wanted to be able to find my way home.

"SHE APPEARED WITHIN ME." That's what Ella Mae said when I asked if she could remember me being born.

"She? Who?" I asked.

"You was within me," she said, correcting herself. "I could feel you there. I dreamed that I walked beside water. There was a wall, and I walked along the wall, and the water was flowing beside me in pace with my steps and there was eyes, wide open, and the body was no bigger than a chicken. You was inside of me. I knew that."

I didn't say anything, but I wrapped my arms around my body, feeling fingers on muscle; trying to know myself as a tiny thing swimming inside of her. My eyes traveled to her midriff where the ring of fat marked the place, and my head went light at the thought of my body naked inside the empty warm place of her flesh.

I carried this memory as the bus took me further away from her into the untraveled streets of Starkville.

THE HIGH SCHOOL backed up to a marsh that smelled like sulfur. I watched the faces of the other students, laughing and talking as they entered the school. Afros and press and curls, platform shoes, white sneakers; no one seemed to smell the boiled-egg swamp stench but me, like the smell of when our toilet backed up on a St. Louis Christmas because Deddy and Grandeddy and all of us kids were flushing the same toilets after turkey, and greens, and way too much cornbread and beans.

I wanted to be anywhere besides that hallway, a row of lockers on each side, the faint smell of urine on ancient tile floors of bathrooms someplace in the maze of slamming lockers and the haze of afro-sheen and after shave. Jovan musk oil hid the shame of new pubic hair, period-soaked pads, and the untamed scent of unplanned ejaculation. I wanted to move my feet, to walk into the current of brown adult-sized bodies or turn and run the path home, but my shoes would not move.

From behind me someone said, "Hey, new gal. Let some light shine through, and God will bless us both."

I turned around, expecting someone other than the thin, dark chocolate girl who smelled like mothballs and black tea. Her eyes were the only thing that let me know the words had come from her; some combination of common sense and recognizable kinship of hurt-girl, a little bit like me, but she was in run-over Buster Browns. My own pair of Buster Browns was one of the new things Ella Mae had bought at full price, polished up the night before with the good brown shoe polish she used for her boots, the white part made to shine with Vaseline.

The girl was confident and sure, like an old aunt. "Come on," she said, and held her hand out for my schedule. I surrendered it to the pink roughness of her palm, dark brown lines like highways on a map. She showed me where my classes were that morning, and at the end of the day she sat in detention hall like a martyr-sage for missing her first class.

At lunchtime, we stood before the chain-link fence at the weedy end of the school yard. The sun seared our bare arms, and the smell of marsh soaked into the sweaters now tied around our waists. She recited some Bible verse that connected scripture to flesh—"Let him kiss me with the kisses of his mouth, for your love is more delightful than wine"—and in that line was something true and holy. Though I had never felt compelled to recite Bible verses or even listen to them in church, I wanted more of the depth of her voice, and I followed her across the playground where she scrambled over the fence like a squirrel. For a moment we stared eye to eye on opposite sides. Then I broke the newness of my Buster Browns, stuck the toes in the diamond chains, my fingers like new claws as I climbed over after her and landed in the part of the marsh that was dry.

We slipped through the tall reeds to the road and into the musty clapboard store for her lunch: green apple, Now-and-Laters, and Fritos. Back in the school yard, she offered me some of her sugar-and-salt treat, and I accepted. The gooey texture kept us quiet as we watched the other ninth-graders run around like children, the upperclassmen sitting in corners and hiding the occasional puff of a cigarette. I tucked my sweater under my butt to protect it from the splintered wood of the picnic table and touched knees with Jamella Nudley.

Chapter 5

I SURVIVED THE WEEK of new schooling and found safety in weeding the garden all day Saturday. Inside the stifling heat of the house, Ella Mae vowed, "I'll get somebody out here for you to hang out with," and I imagined awkward groups of teens standing around staring at one another after being dumped inside the confines of our rickety wooden fence.

"I ain't never bothered with a dog," she continued, "but if you want one . . ."

"No, thank you," I said. I read my math problem over and over, hearing my math teacher's deep Mississippi accent: *Each sad of an equashin mus be ekal to the otha.*

Ella Mae sat at the loom, enduring the additional heat of the lamp. She said, "It's Saturday night. You ain't gotta do homework. Maybe I'll take you to where the high school kids hang out at the Dairy Queen."

She did not know the shame of pulling up at a teen hangout in your folks' old raggedy truck. Besides, I thought the kids at school were all walking facades; watching them in the halls was like watching the Mardi Gras parade.

"Odessa, didn't you say your sister and brother was going to Mississippi State? Maybe you'll be able to visit with them." A false bit of hope leapt like a solar flare; the hope of seeing Lamont and Towanda, then I remembered Deddy's pledge that Mama conspired to keep his secrets, and I felt the scar tissue beneath my glasses from her fist each time I had tried to cross her. No, I had Jamella, and I had the garden on weekends, and though there was loneliness, there was never the fear that peaceful moments would suddenly turn evil.

Sleep came that night, a heavy, dreamless sleep induced by the oppression of motionless heat.

In the morning, Ella Mae announced, "We going to church," to which I replied, "Oh Lord!" Tortured laughter erupted from my throat. Then Ella Mae set the hook: "I'monna let you drive." My eyes and my smile grew wide, and I figured the disgrace of going to church would be worth the stories I could tell Jamella about driving a truck all over Starkville.

I changed into the awkward skirt and sweater Ella Mae had given me, and I sat on my bed while I waited for her to get dressed. I wouldn't be able to wait until Monday to tell Jamella, so I opened the notebook where I kept my journal and wrote a surrogate letter to my big brother.

Dear Lamont,
School started a week ago. I have a new friend Jamella Nudley who says her brother is at Mississippi playing football. Do you know any Nudleys? Other people call Jamella "Fats" because she is so skinny. I went the first week of school responding to my new nick-name, "Ham," until Jamella told me that it's because I came to school smelling like a smoke house. Ella Mae uses wood in the morning to warm the house. Long story. Anyway, guess what I'm about to do? Drive! Big benefit of being in the country, fourteen is old enough to drink moonshine if I want to, till a whole field if you're told to, and drive the family truck.

Ella Mae walked past the bed, looking like a giant in a muu muu she'd found at the dump and fixed up by taking in the waist. It made a silky pink and white shroud for a square-framed six-foot woman with thick, muscled calves that rose up firm out of men's shoes. I looked up and shook my head in disapproval; then I pulled closed the curtain that walled off my little room-space, and I went back to my letter.

Your school started almost a month ago. When are you coming to see me?

I shut my notebook, shutting out the feelings that were buoying to the top. I tucked the pages between the mattress and the plywood frame, where the truth of my wants was near, but could not take over the "me" who had since bucked up. Ella Mae moved my curtain aside. She was in a clean work shirt and jeans.

"Better," I said, and we both giggled.

I hoisted myself into the driver's seat, and Ella Mae lowered herself into the passenger seat. Behind the wheel, my confidence slipped. "You sure about this?" I asked Ella Mae.

"I'm sure I need to try to give you your people. I myself don't like 'em, but I cain't let my problems with 'em be your problems with 'em. People need family like crawfish need mud." She blew a half giggle of air to calm her own nerves. "Being by yoself might seem nice now, but older you get you'll wished you had took care to nurture some kinships. And that church is full of yo kin."

I stiffened my steering-wheel grip in frustration. "Not that! Are you sure about me driving? What if I crash us into a tree?"

Ella Mae looked me in the eyes the way she did when she meant *Hush*. "You've practiced in the yard before. Don't let your mind play tricks on you."

I started the truck and rolled slowly down the driveway with my left foot pressing the clutch pedal so hard that the floor of the truck threatened to give way. "Good, just coast 'til you get up here."

"Brake," she said when I reached the end of the driveway, where gravel and dirt met the asphalt road to town. "To get up on here, just pull out regular, not slow, or it'll cut off." My back teeth tapped together to absorb the anxiety. My heart beat in my chest with the fear that I would surely pull out onto the road and only enjoy a few yards of my first driving experience before ending up like Mama when she was a Mississippi teenager, in a ditch, and later with a metal plate in her head. I imagined that the metal plate was the funhouse mirror that distorted all of Mama's truths; the beginning of her world filling up with unintended lies, lies that she believed because every time she went back to check the real memory, there were contorted truths reflected on her metal plate. *This could happen to me*, I thought.

"Go ahead, pull onto the road." Ella Mae's voice and the smell of exhaust from the tailpipe brought me back to the moment. "Not so slow," she said again.

"I know!" I yelled out over the rumble of the truck "Or it'll cut off."

She nodded for me to coordinate, clutch and gas, the way I had done in the yard, jostling over the dirt and stone. "Well, ain't nobody comin; try it now."

My pulse throbbed in my neck, and I unbuttoned my white blouse. My hands shook as I attempted to coordinate steering and clutch and gas pedal. In the yard my driving lessons had been in bare feet that now squirmed in my school shoes. "Maybe I should be barefoot," I pleaded with Ella Mae.

"Odessa, jus go," she said with one hand on the dashboard.

I swallowed before letting off the clutch, slow and jerky like riding a bull. "Give it gas!" was all I heard above the grind of the engine, and a cloud of dust engulfed the truck. There was the violent crunch of steel-belted radials grinding dirt and rock, and then the high-pitched squeal of hot rubber—and then the quiet of asphalt road; only then did I remember to add the steering wheel to the coordinated dance. I swerved to turn away from the sight of open field, then away from the sight of woods, then the road appeared in front of me again.

Ella Mae hollered like she was hollering for the chickens: "Yee-yee-hee!" We broke into hysterical laughter that slowly quieted as we traveled down the road. The pinched spaces in my lungs had opened. I smelled juniper, the sulfur of hot mud and crawfish, of hot, dry magnolia leaves pressed into earth. I could feel the muscles in my arms and legs, the solid lock that my knee and elbow joints made to hold me in place, the slow trickle of sweat from my underarms. I had shifted, and Odessa Lacey was different from Odessa Blackburn. Odessa Lacey liked to take a salt shaker to the garden and enjoy the taste of salt on tomatoes picked right off the vine; she liked the mineral taste of well water, liked driving a raggedy red truck with no seat belts, the windows rolled down.

WHEN WE ENTERED the church, there was a mumbling that swelled like bumblebees after you took off the lid to their hive. The deacon scooted his chair, wood over wood, as he adjusted himself before playing the light piano tune that held space before worship; the space to quiet the congregation from talking among themselves. But me and Ella Mae distracted them from being obedient when we entered, and the mumbling continued.

The two of us floated in the waking memory of the day the church had held our kin, mourning the loss of Granmama. I did not realize Ella Mae was holding my hand until she pulled on me and leaned in to compensate for her self-conscious discomfort; the lines in my hand defined by the lines in hers, new calluses against the leather texture of her fingerprints. We made a taut extension bridge with our connected hands, lighted by the stained-glass judgment of kin.

We slid into the pew with the end plate that bore Granmama's name, "Elizabeth Lacey." Ella Mae was her namesake.

The deacon hammered at the bass line, playing with his right hand crossed over his left, to get the congregation to pay attention, but there was still a stirring of women's fancy hats; yellow, white, light blue, and straw hats among the cottony black pillows of men's heads. The hats were fancy, but all the outfits on all the wives, husbands, widows, and their children were worn and dingy from well water and field work.

Ella Mae kept her head erect and her eyes on the embossed cross on the wooden pulpit, but I looked around at the eyes, light brown with hazel-trimmed edges, dark brown with blood-shot whites from alcohol and too much cola; light skin, dark skin, some looking so much like Ella Mae; broad head, eyes close, nose narrow. Some like me, with darker skin. All of their disapproving stares harmonious as they crept across the aisle and up my spine.

Ella Mae's breath came short and audible. She squeezed tighter to keep herself still, and she whispered, "You ain't here for them. You here for you."

I whispered back, "I thought you said I *was* here for them. I told you I don't need them." I held my neck stiff to keep from rolling it. "Why did you want to do this at all? You don't even believe in God."

Ella Mae still held my hand, but I felt her travel far away and leave me there on that bench to fend for myself. Behind me, the warm swirling of air, the squeaking of the church bench, and the smells of zinc and sweat. I turned to see my Mississippi cousins: Junior, Agreeta, Dafreeta, and my cousin Neckbone, who our family called the retarded one. He was as big as a wrestler and always had food spilled down the front of his t-shirt. All of their shirts used to be white but now looked yellow from being left on the line, then rained on, then left on the line again. The boy cousins were too grown to still be living at home. Agreeta wore lipstick because she had quit high school and gotten a job at the chicken plant, and Dafreeta was my age, in wedge heel shoes, the heels worn down from walking on gravel. Her stockingless legs were as dry as tree trunks.

From behind me Dafreeta whispered, "What you look'n at, orphan?" Her voice was just loud enough for me to hear, but quiet enough to blend into the sounds of the echo beneath the piano board; hammer on taut strings ringing out the tune of "Walk the Streets of Glory." There was a shuffling as people stood and pages fluttered; hymnals were opened to the correct place; throats were cleared; the song began. Dafreeta didn't stand or sing. She just sat back and giggled with dirt-fingernailed hands over chapped lips. I stayed seated too and kept my eyes on her the whole time. I waited until the song was over, and then I whispered, "You smell like cow manure."

The deacon looked up from where his hands were poised over the piano keys. He cleared his throat and turned his attention back to the embossed cross.

Ella Mae was lost inside distant memories of baptisms and funerals, her gaze still turned forward. The congregation rose and song burst forth again: "Precious Lord, Take My Hand." The cousins' mouths opened in praise with the rest of them. Ella Mae roused from her fog and looked desperately through the hymnal for words that meant nothing to her. My anger flared at the depth of our hypocrisy.

WHEN WE RETURNED HOME, the sun hung just above the trees, promising relief from the thickness of humidity. Ella Mae walked to the shed to get a couple of hoes for weeding and came back to where I still leaned against the truck, no longer amused with myself for having driven us there. She stabbed one hoe in the earth and thrust the other one toward me, knowing I'd open my hand.

I took the hoe and said, "Why did we have to sit there in the middle of a room where nobody even likes us? I don't need them. I don't know what made you think we should go there." I shook my head and took my first stab with the hoe at some innocent weed, then pushed past the dangling fence and flung myself down in the shade of the stairs.

She took small steps toward me, as if she were preparing her response, then sat on the bottom stair with me; her shirt lose and open now at the collar, showing her collar bone and the smooth skin above her breast, which reminded both of us that she wasn't just somebody's discarded daughter and sister, or an awkward mother, but a woman.

"Sometimes, Odessa," she said, looking down and sighing and pushing forward the loose, dry earth with the edge of her hoe, "sometimes you have to try things like a 'speriment, and see if it work or not. I thought of myself at fourteen, when I needed somebody."

My tone was pitched higher than the cicadas, "But you needed somebody other than them. You trying to give me the people you didn't even want."

Beads of sweat burst out on her forehead, and she gripped her thigh and cleared her throat. "I'm just tryin to give you somethin that it seem like you need. It's not like you telling me what you need. You just sit quiet most the time."

She squinted down at me, one hand upraised to block the frustrating sun, and I saw the little girl that she must have once been. The way Grandeddy pushed her away as the child he did not father, even though he always made sure she was provided for. I saw the fourteen-year-old girl of her stories, body like a boy, strong and playing for the men's baseball team until the jealous men of my family ripped her shirt off one day and left her bare-chested and alone.

I put my hands on my hips and thought about that word "need" for a minute, and I let it transform into the clever immaturity of smart-ass argument—a decoy to hide my feelings.

I said, "There is something I want. Can I have a TV?"

She looked down at me as if looking me in the eyes would reveal some spirit who had surely possessed my body and spoken such words, and then she blew spit from between pursed lips unintentionally speckling my face. Above us a hawk dipped for the early evening prey of a careless jackrabbit.

She looked down at me, still with her hand as visor. The involuntary stare to bring equilibrium that only a mother can give to her own child. Gravity pulled me down into the worn dip of the stair, pulling out the truth: *I needed more kin.* Tears and sweat together in a drip from my chin.

Ella Mae looked away to break the spell. She undid the hill of dirt with the hoe and exhaled. "Well, goin to church didn't help. I'm sorry. Guess I'll try somethin else."

I squinted one eye closed and looked at her through the wave of heat. The shadow of the pine tree in the distance fell on me and helped ease the shifted sun. She leaned heavily on one knee to get up. "I'm sorry," she said. She forced herself to look stern, but it made her look worn. Her hair hung in her face as she turned to go up the stairs and get away from the influence of my tears; how tears from the child bring tears from the mother, and once brought the flow of milk that had no direction.

Chapter 6

S CHOOL HAD BEEN IN SESSION for more than a month, and there was the disorder of cool nights and hot days, days that were still too hot at three o'clock to support homework. In the clammy discomfort of the kitchen I sat at the wide planked table. The tree bark chairs had been set out on the porch and Ella Mae had fetched two long back-less benches from the dump. She said it would save space to be able to push the benches under the table rather than bumping into the chairs all the time. There was nothing to lean back on and relax, and I didn't tell Ella Mae what she'd made was a basic picnic table. I tried to concentrate on the square root, but there was the pain in my shoulders, the continuous slap and slide of the loom, more rugs to feed another mouth, to buy school supplies and shoes, socks, underwear. I tried to be still with that, and switched to rewriting my history essay in ink, tried to concentrate on not ruining it again with missing words or transposed letters. Neither of us heard the muffler of the rusting blue Pinto sputtering toward the house.

The screen door clapped in unison with the slap of the loom, and then someone knocked on the table to get my attention, and he was standing in the kitchen only a few yards from me. I jumped up and stood on the shadowed side of revelation before throwing my arms around Lamont. We hugged hard and long. I let him go and let go of a breath that had been stored inside the dank basement of my heart, let go of the tears of missing that could not hit air unless there was some Blackburn sibling to receive them. We stood still, taking short breaths of muggy autumn air, until my tears stopped. "Want something to drink?" I asked, clearing my throat, already headed for the Mason jars.

ELLA MAE AND LAMONT stood looking each other over for the balance of truths and lies in eyes, nose, and mouth before seeing who they saw and speaking.

"Well, Lamont, you done growed quite a bit since last I see'd ya." Ella Mae broke the silence with words that would comfort my older brother, who was shorter than me.

"Yes, ma'am," Lamont replied with a blank expression that he held steady while he probed the snapshot memories of the past for her elusive but familiar face. I could see in his one squinted eye that each memory led him back to the Ella Mae mirror game, long black hair, red eyes, and long, killer finger nails.

Ella Mae leaned on the wall and reached out to shake his hand, but she took hers away quickly once she measured his apprehension. She announced in a stammering whisper, "It's fine for him to take you with him in to town. I'm sure y'all got plenty to catch up on." He looked so different. Nineteen years old now, I thought he would have grown taller, but at least his legs had grown stocky and strong; muscular thighs, legs smoother and more hairless than mine. His new style of track shorts and tight t-shirt showed everything God had given him.

LAMONT DROVE US into Starkville and parked in a weed-filled lot in a dilapidated neighborhood. I counted three buildings, an empty lot, two buildings, an empty lot filled with weeds, broken-down cars, and broken brown whisky bottles. I felt the same depression in my spirit as when I went with Mama to the North side of St. Louis to shop at the meat market; boarded up houses, people on stoops to avoid the roaches and heat inside the house; the feeling that I'd taken the value of shelter for granted.

Across from where we parked were the three structures; a white two-story clapboard that leaned from the weight of too many families in one building. The address was the year of my birth, 1964. Around the handle there were years of fingerprints.

A man sat outside left of the white clapboard eating a sandwich wrapped in brown paper; I assumed it was fried catfish on white bread with hot sauce, one of Grandeddy's delicacies. His saxophone rested shining on his right, his dog on his left; thin black suit jacket, black pants, and black hat bore the heat. The dog waited for the leftovers, panting, then licking, then panting, and I wondered how they endured.

The sign above the man's head read "Good Music, Ice, Potato Salad, Corn, Fish and Tripe Sandwiches." Below it was a window covered with chicken wire except for an opening where thick brown hands birthed the fried food to go. I smelled battered pieces of meat fallen to the bottom of a vat of hot oil, and my mouth watered.

Three kids sat on the stoop of the adjacent building. They shared a push-up pop with a wooden spoon, no older than my little brothers, Benson, Daryl, and Baby Jessie. I hoped Lamont was headed there, but when we got out I followed him across the street to the door numbered 1964.

"Did you check out the address?" Lamont asked as he turned, his face in the white light heat where the sun caught his naps of hair and made them halo red, and I suddenly did not trust whatever he was excited to share with me.

Lamont pulled a single key from his back pocket and undid both locks with some wiggling and jiggling of the handle. Behind the door I could hear the muffled drumming of someone coming down the stairs, the same way us kids ran to get the door first whenever someone knocked.

When he opened the door, a young guy Lamont's age stepped into the sunlight; dark-skinned and thin, he wore the same uniformed look, tight t-shirt and jogging shorts. His hair was cut slick to his skull in a brush cut, the line perfect. A little goatee mustache and beard made his face look angular, and despite their similar dress, this man was like our cousin from Los Angeles who visited one time, bringing with him the feeling that he had seen the world, while we had only seen the inside of a sticky Mason jar.

The two of them embraced, and my frown turned inward as their red lips touched. I was riveted by Lamont's show of emotion for a man I had never seen before. The man reached out to my twisted face and then to my hand, which involuntarily rose to meet his. *Very white teeth*, I thought, remembering Uncle Leland. We followed him up the dark mildew and old chicken-grease stairs to an apartment that was, to my eyes, an oasis. The only piece of furniture was an old upright wooden piano, so much like the one at our old church. Body-sized pillows of yellow and burgundy and blue were strewn about the floor. In one corner there was a fake potted palm tree strung with Christmas tree lights that were the same colors as the pillows; in another corner a boombox sat where the wood floor met the wood molding. Along the bare beige walls were patches of stained, flowered wallpaper, décor that distracted from the smells of damp plaster and Pine-Sol.

We settled in on one of the tight-weave burgundy pillows, and Lamont wrung and twisted his hand inside a back pack until he came out with a small loaf of photos. The first one was of Towanda in a fake fur parka, standing next to a man about her age. Her eyes met mine and a twist of loneliness set into my throat, but I spoke to loosen it. "It's cold in St. Louis?"

Lamont leaned back to look at me, and the sun's light behind his head created the silhouette of the same face I'd put my hand to when I was three years old and asked, *When are we going back to Granmama's house?*

He answered me about St. Louis in a voice deeper, more syrupy than I remembered. "Well, it's cool there, not cold. October there and October here are a big difference."

"When were you there?"

"I just got back from fall break." There was another twist in my gut, this one wrenching on the idea that he had been at Mississippi State for almost two months and had not come to see me until now, and that he had been to St. Louis to be with them, laughing, living, without me; they had all moved on without me.

I forced my mind away from thoughts that would only hurt. I swallowed down the lump in my throat and reminded myself that I was happy and wanted to stay that way, but I imagined Towanda at Mississippi State, not choosing to come see me, standing on a stark football field in green and gold band uniform, happy like in the picture.

I asked, "Towanda didn't want to come or something?"

"Oh, girl, you're behind in the news. She's pregnant so she stayed in St. Louis and is now managing a McDonald's and going to Forest Park Community College. This guy"—he pointed at the photo and went on, even though my thoughts were stuck on *pregnant*—"that's her man, Matthew. They got an apartment on Whittier Avenue and told Deddy to go ta hell for thinkin he was gonna just put her out in the street, but they got an apartment right down the street from the tavern." He laughed with his mouth wide open, the sunlight going orange and casting sunset across the floor. "Some people don't know shit about running away." He flipped his hand and said, "You know I'm just jealous. . . ." I wondered what college mate he'd stolen this new gesture from. "For real, though, Towanda's got more courage than the mean ole lion." He rambled on about our siblings, but I didn't hear much. There I had been, thinking I couldn't get on that school bus the first day because I'd be leaving my siblings behind and they'd soon become a memory, but Lamont chatted about life in their world as if I were dead.

I said, "Do they ask about me?"

Lamont said, "Girl, you been to see *The Wiz* yet? I'll take you."

My heart beat an extra tangled beat, and with it came my request: "Take me back to Ella Mae's." I wanted to run, to get away from the empty feeling.

"Girl, you just got here." He settled the pictures on the pillow next to me, stood up, and walked across the patina of the wooden floor, sound of Mississippi sand under his sneakers.

I said, "You only came to pick me up, and only showing me all these pictures 'cause Ella Mae told you to. I was fine. You didn't come all this time. Why you come now?"

He responded with his old reprimand: "Girl!" He met his friend at a curtained-off doorway and took two glasses of red Kool-Aid. When Lamont's hands were full, the young man embraced him by the waist, and Lamont turned to look at me; and I felt small like the day Mama took me to kindergarten for the first time and turned to look at me before walking out the door. That was the first time in my life that there was more than the space of two rooms between us.

Lamont's friend smiled again, showing those white teeth, but I rolled my eyes and turned to look through the yellowed sheers down to the street, where the three children from the stoop played run-across, using the blue rusted Pinto as one of their bases. The vapor of dirty walls, fried food, and way too much cologne hung in the thickness of humidity and made my stomach turn, the warmth in my belly going cold as I allowed myself to acquiesce to the myth of the stillborn child.

I curled up on the pillow and drowsed to the sound of Lamont and his friend playing Ray Charles songs on the piano. The saxophone man caught the tune for a note here and there, but each time he did, the kids on the street yelled, "Nuh-uh! You cheated." The smell of autumn dusk exhaled the hopelessness of Mississippi soil and opened hope through the comfort of familiar sounds, and the familiar smell of Lamont's sweat on the tight-woven yellow pillow, and I fell asleep.

Sometime later I awoke, my spindly legs extending way beyond the pillow, glasses pressed painfully into my nose. The room looked different. Lamont sat on the floor next to me. Lamplight softened the dilapidated edges of the room. Through the window, the street was dark except for the big orange glow of streetlamps. The kids' voices had been replaced by the bass thump from a piano in the ice-potato-salad-tripe-fish-sandwiches building. *Bobby Blues Bland*, I thought as I sat in the haze of napping.

"You need to eat," Lamont said, holding out a plate with two peanut butter sandwiches.

"Where's your friend?" I asked, hoping he'd say *On a plane to China*, though I could hear through the vibration, the touch of fingers on keys and foot on pedal, just like being in the basement of the church and hearing Sister Johnson's daughter's fingers on the wood of the upright piano, just like I used to easily recognize each sibling's footsteps across the floor above the basement where I once slept. I recognized the pause and rhythm of his friend's piano-playing coming from downstairs.

I sat up against a stiff neck, my arm heavy and numb.

Lamont said into the emptiness of the room, "His name is Richard, Richard Morgan," and he ruined it. Made Richard real, human, with a name.

"Where's *Richard*?" I said with a twist of attitude.

"He had to go to work downstairs."

Sleep helped loosen questions. "Is he your . . . you know . . . girlfriend or whatever?"

Lamont laughed in that deep guttural tone, way beneath the sound of talking, that was always stuck in his throat. I tightened my lips to show that I didn't appreciate being laughed at.

"Girl, you don't change. You just be sayin stuff, and people be like, 'Shut up, Odessa.' No, he ain't my girlfriend, but he is my boyfriend."

He giggled again. In my head, in the places where the blues music came up through the floor and took me back to memories of Mama's and Deddy's club meetings and parties, I heard what Mama and Deddy had surely said: *That's nasty.* Lamont kept his eyes on mine for my delayed response.

"Oh," I said, and I bit into my sandwich, despite the sudden montage of memories of Lamont coming home hours late after band camp; Mama fussing him out and not waiting for him to say where he'd been before scripting a punishment if he was out late again with a girl. Judgment and punishment that came out in a mixed uncalled-for announcement: "girl."

"But don't you like her?" I asked, with bread and the salty-sweet paste of peanut butter stuck to the roof of my mouth. It seemed easier to ask with my mouth full so I could be misunderstood and take back the question if he started to laugh.

"Like who?"

"The girl you were always sneaking to go see in St. Louis."

He laughed again, openly as if something had been freed and could not be silenced again.

"Girl," he said, and paused while he swallowed the peanut butter, "Richard is mine. Just forget about all of whatever you got told before. I moved in here yesterday. Deddy said he and Mama weren't gonna pay for me to be at a school that was turning me into a faggot." He stood up in the middle of the room, using lamp light for a spotlight, and recounted the story like he was recounting good gossip. He mocked Deddy's deep voice and spit with every "sh" sound, the way Deddy did when he was drunk: "Shhhhit. Damn shhhhame." Then he folded his arms like Mama, who always sat ringside at Deddy's tirades, showing her approval and fear in one gesture, and I laughed so hard I almost peed my pants.

"Where the bathroom?"

"That door." He pointed to a door that looked like a closet. Inside there was no bathtub: just one naked bulb over a round mirror, a sink on metal poles, and a shower head over a rusted drain. I washed my hands and looked around, proud of Lamont for finding Richard and the small amenities of a free life over the fake security Mama and Deddy offered as a reward for silence. I released a breath that still held thoughts of homework, and the smoked-ham air of Ella Mae's big room, before returning to the pillows.

Lamont stood and talked to me, and we laughed at the shared kinship, born of the war inside the brick building that was the home we were pushed out of. We laughed until tears came, ebbing and flowing between giggles and grief until we were silent. I listened to more of Lamont's story, comparing all of his words to the catalogue of sixties and seventies television shows I'd stored up in my St. Louis childhood. Beneath our laughter I imagined Lamont moving from college to this apartment with Richard, then from this apartment to some fancy city where Richard was probably from, then from there to Paris, like the faggot men on TV, wearing scarves around their necks, tight pants and berets.

Having exhausted his standup routine, Lamont sat down and got serious again. "Girl, you know me. Me and Deddy were talking in my dorm room when I told him, and I said, 'I was made a faggot in *your* house, not here.' Then I brought it home to the West Side." Lamont rolled his neck, and I saw *us* in the station wagon at the old filling station on the way home from one of our summer Mississippi trips. Deddy's hand grabbing to drag Lamont's yellow nine-year old legs out into the dusty open air where he could wield the length of the belt for a beating. But Lamont's arms were no longer toothpicks; he snapped his grownman fingers in the air and claimed the rest of his story.

"Girl, I told yo Deddy, 'If you don't like what you got from the market, take it back,'" and I slipped away to the childhood memory, the smell of steamed hot tamales mixed with the diesel of bus fumes, and the steaming methane stench that billowed from factory smokestacks outside of Sulard's Market. I saw again the image of Mama and Uncle Leland locking lips behind the cold glass windshield, and the fall of Leland's naps of well-oiled hair on our wooden floor the day Deddy slit his own brother's throat; death premonition mixed with the thought of Lamont and this boyfriend living together, hands around the taut muscle of a waistline, below ribs and above the waist band of track shorts. The smell of tripe battered and fried wafted up to the window, and my stomach turned in fear; a floorboard creaked in another apartment, and my breath caught on the word "Deddy." I had not known I was still afraid—although not of him, but of ever again returning to what I now understood was a nightmare.

I grabbed Lamont's warm hand with my cold one. "It's okay," I said, "don't tell me the rest." But his voice echoed anyway in the room. I looked down to the scene outside his story. Lamont talked the way Blackburns and Laceys did, until the whole story and all of its embellishments were told. "Deddy swung on me, and then I ran down the hall from my dorm room and shouted back to him, to Mama and to the audience of bystanders. I said, 'Fucker, Pell Grant is payin my way 'cause you lied on the application anyway.'" Lamont giggled again, drowning emotion beneath each bout of laughter. "Girl, I had forgot that my room and food came out of Deddy's tavern money." He reached over and took a bite out of my sandwich, and I hid a grimmace at the sight of his lips, Richard's lips, my lips around the sandwich bread, his lips encircling my bite.

I thought about how much Lamont loved activities: football, band, "Don't you wanna go back to school?"

"Nah," he said turning away to the floor. "I got some plans." He bit the sandwich again and continued talking with his mouth full. "I was thinkin 'bout all the shit we all put up with and how they just orphaned you, left you standin alone, their way of dealin with the fact that Mama raised Deddy's bastard like the ole southern fuckin code of secrets says to do. Girl, I was mad." And there it was, the place in a Blackburn or Lacey story where too much had been said, but it was never recognized until it had been enveloped by the air.

Bastard, I heard him say again and felt separated.

Lamont and I were both only a few months delivered from the shame of listening on the edge of sleep for the sound of grown bodies thudding against walls in the darkness, hard enough to mean bruised flesh. Lamont laughed, but I went cold and anxious with a delayed reaction of fear. I watched him throwing his head back like Mama, and I wanted the peanut butter in my throat to go down so I could relax into a bout of laughter too. But laughter did not come, and my brain said *run away*.

"Take me home," I whispered, and Lamont's eyes got larger, revealing all of the sandy brown. He wiped his mouth with the back of his hand.

"Girl, this is how we livin." His tone changed from attitude to anger. "You and me livin the truth while the rest of them sittin up there in St. Louis takin Mama and Deddy's crap. I'm on your side." I turned back to the nighttime outside the window. He blew a sigh of guilt and reached one arm out to me, with the other resting in the peanut butter paper plate. I leaned in to him, my eyes still wide with fear of the man who could not hurt me now.

"Take me home," I said.

He didn't say anything, but chewed fast to swallow the bite, and I followed the old impulse to say the things that would be heard, because the true things would never be honored. "Lamont, me being a bastard and you being gay ain't the same." I froze on those words, feeling the warmth beneath his t-shirt recede.

"No . . ." he said, and pushed me back away from him. "No, it's not the same, Odessa, and I'm sorry they did you like that, then threw you away, but you ain't got the good sense to know when somebody trying to be good to you. And fightin— ain't nothin wrong with fightin. It's a whole lot better than just waiting for stuff to happen to you and then deciding how you're gonna deal with it." His voice was wavering now, "That's somethin you better change, because first you had Uncle Leland protectin you, then me and Towanda, and now Ella Mae, but one day you gonna have to learn to tell people to go ta hell, just like the assholes who raised you taught you. They crazy as hell, but they know how to fight."

Good, Lamont was mad. He hadn't heard my plea to go home, but now maybe he was ready to take me back to Ella Mae. But he did not raise his tone the way I expected him to. "You run away from the facts, Odessa. I'm the opposite. I go looking for facts." Lamont did not know when to shut up. So, I used my last defense, silence. He talked without response from me until finally he smashed the plate and remains of sandwich into a ball of frustration. By the time he was done talking, I understood that mixed in with the crumpled plate and clenched teeth was the fact that I had not said anything to acknowledge the triumph of his heroic affront to Mama and Deddy, and that I had not congratulated him on his new mate; but he had not shut up long enough for the words to surface, and now holding back felt like good punishment for not being listened to.

I did not look at him or send any energy his way, allowing myself a younger sibling's lack of responsibility for the emotions of an older sibling. I kept looking out the window at the pink and purple of sunset that layered itself across the sky in a reprimand and omen.

By the time we were in the darkness of the country, the moon began to rise small; not the awe-inspiring orb from the night before; just small. It jiggled in the side-view mirror like a single street light on the country road where I let my head hang out the window, and the smell of mud meant we were almost back to Ella Mae's.

LAMONT HUGGED ME half-heartedly, almost allowing our chests to meet, and he let go before forgiving my ungratefulness and I stepped into the familiar darkness of Ella Mae's yard. The red taillights trailed into the darkness soon after I shut the passenger door. Rocks pinged against the rattling muffler. The light from the open door at my back and Ella Mae's shadow within it stretched out across the ground.

I stood there knowing that Lamont was right. I was a runaway under the agitated stars. I tried to reconcile my truths; running was my survival tool, the strategy that had saved my life; I knew how to run away in my mind, out of my body, and had somehow learned how to use that compass and run to my real mother, even though I didn't know there was a mother truer than my abuser. I stood, refusing to let go of the broken equation. Something must be messed up inside me if I wanted to have my siblings back more than anything but I couldn't turn the survival mechanism off long enough to trust the gift I had been given—Lamont.

"Come inside," Ella Mae's voice called into the still night, and struck up the orchestra of cicada hums and cricket songs.

Chapter 7

THERE IS THIS WAY that siblings move in formation, angled like geese, with the self-appointed leader taking the journey in hand and the others falling in place according to birth order or pecking order. Ella Mae was right, I needed more kin, because there was the way that I knew myself, and then there was the way that I knew myself because I knew where I fell in the instinctual ordering of family. That was what made me afraid to shift or to see others shift: when they left, I might not know myself anymore.

LAMONT'S NEXT VISIT took us to the Dairy Queen, just him and me, no Richard. I made myself be still there, content to be the focus of his attention beneath the shade of a red umbrella on a wooden deck just outside the restaurant. Our sweaty forearms touched despite the sticky sweat and melted ice cream that tasted like warm plastic. If you lived on a diet of foods that came right out of the garden, then all other foods—those that had been "too long tampered with," as Ella Mae put it—tasted like medicine.

Lamont's head cocked to one side as he watched my effort to look as though I was eating, although I was just stirring the white substance in the paper cup while it melted. "Girl, I only got a little while before I have to pick up Richard, so tell me what you been doin over at your new Mama's house?"

I swatted the persistent fly away from my cup. *Don't call her that*, I thought. The word "Mama" conjured only negative connotations for me. I swatted again, though the fly was nowhere in sight. "I've been being hot all the time even though it's October, and just being bored mostly." I pressed my lips tight in a frown at the thought of him hurrying me through an update so he could pick up Richard.

"Just being bored? No new thoughts, nothing to chat about? How about your friend Jamella? Does she ever come over?"

My eyes widened. "I don't want her to see where we live."

"Girl, she probably lives someplace ten times worse."

His words failed to comfort me; he had opened the door for my complaints, and I laid down my frustrations. "Weekends are the worst. No school, and silence. Ella Mae just likes to garden and weave rugs."

Lamont spooned up his DQ and wiped his red lips with the napkin, which the sun made blinding white. "Well, gardening and those rugs are how you eat, Odessa, and if I recall right from fifteen minutes ago, you were digging in the dirt when I got there. I think you like it more than you're willing to admit."

I looked away, and my glasses slowly slid down my nose until I leaned my head over and rested it on my sweating hand, frustrated with him for hearing beyond what I had been taught: to cover uncomfortable emotions with complaints. What I really wanted was for him to come get me more often.

He shot his crumpled cup and napkin into the red trash can. The careful arch of his throw compensated for the southerly breeze from the Gulf, which brought the smell of salt and marsh to everything that already bore the curse of mildew. The wad landed right in the center, no rim, and took out two of the swarming flies on the way.

He licked his lips again. "Bored is a state of mind, Odessa. Let me take you to where you can go all over the planet right from Ella Mae's backwoods porch." He looked at his watch, held to his wrist with a thick leather band. "But we gotta hurry so I can pick up Richard."

I snorted.

THE LIBRARY WAS IN THE TRAILER that sat between the post office and the green wood-shingled house where the Board of Education was. When we stepped in, the mingled smell of pulp-wood pages, ink, and the dry cool of air conditioning brought instant relief. I went through the tedious process of filling out the form for a card, but the librarian re-clipped it to the clipboard and sent me back to the table where Lamont napped. Three times I completed the form, and three times I started over upon the white librarian's command: "This ain't done, little girl." I went back to the table, and Lamont said, "Odessa! Quit being stupid. Use them glasses and pay attention." Then his head went back down and his voice came from the muffled cave made by his arms. "Hurry up. I have to get Richard from school and take him to work."

"From school? You mean you quit, and he stayed in school?" I rolled my eyes.

With his head still down, he smacked his hand on the table to jolt me out of my stalling, but I talked on, in an effort to keep him there. "What are you gonna do? Are you going back to school?" Maybe he could come and live with me and Ella Mae. Maybe he could quit being gay, go back to school, and be what a big brother was supposed to be.

From the cave of his arms where he tried to rest on the table, he said, "Damn, girl. I got plans for my singing career. I don't need to go back to school."

I blew spit from between my lips before giggling. We couldn't sing, not neither one of us. We had stood in the choir stand mouthing the words to the songs after the aunts had shamed us into being a muted chorus of Blackburns: "Y'all stand in the back. Y'all cain't sing." Our lack of singing talent had been attested to and confirmed often enough that none of Loni Blackburn's children should have been in denial any longer. Lamont smacked the table again, and under the librarian's glare, I got up to turn in my paperwork.

When the woman finally handed over the stiff paper card, Lamont snatched it away and hoisted his bag onto his shoulder. "Come on!" I followed him, feeling five years old.

We went to the row upon row of little wooden boxes that I had avoided at the school library. "Card catalogue" was a term meant for those patiently seeking knowledge. Numbers, letters, and periods thrown together in encrypted codes seemed to jump up and reconfigure themselves right before my eyes. Reading was hard enough, but these little drawers made my neck itch the way the Rubik's Cube did; something everybody understood but me. I used to spend hours locked in the bathroom, just trying to fix the yellow side first, with no success.

Lamont said, "What you wanna read?"

My attitude was fully engaged by now. "I didn't say nothin about wantin to read. I said I was bored, and here you got me filling out some long form, longer than a welfare application."

"Girl!" he said above my tone, then in a whisper through his gritted teeth. "Be quiet. Actin like you ain't got no sense. You cain't be all loud in the library. I asked you what you wanna read."

I mumbled, "Mimosa trees. I want to find out about mimosa trees."

The week before, I had occupied myself after school with the constant weeding of the broccoli that struggled to spring up from the ground. I was invested in what broccoli would look like, having never eaten it in St. Louis; but I remembered Peter Brady pushing the mystery around on his Brady Bunch plate. I came in with the hoe in hand and asked Ella Mae what kind of plant was coming up next to the house. She came out on the porch and said, with disappointment, "Mimosa. That's a weed." I liked the sound of that: mimosa.

Lamont was relieved that his delay in seeing Richard was almost over. "Damn," he said to me. "Thank you." He went to the puzzle of little boxes and came back with an encoded card. People looked up at us, and I returned a glare to Charles Walton, a black boy from my school who acted like he was better than everybody else. That was his cover-up for his shortcomings. His light brown hair was always filled with lint, and his Saturdays were spent in the library, not because he liked to read, but because his mother was a junky and wouldn't let him in the house on Saturdays while she used their apartment as her prostitution station.

I could smell Charles's sour, musty hair as we marched across the carpeted floor to the stacks of books. Lamont fingered the edges of the plastic-covered books as if he was looking for a number in the phone book.

"Here," he said. He stopped and used his long index finger to pull from the shelf a book: *The Mimosa Tree.*

I looked at the front, the drawing of a tree with brick buildings and two children in silhouette. I used my thumb to fan through the pages; no pictures. I looked at the back and did not find the description of a tree but the description of a story.

"No, I'm looking for books that will tell me about the mimosa tree. Not a story with a mimosa tree in it."

"Well, you got what you got. Now, you have a card, come back and read whatever the hell you want. You didn't even say thank you. Come on."

He was mad, and so was I, and I wanted my being mad to be more important than his needing to fetch Richard from class. I looked at the card catalogue wall of tiny, mysterious drawers, and I picked up the book in defeat.

"Shh," Charles Walton hissed as I approached. He looked up from his comic book as if he smelled something more stinky than himself.

"Sorry," I whispered, glaring at him.

Lamont waited at the door while I checked out my first book.

ON HALLOWEEN, Lamont, Richard, and I sat on Ella Mae's steps. No childish jack-o-lanterns; we had pillow cases filled with water balloons. It was a warm night, smell of mildew lingering beneath the porch, in the ease of the setting sun. Our knees touched, the tight weave of jeans over joints that sat ready to spring from the porch; but no one came down the road. Ella Mae told us that the cousins threw exploding bags of flour at her house each Halloween and that we should expect to clean up in the morning. It was Lamont's idea to fight back.

My world at Ella Mae's had seemed flat, but then Lamont and Richard became weekend fixtures. I sat between them as if we were three siblings, and their knees locked me into belonging. We giggled occasionally, inspired by the thought of the Mississippi cousins—Junior, Neckbone, Agreeta, and Dafreeta— running from water balloons like ants running for their hills in a sudden rain. Between the giggles, we were silent, and this was sweeter than trick-or-treating, sweeter than the hope of going to the mall for Halloween gluttony. The clouds moved over fields where the remains of hay lay flat, off to the left of Ella Mae's house, in the direction of Grandeddy's house.

The smell of Lamont's metallic sweat blended with mine, and in the comfort of belonging, I asked Richard, "You have any sisters and brothers?"

He and Lamont leaned to look at each other and decide if I could be let in.

"One sister, one brother," Richard said, smiling and squinting down at me. He was the tallest of the three of us.

"Where do they live?" I ventured to take the next step in my probe. The balloons inside Richard's pillowcase squeaked as he adjusted them and smiled in some comfort of his own, then looked across me to the mowed field for the cousins who would soon disturb the silence.

"I'm from Jamaica."

"Where?" I said when I conjured no image.

Lamont piped up. "Girl, quit being ignorant. Read a book and learn some geography."

"It's okay," Richard said. Behind me, their hands locked on the splintered porch. "Jamaica is an island not too far off the coast of Florida. There are a lot of black people there descended from African slaves just like there are here; old sugar cane plantations."

And with the mention of sugar cane, I saw the ten-cent stalks as tall as me in a rain barrel at Sulard's Market in St. Louis. Whenever we went to the market, my mouth always watered in anticipation that Mama might buy one and strip the cane into chewable portions for the station-wagon ride home. I said, "Did you and your sister and brother eat sugar cane?"

He unlocked hands from Lamont and groaned. Lamont chuckled in acknowledgement of what Richard would say. "Sugar cane and Bible verses are two things my mother fed me enough of that I don't care if I'm starved of stalk and Jesus for the rest of my life." Lamont winced and looked away.

But I hung on Richard's words, his voice so deep from inside some truth that harbored a cave of dark, sweaty stories, so much like Uncle Leland's smooth way of talking that I was melded into kinship with him.

We were silent again, listening to the crickets and shifting of tennis shoes on the sandy stairs. In the light of the setting sun came a cloud of dirt over the mowed field. Grandeddy's truck emerged from it like a black dirt dauber. Halloween orange dirt and black trees in silhouette against the orange sunset sky. "Trick or treat," yelled Agreeta and Dafreeta from the cab of the truck. "Trick or treat," drawled Neckbone from where he stood in the bed, holding on to the top of the cab. A wild turkey in the cornfield gobbled in alarm at their approach. Arms raised up, and paper bags exploded into clouds of white flour where Lamont, Richard, and I sat on the porch. And like the command Lamont once gave me and the other siblings for the attack on our St. Louis cousin, he yelled, "Get 'em!" and the three of us sprang from the porch and into the yard.

We dodged through the clouds of flour, which now looked like clouds at sunset. Coughs and laughter and copper faces in fading sunlight. We ran with the three pillow cases filled with water balloons, deeper into the dead corn stalks, accompanied by the sound of Grandeddy's truck crunching on the gravel driveway. We crouched down in the stalks and waited, holding in giggles and swatting at each other to be quiet, until they raised another round of paper bags; then we fired. The smack of water balloons on truck sides, the smack of water balloons in tight nappy wool hair, the sound of wet rubber against a face: "Damn it! Damn it!" they yelled in their syrupy voices. Lamont approached the truck, and our war of flour and water turned from laughter to the confusing space where humor tightens in tension. The clouds of flour could not be dissipated by the splashes of water, not enough oxygen in the air, but Richard and I followed our commander to the black truck, with more rounds of water balloons.

Out of ammunition and unable to see, our enemies resorted to taunts. Junior yelled, "Nigga, I plugged yo ass. Look at Dessa lookin like a jiggaboo."

I hugged my stomach muscles where they ached from laughter, and yelled back before Lamont could defend. "Look at Neckbone still pickin the rubba out of his hair!"

"Who dat?" Agreeta yelled in that voice that sounded like an open hand smacking bare skin. She pointed at Richard, and there was silence in the moment where dusk turns to night and people and creatures hush for one breath to exchange places with the nocturnal. The moment clapped shut with the sound of Ella Mae coming on to the porch, but it was too late to stop the words from leaving Junior's lips: "Faggot mothafuckas."

Junior had grown to be as thick a man as Grandeddy was, his weight on the earth like the sound of cattle approaching. He struggled to get out of the truck. The intuitive chill of danger went up my spine. From the field the turkey hollered again, and Junior struggled with the stuck truck's door handle, his eye on his targets. "I'll kick all y'all's asses for fuckin with me. Fuckin faggots!"

Then the deafening sound of rifle fire, the way it rips out through the air, tearing through clouds and the flight patterns of birds. It resonated through the fluid matter in all of our heads.

Ella Mae stood on the porch, fixing the rifle to fire in the air again. Dafreeta yelled, "Crazy bitch!" The sudden noises of wheels and dirt brought back the sound of Deddy skidding and leaving me in the dirt of Grandeddy's yard, where I had stood with the rifle still in my shaking hands that day. In unison with the turkey I resounded with the unexpected release of a dry cry, and then tears. Lamont and Richard both came over to hug me, and their arms quivered with a fear that was not revealed in the way they yelled after the cousins.

"You want a piece of my faggot ass, come on back!" Lamont said. Richard shouted something in patois that I only comprehended as the bark of an agitated dog.

"Come on in," Ella Mae coaxed, using the rifle as a cane and holding open the screen door. We were all insane, and I wanted to be someone else, somewhere else.

LAMONT AND RICHARD used the headlights of the Pinto to guide us in cleaning up paper bags and balloons. We were silent and disturbed. Richard knelt where I could not see him but felt his body's warmth. He whispered, "I'm getting the fuck out of the South," and the moment froze there, my mind acknowledging that my heart had let down her guard long enough to want them, to have them, and to lose them.

Lamont and Richard got in the car, but before they left, I walked in the crooked stream of the Pinto's headlights and asked, "Can I come?" I wanted out of who I was as much as they did. "Can I come?" My hands gripped the rumpled rubber on the driver's doorframe, and I looked through the darkness into Lamont's eyes, not having words to let him know all the things I wanted to say, words that were quickly being dissolved by the cold resolve I saw in his eyes: he was going to be the one to run away this time. The wheels rolled slowly.

"Move out the way, Dessa," Lamont said. "We goin back to the apartment, and you need to stay here." He looked away to Richard and then over his shoulder as he backed up. I kept moving with the car, wanting his eyes back, but he cut the wheels in the direction that would not crush my toes and rolled away. The one red tail light was what I focused on. At the end of the long driveway it paused; then there was the trace of yellow breams down the road. Like two shooting stars, they were gone.

Chapter 8

LAMONT DIDN'T COME the next Saturday. The day crept on slowly. I weeded the broccoli and collards, which didn't need much weeding with the cold weather. Ella Mae and I brought a week's worth of wood up from the place behind the house where it was stacked, wedged between the teenaged poplar trees. Our work was wordless.

She finally said to me, "You going out with Lamont today?" I didn't answer, but I told myself not to be upset with her for asking what I had promised myself I would not ask. I hugged the wood to my chest. My red and black plaid CPO jacket hung open, and the wool collar itched where my scoop-necked t-shirt exposed my dry skin. "Don't hug it to ya like that. I got bit by a brown recluse like that. Right on the chest."

Now I was ready to answer her so she wouldn't feel obligated to make small talk. "I don't think he's coming today."

We both looked out at the trees. A few dangling orange leaves, green fur tufts of the pines against clear blue sky, a hawk circled and yelled a long cry. The sounds and colors woke up the smell of cool mud, spicy cedar from the tree that lay where it had fallen in last week's windstorm, the warmth of summer heat still in its wood. There was the memory of a moldy library trailer without the harmony of sibling voices whispering in argument. I looked up at the sky. Cloud cover was moving in, closing up escape routes.

ON MONDAY, I got off the school bus with the smell of the day on my clothes and hair, the dirty fried grease smell of the cafeteria. The crisp, cold November air over the marshes was now too cold for the smell of sulfur to drift. I went to the mailbox as I always did when I came home after school, knowing I could open anything that Ella Mae would think was junk mail. But there was none of the usual junk; just one unsealed envelope addressed to *Odessa Lacey c/o Elizabeth Mae Lacey* in Lamont's left-slanted handwriting. I opened it and wished the sun was shining as I unfolded the paper. I looked down the road on each side of the driveway, and down the driveway to see if his car was there. In the distance, the yellow of the bus turned the curve in the road and blended in with the remaining yellow leaves on the trees. Then the rumble of its engine faded.

The sheet of white notebook paper came out of the envelope word-side down. I did not turn it over, but looked down at the backwards-embossed lettering; only a few lines were there. My two-tone white and brown Buster Browns provided a backdrop for the white paper. The crunch of small gravelly rocks was the only sound as I walked toward the house. I saw my breath and smelled hickory smoke and the savory scent of butterbeans cooking.

Ella Mae had learned to cook dinner on a schedule now, not just when she was hungry, and she looked relaxed in her face each day when I got home from school, instead of a furrowed brow that said *What am I supposed to do with you and how am I supposed to do it?* I told myself to be grateful for what I had, and I imagined myself crumpling the letter and throwing it into the woods, but my shoulder ached beneath the cloth strap of my rag-rug book sack, and my heart leaned into that pain.

I stopped behind one of the thick pines, just before getting close enough to see home through the skeletal corn stalks and naked trees. I leaned against the pine trunk and allowed it to hold me along my spine. I turned the paper over.

Odessa,
Richard and I took the train to New York.

I exhaled and deepened the valley my ribcage had already made to protect my heart and guts from impact.

It might be a while before we find a place. Ask Ella Mae if we have any relatives up this way. We are staying at the "Y" and it's real shady. Richard's gonna apply to NYU if we can get an address. I might get some vocal studio work next week. I'll write when I'm settled.

Love,

Lamont

And there were no more words, no return address, no way for me to be the one extending or refusing touch. The air circled the empty space around my body. The light shifted in the sky from blue-gray to gray, and I did not feel my feet in my Buster Browns now. I started writing my own response to him in my head. I told myself not to forget any of the main points: *I can come and live with you guys. I can go to school there and won't need anyone to be home after school. I can do the house work.* Adrenaline fizzled in my neck like bubbles rising in a soda bottle. I shook loss out of my mind and pictured the train ticket in the mail smelling like ink, New York cigarettes, and hot dogs, and I picked up my step toward the house: *I'll go with them, I'll catch the train too.* I breathed deep through my mouth despite the sudden taste and smell of cow manure in the cold air, then the smell of wood smoke again.

I walked toward the house allowing the memory: the feeling of Lamont's and Richard's knees against mine on the porch. I remembered them rolling away in the blue Pinto, and I slipped into blame, a much more powerful feeling than defeat. It was Richard's fault. *Richard's gonna apply to NYU.* Always a plan for Richard. Lamont, a fool to follow. My decision was to get the train, to catch up with Lamont, extend my touch to him, and my rib cage broadened with my plan.

Ella Mae opened the big door and looked out at me through the screen. The smell of cooked sweet potatoes pirouetted out into the cold air; salt and sweet, warm and cold air moved together, confusing my homing device. "Want somethin to eat?"

she asked before looking at me, and I knew what she saw: me there, black wool handmade hat that protected my puffs of french braids from the cold, the black frame glasses, red and black CPO jacket holding my new breasts and warmth of my body tight, my lips pressed in disappointment.

Blame was more powerful than defeat, so rather than accepting the comfort of sweet potato warmth, I convinced myself that she had already been to the mailbox. She knew. "Come on girl, come on in." She knew. I walked past her, into the warm embrace of hickory-heated woodstove, sweet potato cinnamon, and I disappeared behind my curtained door, before she could offer her tentative touch. The letter in my hand with no return address, no phone number, no place to pinpoint on a map, no destination to give a train conductor. Ella Mae was the only tangible landing pad for my grief. Sometime shortly before dusk, just after my brain exhausted itself with imagined scenarios and conversations, I fell asleep.

IN THE MORNING, I sat puffy-eyed in the lamplight of the kitchen. At dawn, an owl hooted, ending his night. A single cricket chirped. The steamy smell of chalky oatmeal called to me from the stove, but I didn't want the warmth to be swallowed and push out the cold. Hunger was my choice. The floorboard behind her bedroom curtain creaked, and I tipped out the front door, closing it until the swollen wood stopped and I was off and up the driveway. My heart beat in my ears, and at the sight of my breath in the gentle light, I remembered my coat, and cursed myself for having to double back.

"Good mornin," Ella Mae said from where she stood at the sink. "I wish you would talk to me and not try goin off to school with out eatin or talkin. It's best to talk about him leaving." She sounded as if she had rehearsed it all from some book. "You should say whatever you feelin, or ask me any thing ya want to ask me."

I thought, *How could she know that he left? She read the friggin letter, that's how.*

Out loud, I said, "Did he tell you he was going to leave?" I looked her in the eyes.

She put her hair behind one ear, then turned back to the stove. "Sit down," she whispered, after placing my steaming bowl of oatmeal on the table.

Her face looked thick and distorted in the indirect light from the east, refracted through the kitchen window. I shuffled over to the picnic table but looked at the Mason jars of dry butter beans, canned string beans, canned tomatoes, not at her.

"Odessa," she said, "Lamont is smart. If he had stayed, people down here wasn't gonna let him be."

I said, "I wanna go live with them."

She squinted and looked at me with one eye more closed than the other. "New York ain't Starkville. You got to stay here."

She had never hit me no matter what I'd said, and bolstered by that reality, I pressed on. "I'll take the bus and go. I'll be fine." I picked my school bag up and disrobed the chair that wore my CPO jacket, putting one arm and then the other in the garment that smelled of the appeasing dinner from the night before. A confusing desire tingled at the back of my head. *Did I want her to hit me?*

"Odessa, I cain't let you go off to New York."

I needed to walk away. "I'm gonna miss the school bus if I don't go."

Yes, it was true, I wanted her to hit me, I wanted her to stop the unfamiliar freedom, to hurt me with the familiar pain of a slap, so I had the last word. "I'm going to New York. I'll pack my stuff later. I'm just asking you to buy me a fucking ticket."

I looked her straight in the eyes again the way a dog challenges without flinching. She dropped her forehead into her hand, her hair draping over her hand. "I'm not gonna do that. That would be a bad idea." I glared at Ella Mae, her hands over her forehead, still, peaceful. She looked exhausted, and I didn't know why, but I was glad.

I said one more thing from the evil self that I did not recognize. "I'm sick of your weak shit." Whatever reason I had to fault her grew even stronger when Ella Mae still did not move. I frowned and turned to the door, yanked it open, and slammed it, making the front wall of the house shudder.

DAFREETA SAT IN FRONT OF ME and Jamella on the bus that morning. My teeth were clenched so tight that each pothole hurt my jaw. Some of Dafreeta's short hair still held the naps that undid her press-and-curl hair from the Halloween incident almost two weeks ago now. The base of her hair had gone fuzzy, acting as a foam cushion for the straight spikes that jumped out.

She noticed me looking at her, and she got up and stood over me. "What the hell you looking at, sister faggot? Faggot sister?" I eased away from her and I let the space in my chest open to the energy that swelled inside me: hate. Jamella squeezed out between us and scuttled to the back of the bus. Dafreeta let her go with barely a glance. I braced one hand on the metal back of the seat in front of me and the other on the seat behind me, and I stood up, glared without blinking.

The whole bus of kids suddenly swarmed toward us in a mass of plaid, quilted jackets, hunting caps, anticipating a fight. The driver's eyes were in the mirror, squinted in a question as she stayed locked on us. She shouted, "Have a seat, ladies."

Dafreeta's voice billowed louder. "I said, what you looking at you orphaned bitch?" Then she giggled and looked to the three girls across the aisle for approval. From the back of the bus I heard Jamella gently reciting a Bible verse: "Though I walk through the valley of the shadow of death, I will fear no evil." In the rhythm of the sound of the train chugging over rails past dilapidated trailers and abandoned trucks, I heard the Bible verse again, and above those sounds, Dafreeta: "Orphaned bitch."

Despite the gentle eyes of the driver watching me, I balled up my fist, and like the train it traveled past the empty space, and just before the brown dry flesh on my knuckles connected with the brown cushion of Dafreeta's jaw bone, I thought, *No.* But I had already punched her. There was the chaotic noise of kids yelling, the jostle of the bus driver slamming on the brakes, and then the grip of her old thick hands, the smell of her sweat like urine over me. "Gal! Gal!" was all the driver said over and over as she yanked me out of the seat, holding Dafreeta away from me with her other hand. She hauled me through the trail of my own tears and snot to the seat nearest the front door of the bus. Dafreeta held her jaw and yelled threats of how she would kick my ass. The driver perched herself behind the wheel and her expression changed to sympathy as I held my face stern, refusing to wipe away the stream of tears. I turned to the windshield, thinking myself no better than my father: using fists to break tension.

The air that day stayed numb in the classroom, where I did not listen. In the cafeteria, I only ate the tater tots and left the meatloaf and Jello. By afternoon, I had not calmed. My hippie white typing teacher watched me as I hung my coat behind the half-wall in the coat room. He stood, thin framed, long blond hair, in a tie and white shirt that his slouched body carried awkwardly. He waited for me to finish hanging my coat and then stood with that sorrowful Jesus-looking expression that ex–Peace Corp types wore when they assumed that they read "underprivileged" in the eyes of black children. I stared at my chair and walked past him, imagining my open hand smacking that missionary look off his face.

ON THE DAY BEFORE THANKSGIVING, Jamella and I sat out on the cold playground and ate the salami sandwich that I had not eaten at lunchtime. I despised the smell of the lunch room; balogna and bleach, and old apple peels, spoiled milk riding in the odor of it all.

"Talk to me, girl," she said, sporting that grown woman worried look that was always on her face. Her dark skin was so smooth. I imagined my hand lifting to touch her face, but refrained. She didn't seem to mind that the other kids made fun of her for coming to school with her hair half pressed, the nappy side in a french braid like mine, the other side straight spikes; her hairline rough in stark contrast to her skin. She clutched her hands to her chest and said, "Tell me, Odessa."

Jamella told everybody she was practicing to be a minister, which of course classified her as a freak, but ever since the first day of school, I admired her sense of commitment to her beliefs. We sat together during outside time, because no one else would sit with either of us. But this day I didn't feel desperate enough to do what she requested. "Tell me, Odessa. I might know how to fix it." Her eyebrows slanted down toward the middle of her forehead. "Tell me," she kept saying, in a gentler and gentler voice, the smell of her unbrushed teeth caught in the cloud of cold air.

I bit into a pepper corn in the salami, the reality of a sickening cold sandwich on a cold damp gray day. I looked back at her and saw myself in her eyeballs, my glasses defining me; a me that I spoke quickly to recreate.

I told her in as much detail as I could manage before the bell rang. Told her first that I ended up staying in Mississippi to live with my real mother, then told her that I hated the boredom and I missed my sisters and brothers; then I told her that my brother who used to be at Mississippi State with her brother had left and gone to New York—and then the story turned fantasy. I told Jamella that I would be taking the bus for Thanksgiving and visiting him. Jamella put her cold hand on mine to stop me.

"Odessa, I have a confession before you and God. I was shamed of myself, so I lied. I ain't got no brother at Mississippi State like you had. I ain't even got no big brother; just a bunch of little ones. I lied, but I'm confessing now. That means I'm not a sinner."

I frowned at her, sighed at the thought of confessing too, then lied, because I didn't deserve to be left behind, and Jamella didn't deserve to be poor and made fun of without at least a good story to lean on.

"Yeah," I said, "my new mother and I are going to go up there to see him and go to Central Park and all the museums. I might even get a chance to see a show on Broadway. *Cats* or something. We're not sure."

"Where you gonna get money?" she said, her face still holding the same expressions. The other kids were off a ways playing football, or sitting on the tops of picnic tables with their feet on the seat, warming hands on each other's bodies. Mr. Collier, the principal, known as the Pillsbury Doughboy, walked the grounds on duty and avoided that bunch of afro teens. They were the seniors, the smokers, the ones who we were sure were living the mystery of sex and drugs.

"Well?" she insisted.

"My brother is a studio musician now. He played on the Commodores' last album. He's sending us money to get there, then we'll be staying in his penthouse."

"Wow!" Her face stayed the same, and the "wow" was not one of envy but of disbelief.

The fantasy made me feel warmer on the cold playground. Who cared if she believed me?, "Actually, I'm gonna wait to buy my ticket until I see if he wants me to take the bus or fly."

She bit into her sandwich. "Why take the bus if he's sending you the money?"

But I ignored her, lost in my own fantasy. Flying, yes, I liked that; I created what needed to be true until the bell rang. Wednesday would soon be over, and Thanksgiving break would buy me time to explain why I had chosen not to go. In our last class of the day, Jamella asked more questions, so I painted the picture of Lamont's penthouse on Central Park, which I imagined bore a close resemblance to Buffy and Jodie's penthouse on *Family Affair*. The longer I talked, the more the stark difference between reality and fantasy annoyed even me.

I dreaded the end of the school day, because the coming days would be spent having to sit in the silence between me and Ella Mae with nothing but the clap and slide of the loom to fill the space. I'd probably break my standoff and start talking to her; I'd probably get hungry and eat in her presence. My orneriness was all I had control over, and too many days with her would melt me back to powerless.

Jamella sighed on the way out of the building. "You seem unhappy again, Odessa. Want to talk some more before you catch the plane? I can come with y'all to the airport." I looked at her, beyond her performance as a minister in a little girl's body. I reminded myself of what Lamont had said about Jamella probably being much worse off than me, and my New York fantasy gave way to who I really was, and who Jamella really was.

"No," was my deflated reply. "What are you and your little brothers doing for Thanksgiving?" She stared at me, shrugged, and looked away.

Chapter 9

WHEN I GOT OFF THE SCHOOL BUS that afternoon, I retrieved the junk mail from the leaning mailbox and started up the driveway as the early winter sun began to offer the amber light of evening.

I got to the place where the cornfield was, where I could always see Ella Mae's truck and the porch and the billow of smoke coming from the woodstove chimney. The rusted red truck sat in a depression of hardened terracotta mud, but there was no smoke, no smell of beans or salt pork in greens or rutabagas.

I stood in that space and created an equation for what I saw: the truck there, but no sign of my evening with Ella Mae. My toes were cold in my shoes. I felt myself there in the driveway, human and fragile, and then the front door opened. Ella Mae came out onto the porch in her long wool men's coat, her good jeans, her boots polished dark brown. Her hair and the coat made her look ominous, like a faceless raven, as she labored to bring one suitcase then another out onto the porch. Then she held the screen door ajar with her backside while she did a thing I had never seen her do before: she pulled the puckered, heavy wooden door shut and locked it with a key.

"Where you going?" I yelled, but my voice was drowned by the rumble of another truck's engine, growling louder as it ambled up the drive from behind me. I recognized the truck as it went by: Grandeddy's truck, with Grandeddy driving. Its fumes seeped out in slow, caustic clouds. I looked back at Ella Mae. Was she leaving me? A crow cawed as it swooped and flew over the diminished food of the cornfield. Grandeddy pulled to a slow halt in front of the house. Ella Mae did not look at me as she slung the suitcases into the back of his truck.

"Get in!" she yelled over the sound of the engine, which was idling higher and higher. Until now, I had not noticed that her big face was the same shape as Grandeddy's: his hair a head of completely gray naps, hers straight and slowly being robbed of its black. Ella Mae jerked the passenger side door open and stuck the polished boot in.

Grandeddy mashed the gas to quiet the engine, and he said, with more volume than Ella Mae: "Dessa, get in." I did not move from where the cloud of exhaust engulfed me. I had never heard my name roll across his thick tongue before. I was always "that four-eyed one" or "that nappy headed gal."

My name in Grandeddy's voice, Ella Mae's polished boots, the black coat brushed, her hair brushed, on her skin the minty smell of the rosemary soap that she made for me. She sat there in the cab of Grandeddy's truck, motioning to me that I should defy my instincts and join the enemy too. Then she hopped out of the truck in one move that made her body seem as tall as the pines behind her. Her eyes on mine, her face and hair and coat a mass of brown and black against the naked silhouettes of trees and wintry blue sky; she grabbed my hand, hers hard and fleshy but female; mine cold and bony in hers. My nose burned, and she snatched at my arm to yank me away from where I stood—a snatch that I could not decode; angry or hurried.

Ella Mae's eyes stayed on mine longer than they ever had. "You and me goin to New York for Thanksgiving," she said. The heaviness collected from where it had spread out to my limbs, hardened into a tight rock in my throat. I put my hand over my mouth to hide the grin of excitement, hide the guilt, hide the misbehavior with Ella Mae, the fight with Dafreeta, the lie to Jamella.

When we got to the bus station, Grandeddy stared out at the parking lot, picking his teeth, his fat, ashy arms in t-shirt and overalls even in cold weather. He waited for us to get the suitcases out of the truck. Then he hollered "Yep!" with a wave of his fat arm, and he headed back to his house while we headed north.

From the bus window, I studied leafless trees and yards of cold lawn furniture. Dusk and Ella Mae's reflection over my shoulder brought a flash of memory, scent of Lamont's nine-year-old breath warm in my ear when we took the train home from Granmama's funeral. His words: *Granmama's dead.*

I leaned back on Ella Mae, relinquishing the cold rudeness I'd placed between us. The feel of breast and muscle and rib cage on my back, her eyes reflected in the window, her right breast beneath coat and shirt, all of these cushioned the space of my heart and all the arteries around it. She handed me her handkerchief and left her hand there in an awkward clasp. The dusk became night and turned the window to a mirror that my tired eyes could not bear to look into. I slept deep into the tight weave of her good coat and the bus seat that smelled like so many black bodies that had traveled to and away from home. I slept deep in surrender and let myself belong to her. Trusting, if only for a while, that I was hers and she would not betray me.

It was Thanksgiving afternoon when we arrived. The New York bus station reminded me of a larger version of Union Station Bus Depot in St. Louis. People walked past with hurried concern. We weaved in and out of shoulders and arms, using our dangling luggage as a tool to make our path, and we emerged among the noisy gray of buildings that shot straight up, minimizing the sky. Ella Mae paused in the mess of movement and went back into the bus station as if she'd remembered something; through people and past sliding doors we hurried. Signs bore numbers and letters, some circled and some inside triangles. This was some city code that I did not comprehend. The fear of getting lost beat in my chest and in the rhythm of my steps as I tried to remember our path for later retracing, but at some point all of the rust-colored painted cinder-block walls looked the same. We went down an escalator, all faces staring forward, refusing to make eye contact.

When we stepped off into an underground world of electric-smelling dry heat, I saw train tracks in a basement. Phrases:

"Union Square," "Washington Square," "Uptown," "Downtown" on bold white boards over our heads. There was a lit billboard of spiderwebbed tracks in red lines, lines of yellow and green crossing, reminding me of the St. Louis bus route map.

Ella Mae did not look over at me to acknowledge my uneasiness, but she whispered, "Don't look like you don't know what you doing," and kept staring forward. I looked past her and saw others staring forward, some speaking softly to each other in a way that sounded like what they called "speaking in tongues" in church. Some read newspapers; some read magazines or books. I asked myself, *Has she done this before?* A white family in unblemished coats and hats wove in and through the crowd. They were confident as they maneuvered around people. The fresh scent of their soap and expensive perfume temporarily masked the smell of urine on damp cement. They lifted their packages, which smelled like stuffing and cake, high to their chests and perched nearest the yellow line, where they peered like pigeons in the direction of the coming light.

We boarded our train, rode it for a while, got off, and stood still on another platform, just to hop on the next train, which lost more white passengers and gained more black passengers at each stop, black passengers in lint-filled coats, some with children held tight by the hand, others with black plastic grocery bags that they clutched in the same fashion. The subway journey went from being well-lit and smelling of expensive perfume, cologne, and precooked turkey to being lit by flickering fluorescents that cast a glow over the smell of overused toilets. Multicolored graffiti walls replaced the flat gray of the first subway station, graffiti always with black paint as the background color. I held on, swaying with the curving underground motion of the train, and thought about Marvella Proffitt in *The Mimosa Tree*. She had left Goose Elk hoping for a better life, and had ended up in a Chicago tenement. I hoped this part of the journey would bring me to the trees of Central Park, the yellow taxis, horse-drawn buggies, doormen like the guards at

Scotland Yard, and somewhere in the background there needed to be Frank Sinatra's voice tempting me to snap my fingers and do a jazz shuffle.

"Hundred and Thirty-Fifth Street, Lenox Avenue," said a scratchy, robotic voice, and I stood behind Ella Mae at the door of flickering darkness. A man pressed against my back, his smell like the smell of never-before-washed carpeting; feet, whisky, sweat. I was grateful for the blanket barrier of my CPO jacket, but my skin crawled all the way up my back to the french braids beneath my crocheted cap.

We ascended out of the dark tunnel, leaving the smell of urine mixed with unseen water currents beneath us, and out into the light of fall sun, smell of chitterlings from high kitchen windows cracked open for relief, the sound of car horns from loud, rumbly Chevys, Datsuns, vans with airbrushed mermaids on the side, a bug-green Cadillac with horn blaring to draw attention to itself. No yellow taxis like on *Family Affair*, but a rhythm and a smell on the street that made me think of Aretha Franklin singing "Easy Chair." Ella Mae and I stood in the swirl of concrete, chain-link fences, hospital buildings stacked like light blue cinder-block Legos, and brownstones. The train ride had brought us from buildings that loomed and made me feel small to a neighborhood akin to St. Louis streets.

Ella Mae looked at a yellowed sheet of paper, worn and fragile with dryness, then looked around to get her bearings on this corner of treeless Harlem. It looked as if the west side of St. Louis had been squished, all the extra space of gangways and alleys squeezed up, and slowly I noticed the people.

A group of finely dressed black teens, afros on every one of them, was scattered in front of us. Had they been to church? They reminded me of the seniors in the Starkville High school-yard. The girls wore big earrings, coats of thick plaid and short, like their dresses, which seemed too short for cold weather. I looked down and did not realize I was gawking until one of the young men said, "You ain't never seen platform shoes? You all are lost, aren't you, lil' young blood?" I did not answer because now I was stuck on the suit jacket and how well it contrasted with his brown chestnut skin and the chestnut halo of hair.

Ella Mae pulled me by the hand as if she had spotted some familiar landmark, and we walked for blocks that all looked the same: cracked sidewalks, tiny wrought-iron gates that couldn't possibly keep anything out, and tall brick dwellings with the same wrought iron over the windows. Twice we passed the corner grocer where people continuously stepped out with the little black plastic grocery bags, while others turned sideways to slide into the doorway.

"We're going in circles." I complained, the tips of my toes scrunched and contorted with attitude.

"Hush." Ella Mae looked at the paper again, quickly so as not to make anyone think we were lost. "Hey!" The teen I had seen before, the one in the suit jacket, yelled from a stoop where he was clanking his keys, but Ella Mae did not turn to look, and she mumbled to me, "Hay is for horses. Turn yo self around." I made my eyes big to refrain from rolling my neck.

We walked until my two-tone Buster Browns threatened to squeeze the life out of my toes. Finally, Ella Mae stopped, peered up at a door, looked down at her paper, and then ascended the few stairs of an apartment building in her long wool black coat, her dark hair and hat. From behind, she could easily be mistaken for one of the black men coming from church or dinner or wherever all these black people had been going all dressed up.

WHEN LAMONT OPENED THE DOOR, I squeezed him so tight that I will always feel the imprint of his ribs on the meat of my arms when I think about that day. We followed him up a flight of stairs, where smells of food in the dark stairwell made my nose burn, smells like garlic bologna and vinegar, and a gentle smell that reminded me of cinnamon but did not conjure the image or taste of sweet potatoes. There was no familiar smell of Thanksgiving:

seasoning salt or Worcestershire sauce or the simple sweetness of onions bubbling in gravy.

"Come on in, come on in," Lamont said, holding open one of the three apartment doors at the top of the stairs, his whole weight forced against the industrial spring hinges. I didn't want to embarrass him, but I surveyed the locks, of which I counted three: a slide lock, a latch, and a dead bolt.

"Girl, quit actin like you ain't never been nowhere. Come in." I frowned and rolled my neck hard with attitude, enough to compensate for the way I felt about losing a big brother to a big city and about the lost fantasy of Buffy and Jodie's high-rise. Compared to Lamont and Richard's apartment near the blues shack swamp in Starkville, this was down-and-out and no improvement over the closet; no high-rise. But I stood there looking at the backs of Lamont and Richard's heads, both pea-headed men, wearing shorts and short sleeves in November, the two of them to each other what I suspected Mama and Deddy were supposed to be to each other, and I hid my sudden comfort behind a pretend yawn.

There was one window. The walls were brick, and the electric boxes and cords were exposed, some nailed to beams on top of the bricks that were no doubt supposed to support insulation behind smooth, white drywall. "A work in progress," Richard said in his new smoky New York tone. A little table made from a door and two stools stood just beneath the window. I imagined Lamont and Richard talking to each other while maneuvering up the narrow staircase, each holding an end of the found door. In the middle of the table, an empty green Coke bottle was stuffed with small sprigs of spruce pine, a pleasant odor that separated the apartment from the smells in the stairwell.

I recognized the little black and white TV from Mama's kitchen perch; its antennas spread in greeting. My whole understanding of life beyond the Blackburns and Laceys was inside the televisions of my childhood, and I was comforted to see the old thing. I looked around the small rectangle of a room, and I was disappointed that the upright piano from their apartment above the blues club had not made the journey.

Richard said, "This is the big room," gesturing with his arms wide open. Lamont stood behind him in red jogging shorts and a white t-shirt. The two of them always looked like characters from *Three's Company*: too much skin exposed. After the gesture, he left his arms open. "Well, Odessa, I don't get a hug?" I walked slowly across the room, frowning and rolling my eyes. We embraced to the sound of Lamont's laughter.

The course of mine and Ella Mae's journey from Mississippi—sleeping at dusk, waking at dawn, changing busses in stations that all smelled strongly of blue toilet bowl freshener—and my desire to know why Richard and Lamont had left Starkville without telling me first, it all melted away as I fell into the comfort of being with someone who had known me as Odessa Blackburn and who now knew me as Odessa Lacey.

I turned to finish taking in the scene: a lamp on a little wire stand next to the table; two twin mattresses, one on each facing wall, each made up like sofas with the same stained pillows that were in their Mississippi apartment. My eyes landed last on a rectangular door to what must have been the bathroom.

I said, "Where's the kitchen?" Lamont pointed to the poorly lit little space with his free hand. Richard added, "The bathroom is the tiny world behind that door."

"Then where's the bedroom?" I worked to leave any judgmental tone out of my voice.

Lamont turned around in a circle of giggles. "You're standing in the living room, dining room, bedroom. You guys can sleep on that mattress, and Richard and I will curl up over here." They traded a sheepish smile, which instigated a frown from me and caused Ella Mae to start humming something under her breath.

A roach caught my attention as it scurried past Richard. I widened my eyes at Ella Mae, who sat low to the ground on the mattress. She snickered and turned away, the way she did to let me know that I was being "silly," as she put it. She worked her way up off the floor, leaning on one knee, and her polished brown work boot came down on the roach with a crunch.

"That's my kind of woman," Richard said, allowing his voice to break into a Jamaican accent.

I took Ella Mae's coat and hat, and I piled our coats on the edge of one of the sofa mattresses. "We got dibs on this bed," I said, picking up my spirit to hide my concern about roaches crawling over me in my sleep. *Wood beetles, wood beetles,* I said to myself, thinking about the lighter-colored roach cousins who crawled from beneath the wood pile in Mississippi. I would make it my chore to sweep after we ate dinner, and I would insist on wiping down the kitchen. I skipped to the dark kitchen for something to clean up the roach.

Later in the evening, Richard ventured down to the corner store, and Lamont stationed himself in the one-butt kitchen, where he hovered over small pots of food that smelled suspiciously like cans of Vienna sausages. Ella Mae rummaged around in her suitcase and pulled out the small loom fashioned from a picture frame and nails. "I'm making placemats," she said modestly. And I took comfort in the shift from pungent odors to warm, spicy food smells that seeped up from the apartment below.

I went to the single, poorly insulated window and put my hand on the glass to feel the cold. Condensation dripped from my warm handprint. The heat from the other apartments must have kept us warm, because the one whirring space heater only heated what was right in front of it. I pulled the blouse sleeve from beneath my long, gray sweater sleeves, cleaned my glasses, and then I used it to wipe the wet window. There was no sun now, but clouds raced in thin, gray layers over the bit of open sky. I reminisced, thinking about the warmth of Thanksgiving afternoons in St. Louis; the hours before the meal, the hours before Mama and Deddy would fight; and when I came across the gentle memory of LaVern and me feeding our dolls stuffing, I quickly pushed it out of my mind, to steady myself in this comfort rather than that longing.

Across the street was a row of what Lamont called brownstones, but they were made of brick, and some were covered in a red plaster. I liked that these buildings had stoops. As I looked out, a small group arrived for a Thanksgiving feast. Two black women, whose dresses moved with their backsides as they ascended the stairs, were followed by an older black man in coat and hat who studied the steps before trailing behind the weighty women. A paper bag hung from his arm, his other hand caressed the plaster railing, and I imagined him balancing on the train with the bag and aching knees while the two women sat hip to hip, taking up four of the hard subway seats.

"Happy Thanksgiving." Ella Mae startled my thoughts away from the three outside. I grabbed at the table/door, making one end of the door rise up and smack back down on the stool. The Coke bottle mysteriously rose and fell with the door without tipping over. Ella Mae laughed with her hand over her mouth, as she often did, to cover her brown front tooth. Her embarrassed laughter caused me to squeak in laughter behind two hands clamped over my mouth. The two of us let go of tension that had been stored in little pockets of grief since the day Richard and Lamont had left. I saw in her eyes that she needed them, the extension of family, as much as I did.

Just before our revelation of laughter was about to turn into tears, Lamont came out of the kitchen, half grinning, like a little boy who'd just missed all the excitement. "What?" he said. Richard undid the locks and came in, and Lamont said again, "What?" Richard looked at us all and said, "What? What?" Ella Mae and I snickered some more but soon righted ourselves.

Ella Mae finished the placemats and set them on the table, adding color to the blank slate of the room. Without her weaving, she was now at a loss for what to do. She tilted her head to one side, a pair of Walgreens reading glasses perched on the end of her nose, as she looked about for her next project. My own glasses slightly tilted in sympathy. I pushed them up and said, "The placements are nice."

"Mm-hm." The room was silent again except for Richard and Lamont rustling through the paper bag for whatever Richard had forgotten to buy at the store. I frowned to one side and looked out the window.

"Thanks you for bringing me here," I said.

"You're welcome," she said in that monotone that hinted at none of her thoughts, and I wondered about her thoughts, in that moment, when I caught myself looking at her without her knowing. Her shape like solid bone draped in the unexpected gentleness of so much darkness. Her hair now showed gentle streaks of gray, a sort of surrender of her stronghold that I was normally not privy to. When I caught her off-guard like this, I could see past the brick solid woman and see the beautiful girl, the beautiful woman with songs buried somewhere in her heart.

Lamont walked over to the little wire table that precariously held the TV, its antenna, and the phone. He pushed the buttons and handed me the receiver, but I just frowned back at him. Who could he possibly be calling for me to talk to? I did not move from where I sat on Ella Mae's suitcase. The sound of a tinny voice called, "Hello?" through the receiver. It was LaVern, the sister only a year older than me who I'd shared bedrooms and unfortunate matching outfits with. I still said nothing.

Lamont said, "Girl!" and snatched the phone back. "Hey, LaVern," he said into the phone. "Happy Thanksgiving."

My breath caught in my chest, snagged on the word *betrayal*, the betrayal of placing a voice without body on this side of my defenses, like the small cast-iron fences around brownstones, gates that wouldn't keep anyone out.

Ella Mae thunked her boot against the suitcase to get me to come back to the gratification of the moment, and Lamont hung up. It was safe again for me to breathe, safe with what was mine—and the argument ensued.

"Lamont, what was that all about? I don't want to talk to them." I looked him in the eye to get him to see what I could not say: scabs were not meant to be picked. I looked at him as if he surely should have known better.

"Odessa, you're throwing them away like they're all one hurt."

Fucking traitor, I thought silently, my mouth like the grave Granmama had lied me into. Why couldn't he see that having him was a miracle, and that putting myself among siblings who had been taught to think of me the way we once thought of Ella Mae—a mythical freak—was a humiliation that would undo my ability to know myself? The four of us stayed in the suspended orbit silence of the apartment, all feeling in my silence the intensity of some "being thrown away," from the past.

Lamont took the responsibility of shifting us with a sideways apology. "Odessa, come downstairs with me and Richard to borrow some pepper from Ms. Olatunde. You'll get to meet someone new."

I couldn't tell if the suitcase moved because I leapt up, or whether Ella Mae's leg kicked it involuntarily, but it jumped with a sudden convulsive movement, and we all laughed nervously. I was at the door before I could ask myself if we were all okay.

Lamont said to Ella Mae, "We'll be back before you know it."

Richard clicked on the light next to the door for Ella Mae and perched his fist on his hip. He said, "Hey, thanks for suggesting we try this neighborhood. It's perfect, right? Dinner in ten minutes."

"Okay," Ella Mae sighed from the edge of our couch bed, where she was checking the placemats for loose strings, The overhead light diluted the silver of the little black and white TV. Something shook in her voice, a vibration like tears or exhaustion. For one second I had that feeling I used to get all the time with Mama and Deddy: that feeling as if the truth would have to be imagined, because it would certainly not be said. *How would Ella Mae know of a neighborhood for them?* I wanted to ask her, but my curiosity about the downstairs, the location of the mysterious aromas, took me away. I exhaled, and we all descended the stairs.

Lamont said, "Odessa, what, you worried Ella Mae can't be without you?"

"Shut up." I pushed his shoulder, almost knocking him and Richard down the stairs.

"Watch it, girl."

"You watch it." I giggled at Lamont, so newly sophisticated, resisting the crude behavior of childhood in front of Richard.

We paused at the door before Lamont knocked. The little hallway was lit only by the orange street lamp that filtered through the one high, murky pane of caged glass. My shadow elongated on the stairs behind us.

"Look, fool," Lamont said, poking my shoulder. Richard stared at me like he was ready for a story to be told. "Don't act out in front of Ms. Olatunde. She's very dignified. If it weren't for her, we wouldn't even have a place we could afford. So act like you got some sense." He poked me again. "I love you, but sometimes you ain't got no sense." I poked him back to show him that he didn't have any say over me.

"I love you too," I said. "And you are short." I couldn't think of a good comeback, They looked at each other with that couples-confirmation look and giggled before knocking.

Someone came to the door and fiddled with locks and chains before opening it. Then a face peeped out into the hallway higher, taller than all of our faces: round, and sunny-toasted dark and shiny by a type of sun that did not shine on New York. Richard and Lamont said, "Heyyy!"

Is for horses, I thought, contemplating the climb back to Ella Mae and the smell of a Vienna sausage Thanksgiving. The woman at the door was tall and erect in the same way that a preying mantis is poised and confident. She smiled, and I could tell, even in the shadows, that her teeth were not real; all grinded perfectly straight across.

"Come on in," she said with a chuckle. Her smile reminded me of the elf on the Christmas wreath at home in St. Louis. She misread my frown. "Somebody is curious. Come on in." My eyes got big to communicate to Lamont that I was not acting a fool, but rather trying to keep from staring.

Her apartment was so different from Lamont and Richard's. Pictures sat on every available ledge, windowsill, and small table, displaying framed faces. Her walls were not exposed beams over brick, but they were yellowed from fried foods, off white from the steam of overcooked vegetables. She put Richard's head in the vise grip of her veiny brown hands and kissed both cheeks, then did the same to Lamont. By then my discomfort with so much touching pushed me to the door, waiting for the pepper exchange to be completed. Lamont and Richard and this woman chuckled over something about the garbage truck, and then she spoke in a low whispers: "How did her and Ella Mae do on the ride?"

Lamont responded loud enough for me to hear. "She didn't leave none of her attitude in Mississippi, and Ella Mae is just fine." Lamont looked at me and made his eyes big to say, *Come over here and talk,* but I smiled a fake smile and held still in the comforting smell of greens. One of their voices whispered the word, "Puberty," and the six eyes glanced over at me for the visual. I looked away to the shelf of old black and white photographs of men and women in hats and fake furs, until the pepper changed hands along with two Mason jars filled with greens.

"All my love to you and your company," the woman said in a voice as crisp and refined as Richard's new tone. "Tell her I'd love for her to come down too." Something wanting and hungry in her voice made the air tight and difficult to breathe. *Ella Mae's mine,* I thought, wishing the woman could telepathically hear that Ella Mae and I were not to be separated by the newness of New York acquaintances.

We left the apartment and climbed the stairs. Her eyes and the light from her apartment held us in orbit until we reached the top landing, and she was gone.

"Creepy," I whispered to Lamont, who pinched me as soon as the door was shut.

Ella Mae sat up and cleared her throat as if it were some sin to have rested. The light outside had gone, making the apartment look more enclosed. The inside light held us in that space, where we had a quiet dinner of Vienna sausages, collard greens, and box-mix cornbread that had been made in a skillet.

Surprisingly, the food was good. Maybe it was the onions cooked into the cornbread, or the fact that the Vienna sausages had been sprinkled with pepper, or the vinegar smell from earlier that afternoon being cooked into the greens. Vinegar on greens had always been an afterthought for me, but cooked in, the greens opened up the back of my throat and made my tongue ready for the rest of the meal. We each chanted the confirmation of good food—"Um. Um. Um."—each lost in our own thoughts of what had brought us to that moment.

"Wooo!" Richard said, and started to sing real soft: "Shine, shine, shine." He and Lamont's voices in harmony like sibling-voices, and Ella Mae did not look at them, but smiled.

"The greens was good." Ella Mae said, under her breath. "Real good." She went back to the couch bed to sort through all the little remnants and make another placemat. I opened my eyes big again, determined not to speak my critical thoughts: *The food has been eaten. We really don't need more placemats now.* Lamont put his bare foot on top of my sock foot under the table, and I joined in the round, layering in "shine, shine, shine" along with them. I laughed when Lamont and Richard did, tickled that we were again in the mood that we had possessed on the porch at dusk on Halloween.

Ella Mae disappeared into the little bathroom and did not come out until we were silent, watching *How the Grinch Stole Christmas.* In black and white, all the Whos were gray; the Grinch and Max were gray. Without color, the meaning was lost, so the three of us entertained ourselves by changing the Seuss rhyme: "All the Whos down in Whoville, the straight and the gay, they all will join hands and sing 'YMCA.'"

Richard stood up and directed us to stand up too. We obliged him, including Ella Mae. And with that he showed us how to use our bodies to make a Y, an M, a C, and an A to the tune of the song "YMCA."

My arms had not been away from my body for such a long time. Maybe it was the new, musty smell of my own onion-musk underarms that had kept them down, or maybe it was the thought that if my arms ever left my sides, I might be expected to hug someone. But under Richard's direction, my arms came free from my sides, and my mouth opened and sang.

"Not, so loud, not so loud," Ella Mae muttered each time her smile was about to turn to laughter.

"Odessa," Lamont announced, out of breath, "Tomorrow I'm buyin you a coat, and I'm doin your hair."

I was not one to squeal like a girly girl, but I squealed and hugged him hard, completely forgiving him for leaving me in Mississippi and the phone call betrayal. Ella Mae smiled and sat down, and I sat down with her to even out the attention.

THE NEXT NIGHT Lamont held me still between his knees and pressed my hair, long after Ella Mae and Richard were snoozing on opposite mattresses. He used oil of bergamot to soothe the places where he'd pulled too hard with the comb, and while he worked he let me complain about school, Mississippi, and Ella Mae.

I told him the truth, the two of us open without worrying about what we should and shouldn't say in front of the others. "I don't wanna go back." I said.

He pulled my head back, looked at me with eyes that showed alarm and concern. "Is she mean to you?"

I snorted and smiled at the thought that he could possibly do anything to protect me from a woman as thick and strong and Ella Mae. "No, she's really good to me. She doesn't yell, or rush me, or punish me for anything."

He pushed my head back down in a jealous shove. "You mean she spoils you?"

"Kind of, but not with stuff. She doesn't have a lot of money; she's just like you." I picked the dirt from under my fingernails at the sudden revelation that I was equating Lamont with some-one who played the role of mother. "She gives me whatever I need, and she gives me so much space and time to say whatever I need to say to figure things out, and then to apologize if I end up saying something stupid."

He laughed out loud. "Girl, you crazy. What are you com-plaining about then? Don't tell me; you're bored."

"Yeah!" I threw my arm down off his thigh in defeat. "She doesn't say anything bad, but she also doesn't say *anything*. It's like she's being so careful with me that I don't end up knowing her at all. And lately it's like living with somebody that you can tell is having a conversation in her head, but I can't tell what it's about."

I looked at the heap of her body on the living-room floor, and I felt something for her that reminded me of when I looked at the river and knew that at the bottom there was a tempting darkness and beauty that I would never see unless I drowned.

"Like Thursday," I said. "Remember?" I turned around to face Lamont, risking a burned ear. "Something was bothering her. I even think she cried after dinner, but who the hell knows why."

"Shh." Lamont shoved me. "I feel like that a lot with Richard. It takes a long time for people to open up and trust. You were quiet with her when you first got there, but you opened up, and now she's going through her own thing. Ella Mae lived by herself for a long time with no family that she could trust beyond goin to Grandeddy Bo if a storm blew the roof off or something. But Ella Mae is your mother, girl. That means you got as much responsibility to her as she does to you. Draw her out. There's all kinds of secrets she keeps 'cause she think she protectin you."

"So Richard keeps secrets and doesn't trust because he's protecting you? And that's what Ella Mae is doing too?"

He put his hand on top of my head and turned me around like he was screwing the top on a Mason jar.

"Girl, I'm talking about doing for Ella Mae the same way she would do for you. Give and take. Emotional responsibility. Don't act so immature."

I tore the loose skin from around my fingernails while he continued to give unsought advice. "You and Ella Mae just need to be together longer and she'll get comfortable and quit being all closed up." He pulled my head back again and whispered, "You just gotta draw Ella Mae out. Not by getting on her nerves and hoping she'll slap your ass, but just draw her out."

"Okay," I whispered back. "And what are you going to do about Richard?"

He shoved my head back into place. I had exhausted him, "Okay, Miss Odessa Contessa, keep tryin to be cute. I'm tryin to give you some advice."

SATURDAY CAME TOO QUICKLY. Lamont said, "Smile," and the flash of the Poloroid captured me before I could consider saying no. He stood on the stairs of the apartment building, bars on the building's door behind him. His green knit sweater was tight around his torso; his jeans tight and flared at the bottom, with pieces of red and green velvet and little sequins punched in. I envisioned Richard at the makeshift dining-room table under the lamp light, creating the bottoms of the flares that were girly enough that I could only look at them in my peripheral vision. I didn't know about Harlem, but in St. Louis this outfit would have earned him a west-side beatdown. I imagined Deddy's baritone voice: *Faggot*.

Lamont was done shaking the photo, and he handed it to me. At first I did not see myself, but Towanda. The textured fake fur of my New York thrift-store coat made me look so much more mature. I looked at the photo sideways as if the picture would mirror my movements. The hairdo, which Lamont had created the evening before with one of Mama's stolen hot combs and a pair of trimming scissors, made a press-and-curl halo around my half-smile face. We looked at each other in a quick glance that said, *Belong.*

He said, "Did you ever finish *The Mimosa Tree?*"

"No, but I thought about it a lot while I've been here." I slid my hand along the cold stair railing and looked at the pigeons rising and falling from the adjacent rooftop. "Marvella is only fourteen and has to figure in a grown-up world how to take care of three brothers." I looked him in the eyes, seeing the light brown where the sun caught and made him clear and kin. I wanted him to understand the code of my healing, to know that I did not throw my siblings away, that in every face I saw, I looked for them; but that thinking about them on purpose when I couldn't have them was like agreeing to be tortured.

I asked him, "Have you ever read it?"

"Uh-uh." He sat down on the cold black-painted step and leaned on the black railing opposite me. His eyes cast to the street; his thoughts were elsewhere. The sky above us was a dark steel gray, a ceiling of clouds lumpy like the batting inside a quilt. "Snow clouds," he whispered.

Lamont looked at me and spoke louder. "Well, you gonna tell me about the book, right?"

I squinted one eye closed to return to the moment, because my thoughts had trailed away from the book. "It makes me miss our little brothers." Images of Benson, Daryl, and Jessie became characters in the book and I would be sad to see it end. I giggled, the way Mama used to do, to shake away the emotions creeping up. I looked off at the row of brownstones across the constant traffic, static of ragged cars with warm clouds of exhaust blowing in the chilled air.

"When you miss them," he said, "what do you miss?" I shook my head, but he persisted. "I tell Richard all of our childhood stories, especially the funny ones, and I don't miss everybody so much. I call them, but . . ." He looked down at his shifting feet and put his hands in his pockets. "I get it that you cain't do that, 'cause Mama and Deddy built it up for them not to miss you back." He paused for a moment. The gray sky pressed down on us. "You know, Odessa, when I visit and one of them opens their mouth to say something bad about you, I stop them."

I interrupted him, desperate to change the subject. "I never told Mama, but one day last summer, when I was supposed to be watching them, I plotted a day escape. After her and LaVern and Roscoe left for the store, I rushed the boys to finish their Cheerios, and I went into Mama's room, and out of each of the top drawers I took just enough change to keep it from looking robbed.

"I took them down to the basement and dressed them in front of the dryer, then out the back basement door and down the alley so the nosy neighbor wouldn't see us. We caught the bus and rode down Goodfellow to Martin Luther King Drive, then transferred. Honey, we road all the way past St. Charles County to Northeast Plaza Mall on the bus." I remembered the way my chest opened up that day, giving me the appetite for freedom, precursor to running away. "It was so cool watching them stare out the bus window like we were on a ride at Six Flags or something." I blew the memory of diesel exhaust out my nose in a stifled chuckle. "I miss them."

Lamont turned away and looked down the street as if to say, *I told you so*. I rolled my eyes and continued the story, and he turned back to listen. "Benson and them were all excited. I thought their teeth were gonna chatter the way Aint Fanny's cat used to do when he saw a bird out the window."

Lamont laughed out loud in a gut-deep voice through his hoarse throat, always more comfortable with me as long as I was being funny rather than wanting something emotional from him. "Girl, you are crazy," he sighed, and I was steered away from missing the kids by the opportunity to entertain him with embellishment. I told him how I promised them an ice cream at Baskin-Robbins if they promised not to tell, and then I remembered us at the bus stop—sticky fingers, my struggle to get the napkin turned on a new dry angle to catch Benson's drippings then Jessie's and Daryl's, and the bus screeching to a halt in front of us—and I stopped my story, eyes on Lamont's eyes like stopping to remember a dream.

And I remembered: *We'd gotten on the wrong bus. I never imagined Northeast Plaza as a hub for busses that went all over St. Louis. I rode through unfamiliar city streets for what seemed like hours, pretending not to panic, singing to the boys the songs from Gilligan's Island, the Beverly Hillbillies, until finally I told them we needed to move to the front of the bus for our stop. I whispered to the driver that I had boarded the wrong bus and needed to get back to Goodfellow and Martin Luther King. He was this huge white man whose fat belly in his blue uniform pants bubbled over the edge of the bouncing driver's seat.*

Lamont looked away and left me there staring into the remembered moment.

The bus driver looked in the rearview at the passenger in the back of the bus and said, "Hold on. Shhh." I sat back watching his feminine gestures, the way he pursed his lips in irritation with passengers who didn't signal when they wanted off the bus. I heard Deddy's voice again: Faggot! *I remembered the child molestation movie they had shown us at school, the indelible black and white image of the little boy found face down, white dress shirt and black patent leather shoes turned out awkwardly. I looked out the window trying to remember the names of street signs, all the while singing to the boys; the undercurrent in my head a chatter of reasons why this was not my fault, why I shouldn't have been left all summer with three boys, while Lamont, Tawanda, Roscoe, and LaVern had been set free from the house by one excuse or the other. I remembered how the pink and purple of dusk fell over the sky that day while the fear rose in a hard knot in my throat.*

"University City," the bus driver announced, and the black woman who reminded me of Aunt Nell exited the back of the bus. The driver reached up and rolled his sign to "Out of Service," and leaned into where the four of us sat wide eyed. "I have to go back to the garage, right past Goodfellow and Martin Luther King. I'm not supposed to carry passengers when I'm off duty." He looked both ways at the

four-way stop, then turned the big wheel, like spinning a dinner tray.
"I didn't want passengers to hear me. You never know who might tell
my supervisor that I'm being a taxi driver." He flipped his wrist in
response to the invisible people who might tell, flipped his wrist the
way Deddy flipped his wrist when teasing Lamont, just before bringing
the belt down hard: Punk. *Then accusing the son of the father's sins:*
"Faggot, and you better keep your faggot ass away from my other sons.
Fucking child molester." Faggot *and* child molester *intersected in an*
unlit alley inside my mind.

The bus squealed as he pulled up to our bus stop. In darkness these
streets no longer bore the details of garbage blown against buildings,
but it was certainly the familiar avenue of my neighborhood. When the
doors folded open, I released the stale breath that swirled in my gut,
the same breath that caught between my collar bone and sternum every
time in my life that I measured four walls with my eyes to find that
Deddy and I were alone in a room. I released that breath.

Lamont grinned, waiting for me to snap out of it. "Well, you
just gonna stop the story there? You bought the boys ice cream;
then what?" He fiddled with the sequins on his belled pants, and
I did not know I was frowning until he looked up and rolled
his neck in response. I had not realized that in remembering
this, I had paused long enough to skip time, long enough to feel
estranged from him just before having to leave. The light at the
corner had gone green, yellow, red, two times, and I'd almost
mended a circuit between the flip of the bus driver's hand, the
memory of the child molestation movies, and Lamont's fancy
jeans.

"Girl, I don't know who you think you lookin at like somethin stink." He was standing now, ready to fight, as if I was one
of the mean girls on the playground.

I answered with a question I had not intended to ask. "Did
you turn gay because you were molested by a man?"

"Girl!" Lamont said, as he always did with any reference to
the details of his elusive homosexual teen years. He stood up
and looked down the street like he was looking for a bus or

train or stage coach. "You and Ella Mae gotta get the subway and catch that bus back down to fuckin Dixie land. It's a long train ride to Port Authority."

Just like the Halloween night when the taillights of the Pinto left me in the dark, he was shut off from me. Under my breath, I cursed myself: "Shit."

Lamont said, "If y'all wanna get that bus back down south, Ella Mae's gonna have to make her way down the stairs and out the front door."

Ella Mae had once told me that an apology can go a long way to mend hurt.

I stood up too and said, "Lamont, I'm sorry." I didn't fully know what hurt my question had triggered.

He leaned in for a good-bye hug. "Don't worry about it," he said, but he did not fully embrace me. For a moment my big brother disappeared, leaving behind the little boy Deddy had seen defenseless and had preyed upon. But still, I did not mend the circuit between the pause in my story—the frown that carried the weight of molestation fears—and the question of the formula for homosexuality. He left me standing on the stoop, and before I went in to collect my things, I went to the corner store, bought two packs of green apple Now-and-Laters, and left them on the table near the Coke-bottle vase, an altar offering of apology.

I HAD TASTED SNOW, but none like Harlem snow, which set off the saliva on the back of my tongue, snow like the metal taste of the chain-link fence at the far end of the Starkville High field grounds. Jamella had said the iron there would keep me from feeling weak on the day of my period, and so with her as lookout, I had laid my mouth on that gate post, but I didn't taste any helpful minerals; just generations of playground filth on metal fencing.

I did not want to leave Lamont, did not want the flimsy reality of my newfound happiness, to be shrouded in the loneliness that resided at Ella Mae's house. The pace of my shoes on the Harlem sidewalk, two-tone brown and white, gray sidewalk concrete with names drawn there, leaf print in cement, graffiti down low on brick walls, where perhaps no one would catch the culprit.

MY MOUTH WAS WIDE OPEN to catch the steely snowflakes as Ella Mae and I retraced our steps back to the subway station. "Your hair gonna be back like before," she said, looking at me. I imagined myself in the Polaroid and realized that eating snow while walking was a childish thing to do on the sidewalks of Harlem. We walked past the blocks of brownstones, liquor stores, "God's Temple Reading Room," the awkward corner building Lamont had pointed to and said "Schomburg," which I thought sounded a lot like "Humbug," until he called me country.

As we descended into the subway, the smell of wet metal snow was traded for the hot electric-and-oil breeze created by our just-missed train. *Draw her out.* I remembered Lamont's advice. *Draw her out.*

We leaned against the wall, hundreds of layers of spray paint over cement, and I wondered how subways were built so they wouldn't cave in. I watched Ella Mae wedge our two brown suitcases between her boots, which had sustained their polish, and I remembered the question I wanted to ask Ella Mae when we arrived.

"Have you been to Harlem before? You've been here before, right?" I was talking like Lamont now, ending all of my sentences in "Right?" something he must have picked up in New York; but this mannerism seemed to annoy Ella Mae coming from me. I said, "Right? Because you know how to get around. But I thought you lived in Mississippi your whole life."

Ella Mae didn't stop looking at the black wall across the quiet tracks, and I didn't stop talking, because talking kept the anxiety of leaving Lamont at bay, kept me from admitting I had done something to hurt him but could not make heads nor tails of it, did not have the maturity to read what lay in the gaps of sexuality unspoken in the lives of siblings and parents, could not fully grasp the intricacies of silent encrypted acts that at fourteen I was on the verge of understanding.

I chattered on. "Can we stop in the part of New York that they show on *Family Affair?*" She still did not move, and took her hands away from me and put them into her pockets. I wondered if we had time to run back. Maybe I could apologize again to Lamont. Would he invite me to come back? I needed Ella Mae to talk to me so I could read in her voice if everything would be fine.

"Lamont and Richard are in a good place," I said. I pulled the one remaining piece of Juicy Fruit gum from my coat pocket and was grateful for the artificial smell of fruit over the smell of urine on cement. I popped my gum sophisticated; the echo filled the silence in the subway and drowned out the pending chatter in my head. "I can't wait for Jamella to see me in this coat, and imagine me walking through Central Park." I popped my gum again, wanting to show Ella Mae that I was mature enough to understand now that Mississippi could not be home for people like Lamont and Richard.

"This is a good place for them," I said. "I've seen a lot of men here who act like them." I crooked my elbow and let my wrist drop limp. Ella Mae turned to look at me now. I waited for her to laugh, but her words were coarse.

"You need to hush. Everybody don't want to hear you go on and on. For somebody who didn't have nothin to say on the way here, you got plenty to say on the way back."

I touched my hand to my hair where the curls had turned to an afro, and I folded into myself, knowing that whatever I was trying to say about gay men did not reside in my repertoire of experiences. Somehow my knowledge of "the homosexual" gave offense and was mistaken as the insult, "faggot"; my words caused the same turn of moods as questions about being a bastard child, the same shame as the word "rape." I wanted to defend myself, make right my intention, but I did not have the words for that either.

I wanted to change the subject again and ask Ella Mae if she could buy a pressing comb and do my hair back in Starkville, but I had talked myself out. I now hoped for the train as I fought to keep the tears of unclaimed emotions from spilling out of my eyes. That battle was lost when Ella Mae did her thing of saying a few words to maintain her world of silence: "Hush, and wait for the train."

Draw her out. I looked down at the place where her black coat sleeve entered her pocket, and I tried to remember her part of the story about me being born, tried to remember if she had said she'd held me before Granmama took me away. I blew air through my lips to turn sadness into attitude, and I settled in to my mood. I used my rough, furry sleeve to catch the one hot tear that didn't quite dry in the warm air current that preceded the train.

Chapter 10

ELLA MAE CRIED about dreams. I knew, because she did the same things I did to keep anyone from knowing I had been weeping. In the cold dampness of morning, before the sun rose, first light in the sky, before even hearing the rusty squeak of the woodstove door, I heard her slide her shower-curtain bedroom door open. I heard her clear her throat in the bathroom, and the pump water ran, then the splash of water on her face. There was the quiet blowing of her nose; not bold, the way she blew her nose in places where she shouldn't, like at the breakfast table. Then, the water in the sink again, the clearing of her throat again. I reviewed the times I'd gotten on her nerves on the trip home; the subway, the demand to go to Central Park; but no thought produced the reason for her tears. I stayed in bed for a while to spare us from shame.

The rest of that Sunday was quiet in our house. I held on to flashbacks of the YMCA dance, and the spicy walls of the downstairs neighbor, memories of the second hand on the little black and white wall clock while Lamont's knees pressed into my shoulders to hold me in place, smell of oil of bergamot on hot iron comb. I thought I would fold up when we got back from Harlem, but every time I walked through the house my arms were free, above my head or swinging loose at my side. Not like before, when there had been doors and windows shut inside me without my permission. Something about knowing the path to Lamont unhinged my fear that he would stay mad. I'd unnerved him before, and this was not different. The difference between being left three weeks ago and leaving him now was that I knew my way back to Harlem: to the bus station, then the Grayhound, change buses in Arkansas, straight to Baltimore, then to Port Authority, catch the red line uptown to 135th Street. I could remember the bold white lettering on black overhead planks in the subway station. I could remember to board the train that led to higher numbers. I could find my way back to Lenox Avenue if I had to, and that reset a sense of belonging that had been dislodged like loose rib cartilage.

On Monday, I woke up ready to get dressed, catch the bus, and get to school in my new thrift-store coat from New York. I hoped Ella Mae was ready to talk now over a breakfast of grits and sausage. I decided I would apologize for blaming her for Lamont's leaving, and I would thank her again for taking me to New York, set us straight and new, but when I moved my curtain aside there was silence. In the big room there was wood stacked in front of the fireplace, as if she had intended to light a fire to match the warmth of the one in the kitchen woodstove. The logs lay askew as if she had been interrupted. The speckled metal-and-ceramic bowl steamed with my grits, which were going hard, and I tiptoed in my wool socks to the back door to see the truck silently roll up the driveway.

I sighed in disappointment at being alone and turned back to the table, where I saw the brown-paper-bag note: *Dessa I got morning jobs to do. I will be home when skool end.* I imagined her selecting words she knew how to spell, and I took deep breaths of hickory-smoked air there in the kitchen. With every exhale went my fantasy of the new week, with Ella Mae playing the role of June Cleaver, and me as a well-adjusted teen.

Every day that week, when I got up Ella Mae was already at the loom, and she stayed there until I was off to bed. As I drifted off to sleep each night, I thought, *Draw her out*; but I was distracted by Jamella's latest holy advice, distracted by history and algebra, distracted, until new annoyance with our lives took the place of the forgotten strategy, putting Ella Mae and me in the same old standoff. Only this time she was the one withholding, and I was not capable of reciprocating the way she could; a bus ticket, new shoes to draw me out. The only thing I had in abundance for pulling poison to the surface was my attitude.

THERE WAS NO CHRISTMAS. I waited for two days before school holiday started for Ella Mae to mention it, but no mention. The usual silence over a plate of pickled beets, mashed potatoes, fried rabbit, which I always pretended was fried chicken that I ate with a knife instead of my fingers, not wanting to feel the tiny bones beneath the flesh, not wanting to remember the feel of Deddy's kill between my fingers. I finished reading *The Mimosa Tree*. All the Profit children escaped their woes in Chicago and happily returned to the country comfort of Goose Elk, where simple things like foraging for food were possible in troubled times. I shut the book, not convinced of their happy ending. What about Christmas? What would they eat when the blight had killed the crops? Like Ella Mae said, *You cain't cure or can what you didn't kill or pick.*

I SAT ON THE FLOOR on a small rectangle of rag rug in front of the fireplace with my back to the loom. My body held on to the warmth from the fire the way I held on to Marvella Profit before the novel ended, leaving me to confront Ella Mae's silence.

The beans on the cook stove bubbled in a quiet boil; beans I'd picked to steady my mind the day after Deddy left me in Mississippi, beans that had been given all fall to dry and were being softened on the stove. Their steam kept the fires in the fireplace and the woodstove from drying the air of the house. Sometimes, in moments like these, nothing on my mind but the smell of beans, I pictured them: Towanda and LaVern riding on a city bus through the gray streets of St. Louis to the mall, where the smell of food, the sound of Christmas songs and the colored lights, gave a false warmth in the chest that evaporated on the bus ride back to the west side. I lay down on the rug, adjusted my glasses, imagining them giggling and wrapping glass jars of cheap bubble bath.

Through the fingerprints on my glasses, I looked up to where Ella Mae leaned over the table, using a lamp and her one-dollar Walgreens bifocals to assist her in threading the needle.

I tried to imagine her wrapping presents, but the image was as elusive as the thread through the needle. She licked the end of the thread again and concentrated on the precision of making the thin strand fit through the tiny space, a concentration that I broke. "I need new glasses. I think my head grew since last summer."

There was nothing but the simmering hiss of steam escaping the pot top, so I went in with what I really wanted to say.

"Can we go get a Christmas tree?"

She spoke with her eyes still on the needle and her pinched fingers, and answered me with the shortest sound possible. "No."

My brow tightened at her abrupt monotone answer, and I moved my head forward on my neck, not realizing I'd expected a *Yes*.

"Why not?" I thought about the hypocrisy of asking me if there was anything that was gonna help me not miss St. Louis so much, and then just saying "No" in one breath, without asking me why I wanted the damned thing.

"Odessa, I ain't studyin about stuff that ain't real."

I rolled my eyes the way Lamont might have in a moment like this, and I thought, *What's real? Rag rugs, fires, food from last summer, no TV? What's real is boring. Nobody visits us and I'm glad we went to New York, but that was a month ago.* Once I started the barrage of complaints in my head, I remembered that I still had not tried to draw her out without waging war, but now it would be awkward to break the rhythm of my retaliation.

I said, "Everybody at school has people coming for Christmas, or is going someplace or has a bunch of sisters and brothers and is going to West Point Nursery for a tree."

"Hush," Ella Mae said quietly. She still did not look at me. Having successfully threaded the needle, she was now stitching the split in my favorite skirt, and I wanted her to yell at me, to do something to make me feel real.

"No. I don't want to hush." I was up off the floor now, still standing on my rug, but my toes gripped the grooves of the rags to hold me still where I leaned toward Ella Mae's quiet space in her chair. My voice hit the blunt wall. "I said, I don't want to hush. I feel like I'm dead, and you don't care if nobody thinks you alive, but I ain't you. You cain't even cry out loud."

Even with this stab, Ella Mae did not turn away from her stitching to look at me, and I was tethered like a June bug tied to a string. I imagined Benson, Daryl, and Jessie watching *A Charlie Brown Christmas*. The spot on the floor where I belonged was empty, and the three of them moved in tight to fill the small space I'd left.

Ella Mae finally halted with the pull of the needle, but still did not look at me. Having skin was awful in that moment. The steam from the pot of beans made my blood hot beneath my skin, and there wasn't enough air in my body to yell as loud and as long as I wanted to yell. I tried to keep the sound in my mouth so I wouldn't sound like Benson throwing one of his temper tantrums, but the sound came out in peeps that broke Ella Mae's silence, and she coughed an unexpected cough. I stormed away from the lamp light and her apologetic bifocal glance, grabbed my New York thrift-store coat off the door, stuck my sock feet in my untied muck boots, and carried myself out into the cold, damp air that made me sick to smell: too clean, no bus fumes, no smell of urine or cement, no smell of hot tamales mixed with the unidentifiable stench of factory smokestacks on the south side of St. Louis; Sulard's market, oranges, apples, stockings, vendors, all with candy canes in one basket next to whatever else they were selling, while everyone endured the cold of an open-air market; fingers reached from gloves with cut-off fingertips to select the smallest apples, which were priced at ten cents each. There was nothing of Christmas to smell on the Mississippi porch, nothing but dead leaves sweet and decaying in the cold air, and there was silence.

I stayed outside until the sky turned to fruity pink and the brown and gray tree trunks turned to black silhouettes. I stayed until my breath was steady and tight, as the cold inhalations burned on the way down, until guilt and the threat of frostbite sent me back into the house. The lamp light on the table was the only light, and beyond it the darkness of the big room, where Ella Mae's curtain masked her end of the space. I did not move there in the kitchen, not knowing if I was being watched. I did not sniff up the snot that ran from my nose. I did not want it mistaken for tearful snot.

Ella Mae stepped into the darkness and clicked on the light in the kitchen. "You cain't own a person or a thing in this world, so quit tryin," she said. "You cain't make folks talk when you want or answer you when you want 'em to."

I stayed fixed on the word *own;* the rest of her words slipped into a fuzzy background while I counted the things people owned. I opened my eyes for the confrontation. "You own this house."

"Naw. Yo Grandeddy Bo say he own this house but even he don't own it."

I said "What?" indignantly, but the fact was that she had lost me in one of her riddles of half-said things.

"It own itself, just like you own yo self, and I own myself, and that mimosa weed you put rocks around, like it need you to take care of it, own itself too."

I had the thing to stomp her sitting right in front of me. My history book sat open on the picnic table. For us, there were only two small paragraphs, as if our history didn't want to tell itself, the same way she didn't want to tell about herself; two small paragraphs of a half-said thing. "Who owned the slaves and the Indians?" I blurted out, proud of myself.

She did not pause to think, but looked me straight in the eyes. The bifocals magnified the whites of hers, with small bloodshot lines that always made me wonder if she strained them at the loom, or if red lines like highways on the map happened with age. "Same people who say they own that oak tree out there, and same people who hung somebody in it one time." She walked to the solace of her loom, pulled on the light chain, and started weaving.

Draw her out, I heard Lamont say, but I was defeated. With the image of somebody hanging from a rope just beyond the front yard, the innocence of the oak tree ruined, I was done. I could not play this game to win, because Ella Mae, despite her silence, had seen more ugly things than I had. She had stored up more animated images of death and could answer my string of questions with two or three words that would squash my whole day of stewing. All I had to fire back with was images of Kennedy Avenue, the halls of the house, Mama's voice laughing with the gold tooth, images and smells of Deddy, that made my rib cage close whenever the thoughts came close to the surface of my knowing.

But then my mind played hopscotch, cheated, skipped right over the first five numbers and landed where the stone had never been. My mouth opened with a true question that I had not anticipated asking. "I'm your daughter. Do you own me?"

Ella Mae slid slow on the loom seat and glided away from me until she reached the end of the loom and the jarring of the stop almost spilled her onto the worn, knowing boards of the floor that held our history. I could hear my infant voice crying, arresting the silence of the house. My heart thumped in tangled rhythms. The fire popped in the vast space between the picnic table and the loom, her womb only one small cavity that had not been fashioned to hold us both.

"I'm sorry," I spoke helplessly into the silence. A tear came cold and unexpected onto my cheek, tricking me the way the question had. I mumbled under my breath, trying to label the unnamed emotions, "I wasn't . . . I didn't . . . don't answer, I mean." I breathed through my nerves, unsteady in the risky space where I had used my words in such a way that she was shifted, as Lamont had been shifted. When Ella Mae and I had split the wood, she had told me that the stake and the sledge-hammer were the right tools to make perfect wedges for the wood stove, but if I used them wrong; I could knock the cap out of my knee.

Ella Mae reached down and picked up the bottom of the rug that flopped like a weighty sunset on the floor at her feet. She smelled the end of it, and her hair fell like a crow's wing, making a veil between us.

She peeked through the strands that separated us with surrendered eyes, and I saw for an instant the wild woman with glowing green eyes and killer fingernails, the mythical ghost of Ella Mae that St. Louis cousins conjured in dark bathroom mirrors.

Ella Mae straightened up. "Odessa, why don't you stay quiet till you find what you really hurtin over, 'stead of trying to hurt somebody else just 'cause you hurt and bored." Her words came while she cleared her throat and fiddled with the red cord she'd pulled from the edge of the rug, but she still did not look at me.

The smell of last night's pork chops hung in the cotton of her work shirt, and though I felt it was too late, she said what had been unsaid. "When we got back from New York . . . Well, I'm sorry." I saw the little girl in her again, the apology a thread that pulled me back to her.

I opened my mouth, but she shushed me, "Shhh, I'm the grown-folk. I'm not tryin to make you left to make stuff right. I'm just trying to walk back down some road and open up my heart again, but seem like I just stand at the doors scared to move." She began to rock, slow. "I'm still owning the *you* that I was told was dead, and don't know how to make like this be the same *you* right here, and I still got my heart stuck where another somebody left it even though the whole world done moved on. Seem like too much to ponder on at once." She looked away now, up at the hand-placed rafters of our home. "Sometime when you askin for stuff that ain't somethin I can go up to the Walgreen and buy, I feel like you gonna strip away the only thing that keeps me safe . . . quiet." We both coughed out nervous giggles and almost looked at each other.

She walked past me and sat down at the picnic table, and I joined her. We were quiet together; and somehow we would have to eventually leave the picnic table, wipe the tears and do normal things like work on my history project and make dinner, but all that seemed awkward and impossible. I looked at her sideways profile next to me on the bench—we were the same height when we sat—and I wondered if she looked at me as the girl who stole the dead baby that she had curled up with in a grave. Hearing her tell of the born-dead baby was truth affirmed in pain, the way being born affirms pain, the way I imagined giving birth affirms pain; it was true, I was her born-dead baby in the flesh, and she was my mother.

My words skipped the stone again. "I ain't dead, and you ain't dead either, Ella Mae."

She was off the picnic bench, air and space of the dark room between us, and I heard the shower-ring curtain of our bathroom door before I realized she had gotten up. The water ran, the pump handle squeaked again, the water ran, and beneath it, the sound of a girl's voice, crying for something forever undone. I didn't know what to do, so I sat at the table not moving, not moving, not thinking, making patterns out of the places beneath the slate hearth under the cookstove where settled ashes made pictures like clouds: an elephant's head, a whistle from a box of Cracker Jacks, a suitcase. *Why doesn't she have an electric stove?* I wondered, and got up to turn on another lamp, the greasy black metal one that perched on the shelf, a safe space from the heat of the stove.

IN THE MORNING, Ella Mae shuffled into the kitchen, where I sat listening to the sounds of morning and waiting to feel awake. Something in her had surrendered, surrendered and brave in coming into the kitchen with the tears and her glasses still perched on her nose, her hair behind her ears now. I had not noticed the thinning of her face before. I always saw the woman who had approached me in the field of hay, but now she was Granmama, standing there, still in the bifocals, her eyes intent on mine, softened. She did not look away from me. More tears came, steadily, making her cheeks shiny, and I could not look at her; the sacrilege of a crying mother could not be undone if looked upon, could not undo the stepped-on cracks and the breakage in a daughter's spine.

"I think you need to look at me," she said, her voice deep and hoarse. "I ain't a crazy woman with long killer fingernails. I'm your mother."

She held out her hand. Conscious of the strangeness of touch, I put my hand in hers and let her find the way to shape her arms around my body that would allow us to stay in that moment long enough to feel the broken family line of mother and daughter reconnect. The light of the house held us; cookstove, fireplace, lamp over half-woven rug at the loom, white glow of history book pages splayed on the picnic table, the light of day coming into the sky.

WE SAT TOGETHER at the table over grits and skillet bread. Ella Mae sat across from me. The small red rope she had pulled from the rug last night was silky in the morning light that streamed in through the curtained panes of the window. She reached to finger the rope and cleared her throat to speak clear and strong. "I'll tell you about stuff that keep me quiet." She wiped her face with her work shirt and cleared her throat again before sitting up in recitation. "I was in the store one day, a long time back, and a song came on, sound like a bird the way that white lady sang, kind of whispery, and I wasn't paying no attention, just tryin to get some canned beans, 'cause the fungus got all the pole beans, and I was needin somethin other than cucumbers 'cause look like that's all would come up that summer. The song say, 'You cain't lose what you don't own,' or somethin to that effect." Ella Mae lifted her head up like she was going to sing like that bird lady, and I lifted my head up with her, but she didn't sing; she just said the words, in a deliberate attempt to recall. "You cain't lose a thing that you don't own."

She looked back down at the little piece of rope again, tunneling off into her memories. "Something about that was true for me. It was a year and a half after Mama had said you was dead, and I had lost . . ." She stopped and took her hands off the table and put both hands in her pants pockets. "Well, seemed like I had already come out my shell once after you was gone, and wasn't nothin waitin for me, but I understood them words from that one song, and I didn't want to own nobody but me, 'cause wasn't no chance in losing myself." She looked at me beneath her glasses, both hands still in her pockets. "Don't you never get like that. Lamont and folks got to move around and do what they got to do in life. Shuttin the door ain't gonna help nothin. I don't wanna be that way no more neitha." She took her hands out of her pocket and fingered the small piece of red rope again. She exhaled so long, like the women in the movies exhaled their cigarette smoke, relaxation overcoming anyone who watched.

She fingered the rope again and blew the long exhale again. "I could feel affection for a person once. It was the only time since those few seconds of joy feelings that I had when you were born; your eyes in the bloody water in the tub was like the eyes in all the dreams I had when I was pregnant. I still dream that smell of warm water going cold on my legs mixed with that scent of menses, of animal fluid, water that's been run through the body and turned red or yellow."

She went back to fingering the red rope, and looked at me, then back to her own fingers. "Look at my hands. They so old now, like old onion skins. I felt something though with her. You know?" My mind shifted through her words now for the "her." Was it me as a baby, that distant me, that I only knew through her memory?

"Ella Mae," I said. I sat with my legs on the inside of the picnic table to show her that I was listening but that I didn't understand. "You talkin about *me* when you say *her*?" I hoped the answer was yes, and that this would lead to a conversation that would give me more texture of me and her, more reason to stay in off the porch, to stay out of the imaginings of a St. Louis Christmas.

"No, well, I was for a minute." She waved one hand in agitation with her train of thought. "I was tryin to tell you," she created an agitated rhythm with her words, emphasizing each one, and whispering like somebody might hear her. "I-was-tryin-to-tell-you-a-bout one time being in love."

Other people made straight lines with what they had to say, but when Ella Mae *did* talk—she took bits and pieces from here and there, this memory and that thing said, until after a long while I saw it all turn into something. Sentences weaved together like rags until I saw a rug that looked like sunset; but to see it required stillness for some unforeseen amount of time. I sighed and let her voice be the only one while I thought about putting more wood in the stove and opening the door to see if the morning chill had turned to a balmy stillness, or if we were in for a cold, crisp day. The light at the windows and the stiffness of my grits said we'd already been sitting there for at least an hour. I occupied myself with cutting into the hard grits with my spoon until her words shaped into images.

"This was the ribbon off her robe . . . there's a little piece in every rug, but it ain't but this little thing now." She pulled a little piece of light blue rag from the other pocket. "This was a blanket I had made when I knew you was coming, and there's a little piece of this in every rug too, but one day it'll be gone too."

She handed the blue swatch to me, and I rubbed it between my index finger and thumb, smelled it, the same belonging, like the "knowing" my other siblings had through baby photos. She looked at me and then at the wall like somebody might step out of the wood. "I'm so old now I wouldn't know what to say if I ever let her see me. I don't want her thinkin I'm expectin somethin from her." She waved her hand and shook her head. "I done messed that up anyway now. She gonna think I jus got in touch 'cause I need somethin and now I feel like I got to explain stuff that's so old I cain't half remember what was what." She didn't seem to notice that I had stuffed the blue swatch in my overall pocket.

I was not yet able to make sense of her story. Part of me wondered what she was talking about, but somewhere in my brain I understood the confusion of waiting too long to tell about the sins in your heart until no one would believe you because of the passage of time. Somewhere in that place I understood her cryptic speech.

She looked out the kitchen window, where white clouds raced across light blue. "I do still dream, though, and she just be laughin with me in that thin airy way she laughed that winter. I don't know if I want the real life of now to turn that into anything else."

I tried to piece together some images from her rag words. I could see a robe, a red rope tied around it, and I heard a laugh that I conjured from the millions of laughs I'd heard; but the "her" was still without form.

I waded through the quiet that Ella Mae said was necessary sometimes, tiptoed past her to turn on the light in the big room. The fire was practically out in the woodstove. I laid two logs, laid kindling between them, lit it, laid two more logs crossways, and looked over at the rug that lay limp on the floor, parts of my dead-baby-blanket stitched there. There were prominent white people in Starkville who had Ella Mae's rugs in their houses, and their soft, pale feet waltzed on baby blanket blue and mysterious red ribbon.

"Merry Christmas," I said in the space of silence, the sweetness of breath just before words. "Merry Christmas," I said again, placing this Christmas in its own reality, like pasting the evidence of photos into albums. The smell of cedar that usually lingered just beyond the woodshed was fragrant in the red, exposed flesh of a piece of wood in the stack. I laid my hands on the split, dried piece of tree that Ella Mae and I hauled weeks ago. Our sweat had changed us from stranger to familiar, and it was somewhere reflected here in the pulp. I took the smaller pieces into the kitchen, opened the vents on the cookstove, removed one of the plates with the iron handle, and realized that I wanted it this way; wanted the smell of smoked wood in my clothes, the warmth of heat by fire in the bones, the predictability of calm, something that a St. Louis Christmas could not provide. I replaced the lid on the cookstove as morning turned still and peaceful, with the silence of the sun leaning across the floor now. *Round yon virgin, mother and child,* I sang in my thoughts and returned to the eyes at the table that worried over the piecemeal story.

The smell of everything inside the house was awakened, years of hickory smoke in walls, new smell of new daughter, homemade lavender soap, mixed with a scent that had lain dormant; the smell of some other person, of some spice that was familiar on the back of my tongue, familiar spice that lay just beneath the powder of dry tree bark.

I breaded two rabbit legs with flour, salt, and pepper, knowing soon she would do the silent dance of laying the legs in hot oil. I wiped my fingers off and sat back down at the picnic table. My history book was still splayed open. I resigned myself to chores and reading, letting go of the expectation of time or of getting a beginning or ending to Ella Mae's story. I existed on the other side of her memories that finally resumed in words.

"I wasn't brave," she said, looking down at the rope between her fingers. "Lamont and Richard are so brave."

I watched her through my glasses; she glanced at me over the bridge of her glasses that were dirtied with flour, and I looked at my history book and prepared to listen as the pepper dust lodged in the back of my throat.

"Get ya coat on," Ella Mae said. "Just leave all that." She waved at the breaded rabbit legs. "We'll be back before anything can creep out to eat it."

I opened my mouth to question her, but she was already up, getting her coat off the hook, and then she sat at the end of the bench and stuck her feet in boots. Almost left behind, I followed her command, quickly slipping my socked feet into the coolness of my boots, hat, scarf, and one arm in my CPO jacket, the dressy New York thrift-store coat impractical and left behind.

We drove through cold, dry air, leafless trees, blue sky. I didn't have the heart to tell her that West Point Nursery would not be open on Christmas day. We cracked the windows on the truck to keep the windshield from fogging up while we had the heat on. The red, rusty truck switched through the twists and turns of the neighborhoods, where smells of stuffing and normalcy tempted my jealousy. Ella Mae craned her neck to see the daytime decorations outside people's houses. She nodded at one and said, "That looks cute, don't ya think?" I was relieved to be let into her thoughts again.

We pulled into the empty parking lot of the Walgreens. We sat there a moment, Ella Mae staring out, calculating the reality, and me trying to wait, be respectful, not say the first thing on my mind: *They won't be open on Christmas.* A cackling, dark cloud of starlings landed in a swoop of squeaking and pooping. They lifted up in a wave and landed again. Ella Mae turned and grinned at me like a little girl. "Wow," I said, reaching for the crank for the window, then thinking about the consequence of birds overhead. They lifted up and down again in another wave, and did it again, making a black ocean of the parking lot, making the red rusty truck the center, the red buoy in that sea. She put her hand on mine. "That's what I do on Christmas," she said, and I giggled and giggled, feeling discomfort at the way the air entered my lungs cold and exited warm. This was the first time I had ever embodied and understood the word *love*.

WHEN WE GOT HOME, I headed toward the house, bracing against the chilly air, but Ella Mae tugged at the elbow of my CPO jacket, and the softness of her smile said there was another adventure yet to be had. I returned the smile with a laugh that tumbled out easier.

She held up the frame of the hacksaw. "I'll put the blade on this thing. You run in the house and put the rabbit meat and stuff in the ice box, before somethin really do get it." She chuckled, and the sound of her laughter gave me energy to bound up the steps in one leap.

With little clouds of breath in the cold air above us, we walked side by side to the naked trees, through the stubborn green of the live oaks, and to the tiny fir trees that insisted on growing beneath them. Ella Mae handed me the saw and gestured at the nearest fir. I knelt down and held the blade up to the trunk, but Ella Mae said, "Don't hold the saw like that, and let's apologize or something to the tree before you go hacking away at it like that." A chuckle escaped both of our throats, but we were silent for a moment, letting the damp air hold our wishes.

I remembered that I could cut my kneecap off or put my eye out or any number of horrific things if I didn't use the saw right. I bit my bottom lip and worked while Ella Mae coached me: "Now you doin the opposite. Don't be scared of it; just cut."

My chocolate brown scarf became more sloppy around my neck as heat escaped from my body and I sawed back and forth. Little fir twigs fell on my head and face, but I ignored them, my focus full on finishing before Ella Mae could tell me to move and let her do it. But instead I heard her say something that sounded like, "You mine."

I stopped sawing and looked up at her, the silhouette of her face against the lace of tiny green oak leaves and sky. Ella Mae's stern look, as if her face had been molded that way, like the day she had walked me to Granmama's casket, the colors of yellow and black lace veils blending with the oak tree back-drop and the last of the sunlight. She softened into a smile that reflected the lips of Granmama, and someone I did not yet know but whose smile was stored in hers, and she said it again. "You mine."

THE FOOD WAS WELL-DESERVED and tasted better with the smell of fresh-cut fir tree in the house. I was content to start the dishes while Ella Mae sat at the table picking her teeth, and she continued unpacking her suitcase of memories, this time talking *to* me, as opposed to just talking.

"It's too late now," she said. "I'm like a old rusty wheel, set so long I cain't do nothin but stay put."

I did our dishes and didn't turn from the sink until I heard her sniffling and then scuffling to leave the table, no doubt headed for the curtained bathroom, where the water would soon run to mask the crying. *Not again*, I thought, *please don't disappear again.*

But, she bypassed the bathroom and walked past the Christmas tree, sifted a branch between her fingers along the way, and sat down at the loom. A sigh of relief escaped me, and she turned to click on the lamp to compensate for the waning daylight. She looked at me before sitting down and starting the comforting clap-and-slide movement of weaving the rug that had been abandoned for a day.

I put a piece of wood in the cookstove, clicked on the kitchen lamp and sat at the picnic table to begin writing my history report: "The Spanish-American War." I was anxious for us to get beyond the pages in the history book where drawings and paintings of wooded areas and men with beards fought against men in pointy hats so we could get to the last pages, where there was a photo of Martin Luther King Jr.

The loom went quiet. Into the space where I was lost in the slow reading and rereading of pages, Ella Mae said, "Wanna go get some rags from the dump?"

"I don't think they'd be open on Christmas Day," I answered, smiling at the fact that she was like a little girl, energy not yet all used up and looking for another adventure. I sat up from the book to return the conversation and hold her there. The tree sat behind her chair, prominent and undecorated, but we both appreciated it just the way it was.

"I want it to snow," I added, looking up at the window.

"Harumph." She huffed like Mama. It must have been something Granmama did too, because the "harumph" was the sound of all the aunts. With my teeth tight, fingering the outline of Martin Luther King's photo, I promised myself, *I'll never harumph.*

Ella Mae said, "It don't snow here except like a little crop dusting every few years." She slid and clapped the loom.

I put my hand on the lips and mustache of the man in the photo, and I felt something lost and something shameful. I was four when he was murdered. I said, "Did you ever see Martin Luther King Jr.?" Ella Mae harumphed again, and in response to my question her head turned to the loom, and her hair fell, veiling her from me.

She didn't answer, and I spoke above the loom, trying to keep my silent vow to ask what I wanted to ask but not to make her disappear. "Did you ever see him?" I could feel her trying to stay and not vanish, and inside my head I scrambled for something else to talk about. I felt little ants of irritation itching under my skin, the way I felt when I was little and Lamont sat in front of the console TV watching *Star Trek*, and no matter what I said or how I said it, he didn't even so much as flinch. I raised the volume of my voice to reach out past the fireplace and over to where she sat on her perch. "Wow, can you smell how fragrant the tree is? I better put some water in the bottom."

She let loose an unexpected grunt of laughter and we both laughed, me adjusting my tone to see if we were laughing nervously or if something I said was actually funny.

The window shined moonlight through the backdrop of her curtain, making the room look orange. I heard her exhale in a slow, steady stream, then slide, metal rollers on worn wood supporting her weight and carrying her away from the conflict. Her body settled into a slumped letter *C* before she spoke again, slow. "She said things to me like 'open your eyes and be free.'" I sat still, trying not to respond to her voice, telling myself to be quiet and read my book.

Her voice came softly again into the space where I sat at the picnic table, having turned up the volume in my head on the silent reading of my history book; but this time when Ella Mae spoke, I knew she was present.

"When I looked at her, I was afraid to keep looking, but I couldn't look away, the way it was when I saw your eyes in the tub that day, the way it is when I look at myself in the mirror and then make myself look away. When I looked at her, there was more spirit than flesh." Ella Mae stopped and looked over at me, the gray streak in her hair lit by the lamp over her shoulder.

I walked into the big room and sat butt bones on the lumps of the sunset rag rug, streaks of the red ribbon in spare contrast to the orange t-shirt she had found at the dump, hanging loosely on a pole. The light green of a work rag came from a neatly folded pile that had been sitting on top of a black plastic bag in a dumpster. Sky and sunset, and red robe tie against my bottom. The dry heat of the fire promised to hold me there until the story that had forced tears from her every morning since New York had been woven into something whole.

Ella Mae said, "Student Nonviolent Coordinatin Committee. That's what brought her here. She said I was *intimidated* by my circumstances. I didn't even know what the hell she was talkin about. I swear I didn't know I was ignorant until I met her.

"She was in the white general store in town, and I'd gone in there to get good beans, 'cause like I said didn't no good ones grow that year, and I also needed the good thread that they didn't sell at the Negro general store. By that time the store had been taken over by Piggly Wiggly, and they had put in one of them automatic doors that made you feel like God when you approached, and the door just flew open." Ella Mae held her hands in prayer stance then flung them apart. "Negro folks and Indians had to go in past the manager's desk and check out in the line near the manager's eyesight."

She stopped, and the memory on her face made the aged,

tight, yellow skin look young again. She smiled, and like a baby mimicking, I smiled too.

"She was standing there in a brown jockey hat and a short black leather jacket. Weirdest outfit I ever saw a woman have the nerve to wear. Her skin was blue black and her eyes like a wolf, so strong it was hard to look. The three black boys stood proud in the wrong checkout, protesting with her, but the boys were invisible to me. I didn't want to stare at her, but I did. Just stood there like a fool. They had come in for some lunch meat for their travels to Memphis and had just decided to have a little quiet protest right there."

Ella Mae clapped down and slid out of the lamp light. I had not realized the moonlight was gone in the sky. I turned to the window in the kitchen door and it was black, our Christmas tree lit only by the light in the room. I didn't remember ever hearing Ella Mae hum before, but she hummed then, the tune to "Walk with me Lord." I hugged my knees, comforted by corduroy as I remembered Granmama humming that song and holding me, the back of my small skull against her breast bone where I sat in her lap facing a plate of greens and rutabagas.

The humming drifted into story again. "I followed them out of the store after the manager had cursed and told the white girl, 'Just ring the niggers up so they'll get the hell out of my store.' And some bone cracked in my chest. I mean really popped, like when my knee cracks and pops."

Ella Mae touched fingers between her breasts, which were always covered and not calling attention to themselves.

"Outside," she continued, with her fingers still there, "outside she did that stare she does, like her eyes can see through me. She stood beside that old DeSoto with her friends. She motioned for me to come here." I began to imagine the parts of the story that would surely take Ella Mae days to get to: this woman turned out to be her only friend, and she was hung by the Klu Klux Klan, maybe in the oak tree that Ella Mae said owned itself. I had gotten to the scene of the imagined funeral when I felt myself getting sleepy, and a knot formed in the back of my neck signaling the coming of my period. I sat up at the fireplace, my back unsupported. In my mind, her story did not grow clearer, but more obscure, and my eyes grew heavy, like when I was little and tried to stay awake in my bed and listen to Mama's TV, my goal to be awake for Johnny Carson's monologue; but I didn't remember ever hearing one joke.

Somewhere in the space before dreaming, I thought I heard Ella Mae say, "I loved her." Then there was the squeaking of the woodstove door; late-night footsteps and a last load of wood placed in the fireplace to keep us warm. "Odessa, go to bed." Lines of rag rug and crumbs of wood on my cheek.

In the morning, I sat at the table, picking crust from the corners of my eyes, eating peach preserves on store-bought bread. Ella Mae brought her coffee grounds to a boil in the kettle, the smell tempting. The big red-crested woodpecker made that "ye-ye-ye" cry he made when he'd finished beating the cold wood for the bugs that huddled in the dead poplar for winter.

"He's gonna bring that tree down," Ella Mae said. "Then we can split it up for wood." She chuckled at her own joke. I tried to be as awake as she'd obviously been for hours. "Odessa, you wanna walk to Bo's and call Lamont?"

"No thank you, I'll wait till we go to town." Undistracted from the story of the night before, I asked sleepily, "Tell me more about the lady."

She stirred in her coffee cup and did not hesitate, as if she had resolved to tell everything. "We wrote letters straight through the winter. I drove into the post office every day, even if I had just gotten a letter from her, 'cause one time letters did come two days in a row. She sent me pictures of her with this friend and that one, posing at holiday parties, at SNCC meetings, the background just full of papers and ashtrays and Coke bottles. I thought that's what Harlem was: ashtrays, newspapers, and Coke bottles. 'This is where it's all happening,' she'd say."

I perked up. "She lived in Harlem?" Ella Mae did not answer me, but sipped her coffee and continued. "You see, I didn't understand how that could be where it was all happening, 'cause I thought the whole white-Negro problem was down south, and north is where folks went to get away from it. What was I gonna do anyway in Harlem? In every letter, she asked if I had gone and got a TV yet or if I had a phone yet."

I smirked and said, "Ella Mae, I've been asking that too."

She didn't entertain my joke. "Anyway, I told her that if what she say was on TV, people being beaten and hosed down, folks speaking in ways that she said made her hurt in her heart, hurt for being human, then that didn't sound like anything I wanted to be bothered with. She sent me a bus ticket, and I packed on that day in June that was the anniversary of the day I lost my baby, 'cause I just wanted to go somewhere, anywhere. But didn't go, 'cause as much as I wanted to run away from the memory, I got to feeling so heavy, thinkin 'bout that time . . ." She shook her head, and her voice rattled like it was going over potholes in the road. "All the thoughts came again about what I did to make it happen in the first place and what I did that the baby had to die."

She stopped talking and put her hand on top of mine. "That's just how I was feeling then, 'cause I didn't know you was alive."

In the pit of my stomach hot air swirled and cramped at the sight of me, tiny and pruney like the little formaldehyde pigs in science class. Ella Mae took her hand off mine, and it felt like all the fluid in my body pulled with her. I counted the days of the moon: twenty-fifth, twenty-sixth, twenty-seventh . . . it was time for my period, and I could smell the vinegar and warm, stale blood scent that still hung in the dry heat of the trail Ella Mae had wafted into the kitchen. She was bleeding too, and I folded my arms over my gut. I stood up, and her hand reached tentatively for mine. "I got you some pads. They's in there under the sink."

I came back and stood in the space between the big room and the kitchen, watching her. She had changed into a shirt and jeans and cut an onion over a pot of potatoes, and she spoke into the steam, picking up the story where she'd left off. "I didn't even use the ticket, 'cause I couldn't even get out the bed that day."

I was nauseated there in the pit of my belly, but I was determined to hear the rest of the story.

"A week later the mail truck pulled up, the man knocked, and left the letter; 'hand deliver' stamped on it in red. It was another ticket with a note that say, 'Come where you are appreciated for being who you are. You are beautiful.' And I went with that note to that same little piece of mirror in the bathroom and couldn't figure what she meant, but I drove to the bus station, left my truck there. Just let myself stay in the fog I was in. Told myself I didn't want to think. I cain't remember packing, but I did. I remember bein' in the truck and the gravel road, and then next thing . . ." Ella Mae's voice smoothed out. "I laughed out loud when I snapped out of it and was lookin at my red truck in the parking lot of the bus station, and there I was, Mae on the bus, and for the first time was leavin Starkville." She elongated her neck with pride.

I thought about the foolish voices of Mama and Aunt Nelle making up stories about a ghost for their children to have as a horror game, while Ella Mae was trying to live in ways that Mama and Deddy didn't have the courage to live. I said, "That was really brave. I mean, you didn't even know this lady and you just hopped on a bus." I was smiling with her, but then her smile settled into a straight face, her eyes on the unfinished work of red rope threads at the loom. I pinched tight to keep the blood of my period from coming in the gush that would surely bleed past the pad.

I walked across the cool wood of the floor to the kitchen, where Ella Mae sat with a cup of kettle coffee, and our eyes met.

"Mm-hm," she said, acknowledging that a question hung in my eyes.

"Can you just tell me who she was and why you're telling me this story? Did you hang out with her and the SNCC people? I mean, obviously you've been to Harlem, but when I asked you that last night, it was like a secret-agent moment."

"Odessa!" she said above my monologue. "Hush." There was silence between us, the muted knocking of the determined woodpecker on hard wood, his red crest giving him away in the morning light. The sound of steam rose up from the kettle, and right in the middle of the whistle, when there were words I might miss, she offered the important words of her story: "She owns the brownstone." I quickly catalogued the very few brownstones in my memory until I was in Harlem, the two of us in winter coats standing outside Lamont and Richard's apartment. Ella Mae sipped her coffee, and goose bumps rose at the reality of her words. "I sent them to her for a place to rent, but I couldn't go down there and see her." Her voice rose to a whine on "her." She waved her hand like she was waving away the steam of a cup of coffee, and my mind almost saw something there in the curve of her shoulder blades and the tilt of her head. I almost understood something in the puzzle of her words, like almost spotting the likeness of an owl in the camouflage of a dead tangle of woods.

I had to pee, my bladder crammed full and bloated, but I held on, remembering the name of the overly gracious neighbor, Ms. Olatunde. The smell of spices that warmed the blood came back to me: cinnamon, cardamom. And I asked, all of me wanting full understanding. "Ella Mae?"

"What?" she didn't turn to me, but let me view her in profile, in half-presence.

"Why didn't you go to see her? She was your best friend. Her place is nice; she seems like a nice person." I shrugged. Her friend could be someone I could visit too when I went back to Harlem, now that I knew this woman was no stranger. "She probably thought you didn't want to see her. She even asked about you. You finally came, and you didn't even go see her?"

Her shoulders let go, and she looked at me the way my math teacher did when I missed the most basic of algebra concepts. There was a long draw of breath through snot over the steam of a coffee cup held with two hands. The sun broke just above the trees in the door window. The woodpecker's one eye paused on us.

We were all still. I felt some trapped spirit exit the house like a swarm of wasps going up through the chimney, out through the cracks behind the sink where field mice entered at night, through the small spaces around window panes, through Ella Mae's eyes.

She faced the door window now. "Odessa, I loved her like Lamont loves Richard."

Part 2

Chapter 11

I SAT IN BED with Ella Mae in the dim nighttime shadows of Lamont and Richard's apartment. It was long after sunset; we had too much Thanksgiving dinner in our bellies. Lamont and Richard lay curled up like fraternal twins, their breath one rhythmic, sweeping whisper.

I could feel Ella Mae contemplating touch; I sat vigil-like, waiting within the suspended space of a newborn's breaths. My eyelids heavy. I heard her whisper, "I have been a woman," not knowing if she'd actually opened her mouth or if I'd heard her the way she said she once heard me speaking inside her womb.

I extended my foot from beyond the covers to touch her back, to feel if she got up to go do what she needed to do. My eyelids heavier, I dreamed her voice in the recitation of poetry like a lullaby, calling love:

I want you to see me.
I want to be fully visible, fully reconciled.
At this point in my life,
I don't want to be the one they murder.
I want to be the one that lives with intention.
At this place in my heart,
I want to reach into the spaces
where briers and sticker bushes threaten and snag.
I want to bring forth in my embrace the black berries,
the roses, the food and medicine.
At this point in my life,
if you dream of me like I dream of you
and if you are willing to pull those dreams into the light,
I will stick my whole self into the depth of thorns for you.

Above sleep, there was the sound of Richard and Lamont's apartment door closing, then the muted slam beneath me of Ms. Olatunde's door, muffled like the thump inside the chest. Ms. Olatunde's door did not make another sound until dawn's steel blue light shone in the tranquility of the room.

I looked at Lamont and Richard. They stirred, but kept sleeping. I sat upright on the mattress and even in the dim electric light of the sky, even then I could see the clear beauty, the element that had been missing in Ella Mae's face, the bridge between desolation and home that her spirit had traversed. I could see Ella Mae's whole beauty.

In the darkness where I slept, my jaw slack, my mind still in the clairvoyance of dream, she explained her absence, *We were up talkin, that's all. Don't get no ideas.*

I didn't remember her coming to bed or turning over and heavily sleeping, but the rocking of her body made images of blue waves that leapt in inverted teardrops up to the sky until the yellow warmth of sunrise over Harlem consumed us.

Chapter 12

M OST OF MY SIXTEENTH YEAR was sweet and cyclical; me and Ella Mae on a routine that I recognized not as boring but predictable and safe. We had established a tradition of spending Thanksgiving in Harlem, where I could visit Lamont and Richard, and Ella Mae could visit Ms. Olatunde.

On Thanksgiving that year, there was something golden about the light in their apartment. I felt all the bones in my body respond to the rhythm of sunrise, sunset, seasons and belonging. That feeling of being ready to live. And I reached for the sun and stooped with the cold unafraid of dying or losing.

Richard came into the kitchen with his boom box and made an odd request. "Can I just push 'record' and get the real live sounds of our Thanksgiving?"

Ella Mae and Ms. Olatunde looked at each other and communicated something with their eyes, the way couples do. They both sat with their backs resting on the chipping paint of the kitchen cabinet, the five of us awkwardly crammed in the one-butt-kitchen despite the fact that the table made from a door and stools would have provided more space. The two of them stared their answer of *No* with tongues foraging behind closed mouths to search for leftovers. I stood at the stove making frosting for the chocolate cupcakes in the tiny oven. I turned my thoughts away from the imagined picture of their lips locked.

Three years of Thanksgivings had moved Lamont and Richard from Vienna sausage meals to collards, cornbread, macaroni and cheese, canned cranberry sauce, and turkey strips that I teasingly called "almost a turkey." Lamont said with a laugh, "Richard, you don't ever give up the anthropology thing. Somebody needs to be studying you."

Richard said, "Look around. You have the old queer regime," he pointed at Ella Mae and Ms. Olatunde, "and the new queer regime," he put his fanned out fingers on his chest and poked out his bony hip in hip-hugger jeans. I saw Ella Mae's earlobe move the way it did when she was chewing or when the tension of a thing caused top molars to grind against bottom molars.

"What's my regime?" I asked, not turning from the stove. "The 'little straight girl in the queer wood' regime." They all laughed, except Ella Mae. Even I mustered a giggle so I'd be on the inside of the joke, not the butt of it.

Ms. Olatunde put her hand over Ella Mae's hand, and it settled there as if it had always belonged.

Richard put one hand on his hip, and rolled his eyes, snapped his finger in the air. "Okay, I'm trying to be respectful. Can I push 'record'?"

I giggled louder than necessary and stirred the frosting for my still-unfrosted chocolate cupcakes. Finally Richard sat the recorder next to me, pushed "record," batted his eyelashes and walked away. I fell subconsciously silent into thoughts. The two of them had become so much more flamboyant. I guess being the gay men in the queer woods of Harlem made the flipped wrists and the overenunciated s's seem fashionable and vogue. I worked hard to stifle any negative reaction: staring, frowning, or flinching under the spell of my thoughts. I loved Lamont, but didn't want to see him and Richard kiss; nor did I want to think about the possibility of men's body parts revealed in magazines. And more than that, I didn't want to imagine Ella Mae as having any of the same desires that sent my own hands on the journey of an imagined lover beneath the naked warmth of my sheets on cold Mississippi nights. I fantasized about the moment I would feel a boy's tongue against mine, but agitated nerve endings writhed in my belly at even a millisecond thought of men with men or women with women.

Ms. Olatunde swallowed a bite and said, "Racism and homophobia are the same; people have trained themselves to feel disgust at the sight or mention of black people sitting where they would soon sit or sipping water where they would soon sip water." She pulled her long neck away to look at Ella Mae, though Ella Mae looked at the stove, where I frosted the cupcakes, "Richard's research is good. People can be trained toward a good response when seeing a homosexual person as easily as they can be trained toward a positive response at seeing and knowing more black people."

The thought of being "trained" at all made me feel small and ignorant. I just wanted to control my negative responses toward my brother and stop myself from worrying about what would likely never happen between Ella Mae and Ms. Olatunde, who were much too old to act like gay people.

The four of them retired to the other room for the sociology and human behavior discussion, leaving me to finish frosting the cup cakes. I put the spatula down and scratched at my wrist; the pink t-shirt Lamont had bought for me itched where the long sleeves were laced at the bottom. I wasn't one to dress like a black Cyndi Lauper, but liked the embraced feeling I got from the gifts he and Richard got me.

I frosted the chocolate cup cakes slowly, thinking through the shifting current of my thoughts—warmth of family, but not a family I could show to anyone else and still feel that same warmth; my brain still too young to know that houses could be built of blood, straw, or tin. The integrity of the house was in the commitment of its members. I watched them from the kitchen and listened to the ebb and flow of their conversation.

THE EARTH TURNED; frost, spring, summer, brutal gardening and canning, the uneventful seventeenth-birthday trip to the new mall in West Point, the start of school, the smell of gym shoes on persistent boys whom I thought about in my dreams but did not want in the daytime.

I approached the first months of my junior year like a premature baby, behind on so much of my development, but still managing to get A's, some of which were the result of dumb luck. My trigonometry teacher, Mr. Martinez, was the only Latino person in the whole school. To calm his nerves, he rolled the chalk between his hands, and it clicked against his wedding ring; little bits of chalk made his fingers white, the floor white, the air in the room dry with loose particles. He taught the whole lesson, ignoring the kids in the class who talked to each other, played cards in the back, or slept. I got an A in trig on the preliminary progress report after the first month of school. I had turned in all of my homework, but I hadn't understood any of it, so I was certain that my grade was payment for doing my homework and not disrupting his class.

One day someone left a piece of masking tape in his chair with thumbtacks stuck to it, points upward. The class roared at Mr. Martinez's grimace and quick reflexes. He held me after the bell that day, rubbing the chalk in his hands, his tongue seeming too large for the straight edge of the English language. He looked at me over his glasses and said, "No more slack. Bring yourself up to that A, or you get what you get as a grade." I had never received a poor grade in any class.

Fall settled in around the house. Leaves fell on the tin roof like crisp potato chips. Each night at the picnic table Ella Mae gave me ample time and space to complete the homework that she could not assist with. When she wrote her weekly letter to Ms. Olatunde, she would ask, "How do you spell . . ." and I would write the letters out, making sure I had them right, before yelling them in to her. On those days inside the maze of trigonometry headaches, I welcomed the stillness of our house.

I even went to Jamella at the library to try and understand. Her younger siblings were old enough to fend for themselves now, and the library became her after-school haunt. Her homework first, then an activity: Bible study, botany, sewing. It was Tuesday. She had already done her homework and had taken her crumpled paper bag of torn skirts and blouses to the back room of the mildewed library trailer for sewing class. I got the

librarian to help me find a book that would explain trigonometry better, but the confusion of letters was difficult enough
with social studies and English; adding to it the use of x and y
in the place of numbers was the end of me.

Jamella filed out of the small room in front of the three white
girls and one black girl who all used the sewing class to make
clothes that were against dress code: cheap Madonna look-alike
outfits with long lace sleeves, skirts with lace bottoms, chintzy
clothes that affected their attitudes. Behind Jamella's back, they
held their noses pinched and fanned the air, but Jamella seemed
oblivious, and kept her eyes on mine as she approached.

"Odessa, take linguistics with me. Mr. Martinez won't even
miss you in trigonometry. Just go on Monday and Friday; those
are the only days he takes attendance. The other days, come with
me to linguistics."

Ms. Gaines, the linguistics teacher, didn't question my sudden
presence, and soon I was raising my hand and asking questions.
Homework became less stressful. I made flash cards of prefixes
and suffixes: ped = foot. So many words began to unscramble
themselves. I could look now at just a piece of a word and
understand so much about its meaning.

At the end of the first quarter, we received progress reports:
an A in American literature and social studies, always an A in
P.E., an A in chorus (because I knew how to hide in the back,
follow the instructions, and mouth all the lyrics well enough
to never be suspected of hitting the flat note), and an A in
trigonometry, because in my absence I was no trouble to Mr.
Martinez.

Jamella held my report card up and said, "Magic. If you pay
attention and stop struggling, you get what you need. Maybe
not what you want, but what you need." Twice she came home
with me to study at the table, and I borrowed the truck to take
her home.

"That's good," Ella Mae said when she heard the keys return
to the nail in a jingle. "Odessa, one day you gonna ride on

away from here. You growin up." I shuffled away to my room at that startling thought; sharp objects always embedded inside of liberation.

Lamont and Richard came to visit on Richard's fall break, and I listened to peripheral conversations about Richard's success in the anthropology department and his prospects after his last year. The two of them sat on the porch in Ella Mae's cane chairs. I sat on the steps where, three years earlier, we had touched knees, all still close enough to childhood to want to play. I looked over to the side of the house where the magnolia stood. It used to be big and beautiful, but lightning had struck and sheared the tree in half. We hardly even looked at it anymore. The mimosa weed was now a tree that lopped over and blocked the view of the magnolia. The mimosa's pink, wispy flowers showed up all the other bright greens and blossoms in the yard. I listened to them whisper above my head and harumphed, quieting the shifting of my own growing roots with distracted concern over Lamont's being left behind in Richard's wake. When was Lamont going to get a chance to go to school while Richard worked?

I picked up a whisper of "Paris," but when Lamont and I went off just the two of us into Starkville for Dairy Queen and to fly the Frisbee at the schoolyard, he never mentioned it, and I never mentioned the fear of my body turning adult-sized despite my child-sized heart. I told him about my crushes on boys whom I would never approach or let approach me, and he told me about all the music-studio gigs he worked as a backup singer. He teased me about being a heterosexual girl stuck in a heterosexual world. In Madonna's high-pitched voice, he bounced around on the dirt field, and I was glad to have him there, silliness and cartwheels; for a moment we were children.

We would never learn that too much play turned against itself. I teased him back, told him he was letting Richard feed off him like a leech or mosquito sucking his blood, and I sang off key in a raspy Janis Joplin voice: "Take another little piece of my heart now baby." The cartwheel was not turned again.

We walked the raggedy boardwalk over the swamp. He occasionally pointed out the beauty of a lily, the things I'd grown accustomed to and didn't feel awe over anymore. I tried to find a musical medley to bring him back—"Super Freak, super freak, you're super freaky, yow!"—but my jokes bore bad timing and raggedy themes.

Richard and Lamont spent the remaining days of their break in the Holiday Inn, in town with all the aristocratic southern tourists. I asked Ella Mae if she thought Richard was stuck up. She replied with questioning inflection, "Your Mama Bernice was jealous of Leland, but wanted him at the same time. Why are you askin?"

"I'm just looking out for Lamont."

"Hmm," was her reply. She came into the kitchen where I sat. Her voice lower, she said, "Richard is . . ." She slowed down the way she did now each time she was going to use a Ms. Olatunde word ". . . resourceful. He learned to make the world around him his subject for study and his tool for survival. He's smart. What you have against him is about Lamont's attention." She turned to go back in the living room. "Worries me more that he's so smart in that 'survive no matter what' sort of way." She turned to point at me and said, looking at me over her glasses, "Don't distract yourself though, Odessa."

I frowned at the accusation of jealousy. The rest of that day, Ella Mae said I was paying too much attention to other folks' business and needed more friends, that something wasn't right about me spending all my time with Jamella or waiting for Lamont to come visit so I could argue and fight with him. Jealous or not, when I turned my attention away from my business and on to others', there was always some truth in what I saw.

I GREW COMBATIVE as the week droned past with the two of them nearby but not visiting. My one-line responses to Ella Mae's questions were mature enough to get attention, but not the attention I wanted. Ella Mae knew me better than I knew myself, always dismissing my behavior with, "Well, you growin up, and havin growin pains."

Our typical exchange: "Odessa, did you bring home the form for the college fair?"

My response: "The college fair was last week." Then I waited for her exasperated sigh.

When Lamont and Richard stopped by to say good-bye, the morning fog of early fall had lifted and brought bright sun on the spectacle of leaves. Richard got out and stood on his side of the car; a tight red long-sleeved t-shirt hugged his muscular arms. Red shirt, brown skin, and green car blended into the fall colors that surrounded him. He was beautiful, and I stared, and he stared back; then he stuck his tongue out, and I giggled involuntarily, then frowned until he looked away.

Lamont walked past me on the porch, "Hold up, knuckle-head, I'm gonna say good-bye to my auntie." I could hear him and Ella Mae exchange a few words. One of them said, "No time like the present." I listened without so much as moving my head, but the next sound was air escaping their bodies in a hug, and Ella Mae saying, "Y'all be safe getting to the train station."

On the porch I stiffened my arms; my hands almost poked through my sweater pockets. I wanted to steal back from Richard what he was taking out of Lamont, working day and night for dumb, unnecessary things like hotels and rental cars. "Good-bye Richard," I said, rolling my neck and eyes from the space where the rising sun was lifting the mist.

"Good-bye, Miss Odessa Contessa," he said, teasing and letting me know that Lamont shared all of our talks with him. The screen door clapped, and Lamont stood so close that I could see where the Mississippi fall sun had made brown freckles on his nose. I wanted to vent my aggravation with him and Richard, but I aimed my crooked blame at Ella Mae in a whisper: "I don't know why I despise her sometimes."

Lamont moved his head back on his neck. "You'll get it in a few years when you're not a teenager anymore." He looked out on the orange and yellow clusters of trees and took a deep appreciative breath. "Thank goodness you get to be a regular teenager, despising your mother for no good reason while she waits for you to have your few shining moments per month of mature young womanhood."

I recognized the embedded insult. Our breath caught there between our shared glare. The smell of garlic and peppers, likely an omelet they'd eaten for breakfast. I wondered if there would be enough remaining from Richard's splurge to pay their rent, and I returned an insult. "Shut up, love slave."

He just shook his head. "Give me a hug, fool." We embraced long enough for me to relax into the sadness of him leaving. The muscle of his grip sent the signal of safety. "I love you," he whispered, and my ear went cold, paused to weigh that moment. Words never shared among Blackburns and Laceys echoed as they descended into troubled waters where suspicion and instinct had not yet merged into wisdom. "You too," I replied in the scratchy voice of a sleepy child.

Chapter 13

THANKSGIVING BREAK APPROACHED, and I felt the tilt of the globe on its axis, the view of things from a skewed angle in which life was bound to shift. I watched for the moment when Ella Mae and Ms. Olatunde would exchange a letter that would speak of Ella Mae leaving me in Mississippi for a life in New York. I waited for the letter from Lamont that uninvited us for Thanksgiving, because he and Richard were moving to Jamaica. When I was growing up in St. Louis, I would have moments of consistency, forgetting about the troubles of my reality, settling in, and then I would find myself on the receiving end of Mama's or Deddy's pain. The blood rushed to one side of my tilted head. Behind the thick lens of my glasses and inside the memory of my iris, I sensed a peripheral omen of change, and knowing no better, I watched for betrayal.

ELLA MAE AND I boarded the train instead of the bus when we went to New York this time, the comfort of our Thanksgiving tradition slowly pushing away the cloud of suspicion. I frosted the chocolate cupcakes as usual; my specialty by now. "Lamont," I said, "you wanna lick the spoon?"

Richard yelled back on his behalf. "He in the bathroom again. I don't think chocolate anything is gonna work for him." He giggled, and Ella Mae and Ms. Olatunde said in gentle unison, "That's not funny."

Lamont came out of the bathroom and placed himself in the center of the action in a fashion that seemed awkward. He walked toward the kitchen with his arms outstretched and said, in a voice mimicking Julia Child, "For dessert, my sister's soul cupcakes. Notice the Negro frosting, with Negro insides. Negro through and through." Not even Ella Mae could resist the open-mouthed laughter that followed.

We ate the cupcakes sitting in front of the little TV stolen from the St. Louis kitchen. The O-Jays sang "This Christmas," and at each commercial Ms. Olatunde and Richard criticized Macy's for taking up airtime with Christmas shopping promotions when Thanksgiving was barely over. The daylight faded to orange streetlights, and the TV light illuminated our faces as we competed for the best joke about the aging O-Jays, the amount of Grecian Formula necessary to hide four gray heads of hair, the tax deduction they'd get for all the Milk of Magnesia and Ben-Gay.

Lamont went to the toilet three times, each time making a joke on the way out. Ella Mae and Ms. Olatunde glanced at each other, and I wondered what secrets they held that couldn't be told to me.

Ella Mae scooted her stool closer to the TV to turn the dial. Our laughter died down to a silence that was unbearable. Lamont's shuffling around in the bathroom was something none of us wanted to pay attention to. I remembered the Saturday all of the kids had stomach flu. Mama the one left to unstop the toilet and clean up vomit.

The thud of the TV knob landed us first on a fuzzy scene of Sanford and Son's junkyard. Redd Foxx reared back in suspenders and used gestures to say *He must be "funny,"* his flat hand stretched toward his son and rocking back and forth to show the unsteady reality of a gay man.

I quickly shut out the implication, and Ella Mae turned the knob to keep from having to hear Richard or Ms. Olatunde deliver a diatribe about homophobia. She landed on *The Jeffersons*, but there again was a hand outstretched, rocking from side to side as George told Louise his greatest fear for Lionel. This time I reached for the TV and turned it off to endure the silence until Lamont came out of the bathroom. In the stillness there came the revealing click of the "record" button; sixty minutes of taping. This year we were so distracted by Lamont's trips to the bathroom that we hadn't paid Richard's guinea pig recording session any attention.

The next morning, Lamont asked me, "Wanna come to choir rehearsal with me?"

I leaned back, uncomfortable with the imbalance between my new height, thin frame, and large breasts. "Boy, you mean you still trying to sing?"

"Girl! I sing and teach other people too. It would do your tone-deaf butt some good to come with me."

I went with him to the African Methodist Episcopal Church for his choir rehearsal. I sat in the pews and looked at his back in a black waist-length jacket. He was a deity, blending the voices that rose in a swell of breath and body heat into the high rafters. The top of my head tingled like a hand or foot fallen asleep; my soul not able to stay in my body. Lamont's arms flailed the musical commands, a translation of the harmony, the melody. All the voices from single open mouths, a swell of one forceful wave, and I wanted to be swallowed by that sea.

When we were children, we'd stood in church like hungry stick figures while others caught the Holy Ghost. I remember our cousins in the choir stand glancing back at us from where they stood singing lead, their stares accusing me or him or some other Blackburn sibling of hitting the flat note that rang out in the offended rafters of our church. The tension of shame held cross beam and joist in place above us.

But this day Lamont was a man, flown far from our nest of judgment. His arms confident like blackbird wings, commanding as if the words of childhood had not weighted them down. Heads bobbed on the same chord, the feet of choir members beneath burgundy robes patted on the same beat, hands in fists, but I sat stiff, aware of my coccyx bone on hard ebony pew. I was just beneath the glow of yellow light. I was just before the shame that would stop my impulse to stand up and sing with him.

AFTER CHOIR REHEARSAL, Lamont and I sat like pigeons on a wire soaking up the cold air of Harlem, the uneasy task of breathing first the stench of bus fumes, then the warmth of gingerbread cooking somewhere in the distance. Darkness fell and streetlights, fluorescent church signs, and liquor store signs illuminated like separate moons. The train was leaving Port Authority at 9 p.m., and like every year, we had our last moments on the stoop while I waited for Ella Mae to pack. This time we didn't share stories. This time we didn't talk, just sat. Lamont still wore flared pants, but there was something loose about the fit. This time he wore a turtleneck beneath the great dumpster-find burgundy J. Crew sweater. This time Ella Mae came out in her long black men's coat and a new fedora from the vintage shop down the block, her hair hanging beneath, a few more gray strands among the black. This year, in an old derby hat, a brown leather jacket the color of her skin and the dark chocolate night, Ms. Olatunde came out too, and I stood, as if receiving mourners at a funeral. Comfort shifted; she was coming with us.

I DID NOT SPEAK on the train, though it took almost twenty hours to get home. I did not come out of my room until time to eat.

"Shame," Ms. Olatunde said at the picnic table, the middle of some conversation she and Ella Mae were having. I harumphed at the reality of Ella Mae suddenly having words for conversation.

"Shame," Ms. Olatunde said, chewing her collards with her mouth closed, her back erect and head high like Sydney Poitier. Ella Mae kicked me under the picnic bench to remind me to chew with my mouth closed too.

"Shame will keep you from being you," Ms. Olatunde said, "especially if who you were born to be is somebody other folks are afraid of. Shame will keep you a prisoner while the people who think they better than you flaunt they stuff; you'll be all caged up in yourself thinking and rethinking your every move."

I rolled my eyes and went off to bed, and woke up the next morning grateful to head out for school before seeing either of them.

"Good for you," Jamella said when I told her the bad news.

"Good for me? You have no idea. Now there's the one with something to say about everything paired with the one who has nothing to say. Where am I supposed to fit?"

Jamella tore at the rubbery cafeteria pancakes. "Like I said, good for you. Both of them think the world of you. You the only one I know with two grown women to look after you." She chewed and stared off into the chaos of the cafeteria. "You just scared to have it good."

I heard the sounds inside the St. Louis house, the chorus of constant voices yelling because they had learned to yell from Mama and Deddy, and I heard the moans of the house's red brick and mortar; heavy teenaged feet thudding up the steps two by two, the basement door slamming, the front door slamming, the clicking of the ignition on the gas stove, the agitating rhythm of the washing machine that could be heard from any place in the house if your put your ear against any piece of furniture, and Deddy's elbows and fists in walls in the middle of the night, a sound all ears had learned to sleep through. Jamella was right. I slumped into acceptance.

I took a piece of her pancake. "Jamella, you wanna come over tomorrow?"

But Jamella was like a feral animal; it would take months for her to trust being around a new grownup.

"No thank you," she said, looking at her Styrofoam plate.

MS. OLATUNDE BROUGHT MUSIC into our house, the freedom of words, like poetry, truth all the time from her lips. Music like I saw in Lamont's body. I wanted to know who I was and be free too. I wanted to know how Ms. Olatunde knew herself, and at the same time it made me uncomfortable to know that because she was free, she knew me, when I didn't even know myself.

I had not written in my diary since I had first arrived at Ella Mae's years ago, but I dug around and found the old thing, straightened out its pages and tried to free my words the way Ms. Olatunde did:

There is a visceral uneasiness of seeing a bird flying inside of your living room. There is allowance for their flight when it is just beyond the window, the TV-like quality of their flight and the beauty of their song framed by the comforting separation of window. But inside the house wild eyes bring a current of fear up the spinal cord.

This was how I felt about Ms. Olatunde being in our house. She knew something about anything you could bring up in conversation, and she had a way of coming up with new ideas from old ones that Ella Mae had long since rejected, and she put the ideas into action. In just weeks, we had a TV in the big room next to the fireplace, a wall and a door for her and Ella Mae's room, a wall and a door for the bathroom, and a wall and a door for my room. The big room used to be the whole house, aside from shower-curtain doors, but now it was a house with rooms.

One morning Ms. Olatunde put on a gray skirt, a white blouse that buttoned up the neck, and a gray blazer, and she went to Jackson. She came back at the end of the day with big news: a deal with a bunch of home department stores to carry Ella Mae's rag rugs. The next month, the rugs were featured in the *Starkville Home and Garden* circular; the photos rustic with bright sunshine in the big room. The photographer came with a vest full of lenses and film. He was a young white man who smelled like coffee, unwashed hair, and cigarettes. He went around the room in his floppy hair; the big black lens made him look like a one-eyed fly. He stood on the picnic table, fussed over the loom, lay on the floor, and as a result, photographs were produced where the sun dispersed across the red, green, and yellow of the rag rugs and made the house I had taken for granted into art.

Something about Ms.Olatunde's pointed body, thin limbs, and high-held head commanded attention and action. I had never known a woman like her. For all of Christmas break, I set about trying to show her that I was not backwards and southern, but capable and smart like her. Over sassafras tea or cups of cider we engaged in conversation where I misused half the words I learned in linguistics. Her favorite faux pas of mine was, "Do you think that Alex Hailey's *Roots* was better received as a novel or as a film adoption?" She never criticized me, but the way the sound of laughter stayed muffled in her chest always brought me close to tears and motivated me to study harder and figure out what I'd screwed up.

I was allowed to officially spend the next spring semester in linguistics. I began to read more fluidly, pausing less often to unscramble words, and I was able to carry conversation with Ms. Olatunde without using a long string of little words to represent one good vocabulary word.

In geometry I learned that the triangular prism is the strongest geometric shape. The winter and early spring were solid and safe with routine and the wholeness of three people in our house. The only instability in the structure was the absence of Lamont's letters and visits. There had been one worn-edged postcard over the winter; the red scripted neon of Radio City Music Hall on one side, and fast scratchy writing in a staccato ballpoint pen:

> *Hey Odessa. Hope you and E. M. & O are good. Working at Express Credit Card Company all week, studio gigs at night, ushering Radio City on weekends. So many expenses before Richard graduates. I'll write soon.*

That spring Starkville High School juniors scored lowest in the state on the basic skills pretest. Our new principal, Mr.

Flagstone—whom we affectionately called Mr. Flintstone—stood at the microphone in the auditorium and addressed the juniors, who had been assembled for reasons unknown to us. His skin was a sun-deprived grayish brown. He was always in a black suit and tie, but the air within four feet of his body was rank with the smell of old laundry, something akin to the smell of Jamella's clothes; but on her, the familiar odor was pleasant. He tapped on the microphone with his thick dark finger, and the auditorium of rising seniors hushed.

"This year," he said, "your spring break will come later than that of the seniors, sophomores, and freshmen." He looked up over his smeared glasses and tapped the mic again to quiet the rustling of questions and high-pitched complaints. "Over the break, when the school is quiet, and you can focus, you will study for the basic skills test, then take a short two-day break in addition to your weekend." He raised his hand and added, "Be prepared to raise your performance for the actual test on June first through third."

The remainder of the day was filled with the slamming of lockers, cussing under the breath, threats in the cafeteria to dump syrupy fruit cups and cottage cheese on Mr. Flintstone's new green Chevy, plans to paint school-spirit gold on Chevy green. "Mr. Flatulence" became his new name, scribed in red lipstick on the bathroom mirror by one of the afro-wearing, pot-smoking junior pep squad girls who raged at her locker, with purple, oxygen-deprived lips: "That will teach him that we have a high enough vocabulary to pass the language skills portion of the test." The halls roared with vengeful laughter. I laughed too, but Jamella said, "God punishes those who seek vengeance on others for their own wrongdoing."

I paused and looked at her sideways before slamming my locker. "Girl, loosen up."

When I told Ella Mae and Ms. Olatunde, they both harumphed from their separate perches of loom seat and picnic table sprawled with ledger sheets. "Don't seem like fair reward for your hard work," Ms. Olatunde said. I did not tell them that most of my hard work consisted of being good and remaining unnoticed so that I'd receive A's that were basically given out for good behavior; a skill I'd learned in the crowded St. Louis house.

When the skimpy four-day weekend came, spring break came for us juniors, and Ella Mae sat me down at the picnic table, my long legs barely able to fit under it comfortably. She looked over the edge of her glasses, and I pushed mine up to see better what was coming.

"You been watchin that mailbox like a hawk for months, and I feel like I can splurge from the rug money. You seventeen, almost eighteen. You old enough to go by yoself," I hopped in my seat and bared my teeth in a Cheshire cat expression, and she swatted at me to get me to be still until she finished weaving her words. She pulled the bus ticket out of the breast pocket of her work shirt. "It ain't no train ticket, and you only will end up with two days to really be there, but here."

I grabbed hold of it, but she didn't let go before looking me in the eyes. "Just don't be looking like you don't know what you doing and getting yoself mugged or somethin. Walk like Olatunde."

I boarded the express bus for the eighteen-hour trip to reach Lamont. I imagined me and Lamont and Richard catching the subway to Central Park, or maybe finally I could get the two of them to show me Coney Island. To help me get through the journey, I replayed in my mind the words to Brenda Russell's "Get Here."

You can reach me by railway,
You can reach me by trailway
You can reach me on an airplane,
You can reach me with your mind . . .
I don't care how you get here, just get here if you can.

Nightmare bus ride; each time I fell asleep, I awoke with the thick smell of my own sweat like the smell of urine, soaked into my sweatshirt turned pillow against the nighttime bus window. I comforted myself by holding my own hand and imagining the touch of Lamont's or Ella Mae's hand in mine. I checked the fanny pack beneath my sweat shirt over and over to make sure I had not been mugged in my sleep. All of Ella Mae's and Ms. Olatunde's warnings swirled in my sleepy head. *You should wash your hands every time after you've touched anybody's hand. Even Lamont's.* I woke up as we passed the fluorescent street lights of some little town, and thought, *Even Lamont's?*

WHEN LAMONT GREETED ME at Port Authority, his words had sorrow inside of them. We hugged long and hard; the feel of his clavicle against mine signified that he was overworked, overtired. We rode the sleepy rhythm of the 11 a.m. Saturday morning subway to Harlem. The trains were almost empty, as the exodus was out of Harlem on Saturday morning; it was only into Harlem on Saturday night. In my mind it was 4 a.m.; the groggy night of catnaps still with me. The comforting image of the mattress and the safety of him and Richard sleeping across from me drifted in an out of my weariness.

When he unlocked the apartment door, there was a sterility in the air, something of skin and hair and warmth extracted. "Where's Richard?" The waxing and waning of sunlight behind clouds made its pattern across the twin beds. "Where's Richard?" Lamont walked to the kitchen and filled the tea kettle without speaking. We sat down on the floor between the two mattresses, where the daylight held us center stage and the black tea could prepare us for the length of the day.

"Odessa, I have begun to hear the rain. The past few years with Richard have been all about the power of the two of us together."

He was talking to me the way Ella Mae used to, in circles; something was obviously eluding his ability to tell it, but he spoke anyway, and I sifted through the words to find two or three pieces that matched. He sipped the tea, and I mirrored him.

"Odessa, remember that old Ann Peebles song Mama used to play over and over until the needle wore a groove in the forty-five?" We both chimed in with the eeriness of sibling stereo: "I can't stand the rain . . . against my window . . ." Our voices swung high on "rain," and we laughed at the coincidental accord.

"All right, Miss Serendipity," he said, his face smooth and boyish in the light for a moment; then the skin fell loose from the muscle of his smile. Lamont's stare returned with the blank look of memory.

"Odessa, he went home after graduation."

"Who went home?" I said, rolling my eyes, thinking he better not mean Richard.

"Richard left yesterday." There was silence, the way there is blunt silence after a child falls and hits his head; the moment before wailing cries. Lamont said, "I remember us yelling. I remember Richard telling me something about Deuteronomy, then something about gentiles and 'homogenitals,' whatever the hell that is; the word 'disgrace' was mixed in there too."

"What?" I replied, clutching my tea cup with both hands now. "I fucking knew it." At this, Lamont sank. I had never seen him defeated. He was the family fighter, prepared to stand up for any cause, something he had been taught by having to constantly stand up for himself on account of being small.

I wanted to touch his hand, but I pushed back the image of things he and Richard had done with their hands, and then there was the arresting sound outside the window of the bus squeaking to a halt below us.

Late afternoon came in the midst of our sitting, talking, and silence. I refilled the teapot three times, and each time I returned to the floor between the mattresses with him while he looked at pictures of himself and Richard together, and told me of his dream for them to move to Paris.

The orange lights flickered on and left us sitting in the

weary, ambiguous blue-gray of dusk. I imagined Richard in a yellow polo shirt with the collar turned up, brown leather belt, tight Jordache jeans, his goatee trimmed well, Adidas bag in hand as he stepped on to yesterday's dawn bus.

"I'm sorry," I said there on the floor where Lamont and I sat Indian style. My timing with apologies had finally matured a bit. I put down my cup, and after too much thought touched his hand, tenuous the way Ella Mae used to hesitate before touching mine. His skin felt hard like lumpy Cream of Wheat, and my stomach turned as the textured message went up through my arm to my gag reflex, and I pulled my hand back to my cup for the excuse of another sip while I worked to keep my sorrow for him at the forefront.

"Odessa." He looked past me to the window. Snot streamed from his nose, and he did not bother to wipe. "Odessa . . ." I saw time and worry worn on a face much too withered for a man of twenty-four years.

"Odessa . . . The worst thing is being left, 'cause all the energy of how things were is all around me. Worst thing is being left when I need him most." His voice disintegrated. "I cain't tough it or fake it on my own."

My teeth scraped together, and a chill went up my spine. "That fucking asshole. Lamont, I knew he was just using you. He got what he needed, and—"

"Girl," Lamont said, shaking his head, "I'm not telling you this to sit here and dis him. It's about a whole lot more." He leaned forward as if the weight of his head was too much to hold up. He fell onto my shoulder.

The discomfort I felt; he was my steady rock, but not in this moment. I scrambled to get up. "I'm gonna get you some tissue."

We sat quiet as the sounds of more cars and busses filled the streets, horns tooted, the sounds of distant sirens wailed, and the reality of Saturday night in Harlem brought the first day of my spring break to a close. We moved to the two folding chairs that faced each other in the one-butt kitchen, using our laps as tables. Lamont got up and turned on the stove to boil water for oatmeal. "Let me make you some food," he said, and my next thought was that Thanksgiving here would never be the same.

I asked the questions that Lamont had taught me to ask Ella Mae, asked the questions to draw him out. "Did he say why he was leaving?"

Lamont's voice was scratchy and stressed. "His mother came from Jamaica for the graduation. Richard had to meet with his thesis professor one more time and turn in some stuff at the library. So he was uptown, and I offered to be here to help her settle." He shook his head and blew the remaining moisture from his nose, his tone more sober.

"Three years that boy talked about how 'out' he was to his mother, to everybody. But Mr. Gay Rights Anthropologist had lied to his own Mama about us." Lamont's indignant attitude returned and he rolled his neck and smacked his lips, wavering between being pissed at Richard and calming into the grief of losing him. I stayed still, trying not to show emotion on my face for fear that some hurtful truth—like me being glad, like hoping Lamont would now be straight—might come seeping through the angle of my lips.

"When she got here, she said in that accent, 'Thank you for taking care of my son. You can go home now, I'll settle in.' I said, 'I live here,' and you know me Odessa, my hand flipped and flew to my chest when I said that, and it was like she hadn't really seen me until then.

"She looked me up and down, and Miss Thang loosened her Queen's proper stance and was ready to let loose, but I was gonna cut her off with a bit of truth. Of course Richard walked in right when I pointed her down, just when I said, 'Oh no you don't Miss Jamaica. I'm Richard's honey. Get tamed with that.'

"Richard stood there with the door knob in his hand, all brown boned, staring me down like I ain't never seen him stare. There I was with the two of them and nobody to stand up for me, and Miss Thing let loose about all her sacrifices, and more family history than Alex Hailey. She was yelling, 'I did not stand five hours in da Jamaican sun hiding six months of pregnancy beneath fat and all dose shirts, trying to make my top match my bottom . . .' Odessa, she shook her finger in Richard's face, the dirt of other people's house so deep beneath her nails that it became one with her skin. 'I did not tell dat lie dat I was goin to da American conference for my church, did not cry and beg my minister to write da letter for me to go . . .'"

Lamont spoke on, and I could see Richard's mother there in the Jamaican scene, then here in the spot where I sat in Lamont's apartment. I saw her finger lower to Richard's face, and the weight of time and loss settle into the sun-wrinkled corners of her eyes, her voice softer, breaking like her heart, and Lamont continued his theatrics.

"'I did not let dat minister fondle my breast . . . I was so angry I could have put dat golden cross from the wall through his skull . . . I did not leave your baby brother behind so you could be U.S.-born, an American citizen . . . all of dat,' she raised the pink palms of big hands, brown life lines like dirt roads lifted up to God, 'I did not do all of dat for you to turn out like dat.'"

I could see her lips turned down at the corner is disgust, hear her saying, "No! No!" I could see her swatting at Richard, see Lamont go to swing on her, then Richard's hand severing the connection between non-blood kin with a punch to his own lover.

Lamont said it was not Richard's fault. "It's his faith and his family over his relationship with me. When Mama and Deddy came to Mississippi State, I wished that they were coming to take me home rather than coming to throw me away." I could feel his anger and grief battling for primary position, and I saw the ghost of the suppressed words in the dark cradles under his eyes. His eyes said, *Fucking asshole,* but his voice said, in an anemic tone of abandonment, "It's not his fault."

I saw Richard's lips, always so red, always looking like toddler boy lips red from sucking mother's milk, saw his shiny naps in the Jamaican sun on the shoulder of a woman in mismatched plaid, comforted, and I was angry for Lamont.

We stayed in all night, watching TV, looking at all the Polaroids of the two of them, and talking about Richard, Richard, Richard. It was more depressing than a black Baptist repast: body laid out for everybody to cry over in one room, buffet in the next, the meal going down hard as family rehashed the best of times.

The cloud cover was unbroken the next day, but the air held the balmy humidity of spring. For breakfast we ordered pizza, and for lunch we caught the subway to Chinatown, a meal of meat for him, vegetables and bean curd for me. The setting was industrialized, open walls that did not separate us from sewer steam and pigeon feathers.

"Odessa." A warm, ominous breeze of street warmth blew up my spine. Lamont took a sip from the little white ceramic cup, something about the handheld mouthful of tea reminding me of communion. "Odessa," and he looked off at the tops of buildings, where banners and rags hung from windows. Then turned back to lock his brown eyes on mine. "If there's something you wanna do with your life, do it. Don't sit around pretending like people and obligations are getting in your way, because if you're not doing what you love and enjoying being here, you're not really living."

"Okay," I said, rolling my eyes at the sudden declaration, but the space where the solar plexus braces for impact twisted, despite my flippant facade. Lamont did not change his stare into my eyes; he just waited for me to settle.

"Do you understand? Just tell me you understand, because if you can hear me now, then you'll remember what I'm telling you when you need it." He sipped from the little cup again, his fingers looking thinner than I remembered them. "It will be like time-release medicine," he said, smiling just enough that the corners of his mouth moved away from the straight line of his expression. "When you need it, you'll remember."

"I understand," I said with more calm, "like I'm thinking about going on this freedom campout for spring break next year. It sounds kind of nerdy and hippy, but all the female seniors go to a women's camp, learn survival skills, cook their own meals outside, hike, everything."

"Right," he said, no longer looking at me, but staring at the pigeons on top of the buildings again.

I sat in the moment, knowing that there was the intellectual way that I understood his words, but there was some other part of me that could not possibly understand what I did not yet need.

After lunch, we caught the subway to Port Authority for the 2 p.m. express bus that would land me home in time for Ella Mae to drop me off at school on Monday morning. I did not want to leave Lamont. His refrigerator was empty except for something in a can that was called Ensure, and margarine with bread crumbs in it, and the half-eaten pizza we'd ordered. I did not want to leave him in the skeleton of a home; Ms. Olatunde not downstairs, Richard gone. But I also could not stand to sit and sleep in the darkness of his mood, in the quivering reality that something loomed heavy over him, a sadness that brought the premonition of a depression familiar from St. Louis days; clothes strewn all over the house, years of hand prints on walls beneath ugly wall paper that covered bloodstained wall paper. In the two days we spent together the new light that I'd taken for granted in my life with Ella Mae and Ms. Olatunde called me out of the darkness that Lamont and I had entered.

We held hands in the familiar depressive space of our childhoods, like the children on the cover of *The Mimosa Tree*, comforted in the urban filth by the familiarity of sibling touch. We hugged long and hard, but I'd already thrown up a shield between our warmth to keep the darkness from flowing from his chest to mine; thrown up a shield to keep my face normal and straight, though I wanted to cry and tear myself from him and head for the new safety of trees, earth, and the uncompromised love of home.

We stood in front of the bus, my eyes locked on his. He turned me around and stuffed something into my back pack that I would forget was there until someone else retrieved it. "Is that money?" I said, grinning to lighten the moment, and I turned to see the microscopic void where light enters the eye and casts new images on the retina wall, but inside that space of Lamont's eyes there was a slate barricade.

The driver released air from the brakes and called, "Memphis," my excuse to run now before the guilt of leaving him in his sadness set in, and before the ominous feeling that crept up my spine could reach my logic center. I turned to board the bus without waving from the window. I slept until the exchange in Memphis and slept again until I was almost home, the driver calling like Sam the watermelon man at the market: "Tupelo, Tupelo, Tupelo." I was back where green takes over and creeps up and between everything, and things are dirty with earth, not with filth. We rolled up at the bus station in Starkville, and I almost went out in the green field and grazed. Even the big ugly turkey buzzards were beautiful to me.

Chapter 14

THE WEEK WAS FILLED with academic demands to do well and be prepared for the basic skills test. I barreled headlong into the reality of things; not a moment to stop and think about my trip until the following weekend.

Saturday morning, I slept in. Near noon, I left the privacy of my room to where the house held on to the spring coolness of the night before. The bumblebee sounds of Ella Mae and Ms. Olatunde talking as they planted cucumber, tomato, and pole beans that in a couple of months would be rinsed in the blue and white speckled enamel bowl; the sweat of our labor all over the wax of the beans. Thoughts crept in over the pastoral sounds of spring. *Who will take care of Lamont?* The odd directions remembered again. *Wash your hands, Odessa.* My nerves fired to parts of my brain where words might connect understanding, and before I could break the circuit, I realized that with the refrain in my head, *Wash your hands,* I had washed the film of New York off my face each time we went out, and washed my hands after each time I'd touched Lamont's.

I went to my room to root through the crumpled papers and crumbs at the bottom of my backpack, clean out the week before so I could start my new week, get my homework started and completed before the weekend was over. I needed to finish my history paper, do my geometry homework, but I was distracted. I thought about Lamont's hands, hard and lumpy, thin and old before their time. I thought about how our next Thanksgiving would be more silent. Ella Mae's warning, *Wash your hands,* and my thoughts that almost transformed into questions, but the weariness of sleep fell away, and the demands of the week called. I pulled the remains of the things from my bag and piled them on my peach-crate dresser for later sorting.

The crumpled paper Lamont had stuck in my bag was not money but the stub of a bill or something; the tattered bus ticket, the subway tokens, all made their home in the pile on the peach crate, where they could keep me from returning to Lamont's grief. Some broken instinct; I did not open his next three letters.

END-OF-SCHOOL DANCE, junior tests, and rug deliveries. I could not right my mind since my visit to Lamont; could not allow myself to lift up the corner of the rug of my emotions and examine what lay beneath. Along with the demands of school were the boys who smelled like cologne and gym socks, and who followed me down the hall, leaving notes in my locker about the school dance.

Ella Mae and Ms. Olatunde persisted with questions about my studies for the basic skills test: "Has the test come yet? Did you pass the test? Did you fill out that North Carolina A&T application or the one for Norfolk State?" I needed the world to stop turning for Ms. Olatunde to stop preaching about the value of a black college education. My insides itched to get out, while the world around me itched to get in. In response, I slowed and silenced the world, and the power of that felt right.

In the middle of each dinner, I excused myself with a list of homework tasks, but I did my homework only if I had the energy. I ignored the boys who acted like hungry dogs, answered "mm-hm" to any question Ella Mae or Ms. Olatunde asked, and spent endless moments as one of the upperclassmen who lounged on the far picnic tables on the school grounds, "talking junk," as we called it, and taking the speed of our lives into our own hands.

Lamont wrote quick postcards:

All is well—working hard to pay bills—write soon.

I intended to write soon, but writing letters was on the long list of things I did not do.

I did not know the source of my descent. I did not know what the catalyst was. In physics class we learned that there had to be a catalyst to send potential energy down into some teenaged abyss. I did not attend the orientations for senior year. I retrieved mail and stuffed it away; forms requesting Ella Mae's signature piled up on my peach-crate dresser along with all the other demands. Ella Mae's refrain: "I don't know what's gotten into you. I wrote your brother, and he's thinking about coming down here to figure you out," but her lie fell on deaf ears. There had been no letter recently from Lamont, who had given up on my silence. "Mm-hm," I answered her, and shut my door.

SLEEP WAS MY DRUG. I wanted it all the time. Sleep kept change at bay, kept thoughts at bay. "Stand up straight," Ms. Olatunde coaxed, but I was tall, lanky, tired for reasons I couldn't explain, so my body tilted always toward the safety of sleep.

Summer came with the gardening chores that didn't bring me solace like when I was a kid. I pulled weeds and planted and fertilized with frustration over having my sleep disturbed. At night, I fled the house in the rusty red truck for the hideout of the school grounds. Friends offered beer, where we sat with the sulfur stench of the marsh in the air. Summer nights, we were the terrorist rising seniors at the playground picnic tables. None of us knew our basic skills test scores, and none of us cared.

"Beer?" they offered, but I remembered Uncle Leland's words: "I got enough things in this world chasing after my life, I don't need liquor, too."

That night, Jamella stood taller than I, lit only by the red glow at the ends of cigarettes and the one street lamp that one of the boys tried unsuccessfully to shoot out with a sling shot. Her breasts spilled out of her sloppy off-white blouse that glowed in the eerie silver luminescence. She handed me a used zip-lock bag filled with bergamot leaves. "This you can make into tea and feel better." The others at the picnic table tumbled over each other; large bodies of breasts held tightly in tube tops, and hidden erections in jean shorts; children in adult bodies laughing in big coughs at what we thought was a bag of pot that turned out to be simple flower stems to make me more alert, less numb.

"Who would want a bag of that magic? Bring me the good stuff," I said to impress the others.

ELLA MAE DECREED that I was no longer allowed to sleep in the day. "Odessa, now you are going to have to either help in the garden or study for your SATs." I went to the library trailer to pretend to study for the SATs, and by night I joined the congregated at the picnic tables, where even mosquitoes were too suspicious of us to bother swarming. Ella Mae thought she'd discourage me by saying she needed the truck, but I walked to the road to wait for Charles Walton. She yelled after me, "Make sure you get a ride home by 11 p.m., and don't drive in the car with nobody drunk." The freedom that Ella Mae gave me was like having a pocket full of change with no place to spend it. Ms. Olatunde warned, "You need to reel her in."

All summer, there was no letter from Lamont, and the more the silence grew between us, the more oblivious I became about why I did not want to hear from him.

I walked lazily into the fall of my senior year like stepping on a conveyor belt that took me without the insistence of any footsteps, shuttled me through the year without leaving time for me to assess my feelings, my future, to answer any of the questions from Ella Mae, from my principal, who asked, "What you gonna do? Why haven't you applied to college?"

Some days after school I squatted down in the cornfield and made myself small, like a fourteen-year-old again, until my thoughts slowed, until the feeling of sorrow sank just beneath my skin and the sun dipped just beneath the tops of the stalks, and each day I emerged just before the sensation of emotion.

The days of hiding in the corn brought resolve. One day I decided I ought to finally stop bragging about the wet sloppy kisses I was capable of giving and kiss some boy, and I did. I let the Jemison boy corner me between the gym doors and the hallway doors. He squeezed my breasts and forced his mouth on mine in what felt mostly like teeth and gums and spit, and it was over. Another day, I decided that I was going to work at the McDonald's in town after school until I had enough money to buy contact lenses at the new strip mall off the highway, and for the month of October that's exactly what I did. On my break time each day, I hid in the walk-in freezer with the DePaul boy and we kissed until our teeth chattered. When I had enough money, I didn't even call in sick. I went to the Lens Factory and got my contacts, swore off eating cow after spending weeks smelling seared flesh, and forgot all about the DePaul boy. My glasses sat ignored on the towering piles on the peach crate.

The cornstalks browned and rustled where I watched from the cane chairs on the porch, ignoring Ella Mae's worries. It was the first week in November, and that day I stood up and walked out past the corn toward the mailbox without thinking, until I heard my own voice exhale in a sigh, "I miss Lamont"; a thought that had waited until I did not suspect or guard against it. I dusted off my new cowgirl skirt and walked in my new boots with the wedge lift over gravel to our mailbox, and there in the box, left each day by Ella Mae, was the accumulation of three letters from Lamont that had all come during my McDonald's job.

Can you come this Thanksgiving? The next letter: *I haven't been feeling too well. The choir asked for a new director.* Thoughts of him weak and not standing up for himself brought the cloud cover over my thoughts again, the heartache, but I stood with my back to the road. I wished he'd get over Richard, tell the choir to go fuck themselves, and turn back into my big brother. His pain was hard to witness, the way it's hard for a child to witness her own mortality in her mother's tears. The occasional truck or car moved me with its speed, the sun set in the distance, smell of fallen leaves decayed, and I read the letters three times before admitting that two things were true: I wanted to be near him, and the thought of being near him was wholly frightening.

I SPOKE MY TRUTH as I entered the house. "I'm thinking about visiting Lamont." Ella Mae and Ms. Olatunde were in silhouette. They unlocked lips as I unexpectedly entered, but I wasn't startled. Kissing seemed to be the way they comforted each other, but I had decided after my encounters with those schoolboys that kissing was just an unfortunate ritual before sex.

My comfort was found in imaginings of tender lovemaking inspired by my own obedient fingers, and the grounding knowledge that I was not alone in the ambiguous place of departure from childhood, because Jamella walked through the same purgatory of her eighteenth year; all of the adults expecting us to behave like them, when the only experiences we could draw on were those from childhood. All night I sat with the letters, contemplating the distance between Mississippi and New York.

Jamella occasionally spent the night, fretting over her studies and straightening my room, while I listened to Michael Jackson's *Off the Wall* and painted my nails. When Jamella didn't spend the night, I drove to town before school and met her at the diner shop, where I told her all of Lamont's business, all my escapades. I bragged about experimental kissing, going off to colleges that I had not applied to, and we sneered through the window at boys who were on their way to school. Their sudden attention to the girl who no longer wore glasses incensed me.

The Harvest dance was scheduled for Saturday before Thanksgiving, in the gym. Jamella and I sat with our backs against the cinderblock wall. Our punishment for being tardy fifteen consecutive mornings was to decorate the gym, a task some girls would leap at, but one that Mr. Flatulence knew would humiliate girls like us. We looked over the vast gym, newly shellacked wooden floors with thick yellow lines drawn over white and green lines to demark the boundaries of one sport or another, and Jamella proclaimed, "We'll make it look like Jamaica."

"Oh please no." I rolled my eyes and my whole body away from her. "Any place but Jamaica, where Judas is holed up with his mama. Anyway, why aren't the cheerleaders or spirit club or somebody else doing this? You're in the gospel choir, and I'm the silent poetry-writing type, who never writes a fucking poem. We're not decorators." I stood over her, hoping the trailed scent of my period had not hung in the heated gymnasium air.

"Odessa, it's this or sit in detention for the rest of the year. Can we just enjoy it? Or if you'd rather be in New York than at the dance, then go!" She stood up too, her hair in two pointy ponytails as if she was still fourteen. I never allowed her to think that her intuition was right. I hated the invasive feeling I got when she responded as if I'd told her something I hadn't; responded to things I had not brought to the surface of my consciousness.

"Other people don't know, Odessa. What Lamont got ain't no worse than the flu, except it can kill you faster. People think AIDS is a curse or plague from God, but it ain't *my* God's fault."

I pushed her back to the wall to silence her. "AIDS? My brother don't have AIDS. What the hell you talkin about?"

She put her shaking hand in her dirty red backpack and pulled out the crumpled paper that Lamont had given me as a send-off offering, which I had discarded among the piles of debris on my peach crate because it was not money. The piece of paper said *New York Health Department* across the top. The POSITIVE box was checked next to HIV/AIDS.

Before I could tell myself not to, I raised my hand and slapped Jamella across her face, then clasped the same stinging hand over my own mouth, the way I had only done twice before: once when she had quoted scripture to try to explain that masturbation was a sin, and another time when she did not see Mr. F standing behind her and she was about to repeat her famous quote about why obesity was a sin against the temple of the body.

The two of us breathed heavy, and I waited for the damnation that ought to come, but her eyes did not panic or anger; they stayed soft and still while the revelation came to me, the lumps under the skin of Lamont's hand, his trips to the bathroom, his face aged, and the lament that he needed Richard now more than ever.

Jamella put her arms around me. An unmuted cry echoed in the gym.

"He has AIDS, Odessa," she whispered, rubbing in the salve of reality.

I did not help her decorate the gym. Instead I walked the four miles home, welcoming the chilly air on my hot face.

Without showing emotion I walked through the door, past Ms. Olatunde, right over to the loom, where I asked Ella Mae, "Do you think you could buy me a ticket for New York?" Ms. Olatunde sat in the new armchair fetched from the dump, reading under the lamp she'd dragged across the floor to be nearer the fire.

"I don't have the money, Odessa. Maybe Lamont just needs some time to do his own thing anyway." I knew that would be her answer, and I had prepared my attack.

"Why did you tell me a million times to wash my hands while I was there?"

The saltwater fizzled as it tried to reach my nose and eyes. I let the heat of anger evaporate tears; but she did not answer me. Her brow furrowed, her eyes searching under the loom light for the meaning of my words, and the tears finally welled up in the quake of my whole body. "You could send me if you wanted to. You could find the money if you wanted to." She and Ms. Olatunde kept the silent pact to protect me from the news Jamella had already delivered. I went to my room and slammed them, Jamella, the kissing boys of Starkville out.

I spent the night adding and subtracting from the twenty dollars that I had to try to equal the fifty dollars for the bus, but twenty dollars was always the total. Late in the night, I thought I heard Jamella's voice on the porch with Ms. Olatunde. I woke to the scraping sound of Jamella sliding a piece of paper through the vented slots of my bedroom window: "I'll loan you the money." Her martyrdom made the congestion in my head worse. She would loan me the $100 that she'd saved sewing clothes? Her "book money," she said, for Mississippi State.

I woke up surrendered. It was already the Saturday before Thanksgiving, and I settled into the lead weight of attending the Harvest dance at the school so that I would not have to be in the house with Ms. Olatunde and Ella Mae.

THE DRY COLD WAS SO CUTTING that night, the sky dark and without clouds. When I inhaled, the air went parched and biting into my lungs, and I didn't care that Charles Walton was a long, spindly-armed boy—a boy like man in his height but in no other way, nothing with which to protect himself, no wisdom; but at least he had common sense. He smelled like beer and sex. We slow-danced to Isaac Hayes under the disco ball with missing reflecting chips.

Charles Walton was the only boy at school who insisted that he was getting out of Starkville. He was also the only boy who lived on his own and skipped school so regularly that he was practically never there. The year his mother overdosed, no one knew what happened to Charles, but when he showed up working at the Walgreens, the principal didn't question; just felt sorry, and let him back in. Ms. Olatunde, ignorant of the real world I walked in, announced the week before that he would be a good catch.

"Who's that one boy who rode all the way out here to return your math book? Charles Walton? Is that his name?"

I was repulsed at myself for pretending to be a shallow girl who liked him, when he was really just the driver of the Saturday night getaway car. I hid behind saying "How you doin" to him, faking a Mississippi accent to belong somewhere, to belong to him under the darkness of the high school gym turned high school dance, Jamaican theme done up singlehandedly by Jamella, who was nowhere in sight. The bass of the stereo rumbled in the rafters in the shadows of the dance floor; his arm stayed around my shoulders no matter how sharply I turned on my way to and from the punch bowl.

We slunk back behind the bleachers and endured Elvis for the white teachers and Fats Domino for the black teachers in polyester, their aging joints protected by cellulite. We stayed where metal and wood hid us from embarrassment of their bad wigs and run-over shoes. He leaned in with one hand over my head to support himself on a steel strut. The smell of his onion underarms reminded me of Lamont. The light shined through the shadows where Charles's lips pressed warm pillows against mine, not teeth and muscular tongue like the Jemison boy; his body was warm where his heart beat quickly beneath his ribs. The music changed to the Sugarhill Gang, and everybody resounded "hey" and emerged from their kissing corners, but beneath the rafters, lips and the soft terrain of tongues made Charles Walton and me a couple. I called him Chip now and he called me 'Dessa, and our shared miseries of childhood made us kin.

Thanksgiving came and went with Ella Mae and Ms. Olatunde shut out in blame for the fact that they knew Lamont was sick and didn't tell me, but in my mind, I didn't frame it that way; I blamed them for not having the money to send me to New York—denial that Lamont had the virus that the world associated with the bad people, the damned ones.

Through the winter the questions, "What are you going to

do after graduation?" became a muffled sound above my head while I drowned in Chip Walton and other distractions. My grief was smothered by good makeup and the comfort of sweaty, syrupy Mississippi sex.

Cars and people hummed beneath where Chip and I hid, one story above the street in his efficiency apartment. The smell of beer, the scratch of his nineteen-year-old beard, the static image of the Monopoly board on his dresser, the continuous afternoon episodes of *The Lucy Show* and the early evening reruns of *The Lone Ranger* made for days of stasis. Before school and in the evenings I sat at the picnic table and did my homework, to keep Ella Mae and Ms. Olatunde's inquiries at bay. Their questions met with a response of "fine" or "I got plans."

"What you gonna do?"

"I got plans."

Ms. Olatunde pried. "You think about that HBCU in Virginia any further? You finish the application?"

"Yeah." The application was somewhere in the dust on my peach-crate dresser with my diary, my Polaroid snapshots; where my whole childhood had been abandoned under an even layer of dust. The two of them had betrayed me by withholding information the way Mama or Deddy would. Faulting them kept me from the nightmares in which Lamont was one of the zombies in the *Thriller* video. I filled out the application the next night and returned it to the pile, to throw the two of them off my trail. My plan: to graduate, by the skin of my teeth, and go with Chip wherever he was going on his way out of Starkville.

The next night, more questions: "You still trying not to eat cows and chickens?" "You still friends with Jamella?" "You still dating Chip Walton?" Both of their voices came from the big room, punctuated by my long sighs between questions. I refused to look, not wanting to feed either of them with eye contact. Answering would mean I could no longer hope for privacy. Getting up and going to my room meant I had something to hide, but I needed them to hush.

"Meat is not necessary in a human diet. Jamella says hi. Sometimes I see Chip at school, but I'm mostly just busy with school and poetry club." My only busy moments with school were at that picnic table in the evenings; lunchtime and the free period that followed, plus any available time after school, had been filled with a combination of elusive sex in Chip's apartment and elusive sex in Chip's truck.

One day I decided to let Jamella back in my life. At lunchtime she agreed to drive with me in Chip's truck so we could go to the clinic in Columbus. During school hours we wouldn't see any classmates while we got our first birth-control prescriptions. Jamella expressed her philosophy: "Now you can be with him like man and woman supposed to, on the inside, rather than all that messing around on the outside, and I can go on and be prepared in the event that I get with the Jemison boy."

"Shut up, Jamella," I pleaded, as we rode fast back to school in Chip's truck. His muffler dragged worse than her reasoning dragged through religious texts for birth-control justification. In reality, I was already deeply "on the inside," where questions from Ella Mae and Ms. Olatunde, and the mysteries of Lamont's illness, could not affect me; so far inside until it was strangely and suddenly the month of March.

ON THE MORNING we were to pose for senior pictures, I caught the bus to school and then walked to Chip's apartment to get my laundry from the downstairs laundrymat before homeroom. I brought a surprise of biscuits in foil paper. In the laundry room was the crocheted brown tank top that Ella Mae had made to go over my t-shirts; the one I hated because as clothing it made no practical sense and looked too much like a throwback to the sixties. I put clothes in the washer, keeping the ugly crocheted top. In the dank hallway, before climbing the stairs, I slipped the black t-shirt from under the tank top, leaving brown knit mesh over my brown flesh, the nipples of my breasts slightly camouflaged in the weave. *Sexy*, I thought, as I crept up the stairs in sandal feet.

I used my key to go inside, but he was not there. I ate the biscuits, watching the clock, then went down to the washer for a basket of wet clothes. I changed into a wrinkled, wet blouse for picture day, watched the broken sidewalk below for his return. Ten minutes, twenty minutes: and I walked swiftly through the mix of pink and white dogwood blossoms, squatted beneath pines, up the small hill to the back of the field-ground fence, and into the fieldhouse door before second bell.

Three days and no Chip. He was not missing, he was not kidnapped, he had not packed anything; so I thought. I took Jamella with me, and she examined the crime scene like the woman on *Murder She Wrote*. She noticed Chip had taken his razor and his tooth brush, and he'd emptied the socks, underwear, and condoms from his dresser drawer.

When the landlord posted the carbon-copy yellow eviction notice and bolted the door, I did not care that my basket of stale laundry still sat in the wicker basket on his bed, or that the brown knit tank top lay on the bed, waiting to cover me partially before quick sex and homeroom.

IT WAS LONG AFTER MY GRADUATION, which I refused to attend, that I let myself believe what Jamella concluded: that Chip had touched the back of my neck, the top of my spine, noticed that he did not feel the knot that formed there each month, and figured out that I was pregnant.

My diploma came in the mail. I did not want the lecture from Ms. Olatunde and the awkwardness from Ella Mae, so I said all that needed to be said in one breath: "I'm pregnant. It's Chip's. I already know about birth control, just waited too late to get the pill. Yes, I'm sure, and yes, Chip is gone." I went to my room and slammed the door, and I was not disturbed by either of them.

I turned nineteen that summer, and I appreciated the rhythm of the garden again. As summer turned to fall, my belly grew ripe in the sun like watermelon, squash, and pumpkin. Ms. Olatunde's and Ella Mae's silence offered me safety; my pregnancy became the diversion we all needed to justify our denial of Lamont being out there somewhere, reaching for us with hands we were afraid to touch. The three of us were content with the trips to the shed for early wood-stacking, the turning of the garden for fall planting, the anticipation as my womb grew with life that would interrupt the silence.

Ella Mae and Ms. Olatunde planted the collard starters that we'd begun in egg cartons a month earlier. I packed the dirt tight around the plants on hands and knees, the sun beaming down on me, and Ella Mae spoke her mind into the calm moment. "I still think you should go to that school in Virginia."

Ms. Olatunde piped in. "They have an open-door policy—not like Mississippi State, with its old southern guard—and you won't be the only college girl with a baby. They accept folks in January, the baby'll be here by then."

Ella Mae finished their shared thought. "I'd just hate to see all that hard work of your schoolin go to waste."

I blew air through my swollen, flattened nose. Autumn coolness turned warm breath to clouds. Ms. Olatunde added, looking over her reading glasses, "If they accept you, you should go. Take the baby with you. Just do it. With the baby on your hip, just keep goin, don't let havin a baby stop you, 'cause once you stop moving and start getting scared to do for yourself, then it's just about impossible to move." They both looked at me over the tops of their glasses, afraid I would bolt and lock myself in my room, but those days had ended when Chip left and the reality of responsibility grew inside me.

I didn't look up when I told them the truth. "I never mailed the application." I plucked a collard plant from the egg crate and packed dirt around it. The silence was filled with a deep breath from each of us.

"Well," Ms. Olatunde said, "I shouldn't have been messing in your business, and I don't want you to think I've ever done anything else like this, but I mailed the application that you left on the peach crate."

We all held still there, hands in the dirt, making the reality of change hold still. Then I plucked another starter from the egg carton, black dirt landing on the t-shirt that stretched tight like cheese cloth over my already-bulging belly. I was grateful. "Thank you."

"You're welcome."

With knees cracking, Ella Mae knelt down on the ground next to me. "Don't worry. You don't have to go. You can go to a community college down here. I think you gonna need to be near. Besides, baby due in two months, school starts in three months. It's gonna all be a mess." She put her arm around me where we knelt there on the ground like kneeling before an altar. Then she put her hand up as a visor as she looked up at Ms. Olatunde. "Olatunde, she gonna need her mother around, with a new baby." Ella Mae took both my hands to pack the soil around my starter plant, pushing the energy of want and memory down with the damp compost. I sat up on my knees and spoke an unexpected request.

"Yeah, I really want Lamont to come down and be here too."

Ms. Olatunde knelt down where Ella Mae and I knelt, her hand a visor over her erect head with peppery grey. Ella Mae spoke to me and to Ms. Olatunde, whom she'd already made a pact with to protect me and the baby. "Nah, Odessa, they don't know enough about that virus, and Lamont busy workin to keep up with his own health, bills and medicine; you cain't be exposing the baby. And I should have said somethin before, but Olatunde and I couldn't send you to New York before 'cause he moved downstairs to O's old place, and we been paying his rent and utilities for now, 'cause all his money goin to AZT and doctor's visits. There just wasn't no money for all that."

I rubbed my hand across my newly acquired natural hair, a short afro like Ms. Olatunde's. The baby punched out my frustration, and I rubbed my belly to calm the life there. I didn't want to talk anymore.

We tended the garden, all three of us, straight through fall harvest, and we canned our produce and planted a second round of late collards. I welcomed the cooler weather as my whole body swelled. The day after a Mississippi Thanksgiving, I sat on my knees leaning sideways over my belly to spread leaves around the base of the broccoli. High, white clouds raced across a periwinkle blue sky. The last red maple leaf drifted down to where I knelt. The baby jabbed with a sharp kick, and without the pleasurable tension that comes before peeing, water flowed from beneath my skirt into the garden.

Chapter 15

I should have called him, but the pasty green of the hospital wall, the smell of alcohol and bleach on my tongue as I panted and endured each contraction, confused my impulse to call anyone. Sometimes I wanted Ella Mae, sometimes even Mama, and sometimes Lamont. I wanted to call him between contractions, but I didn't know how much worse the pain would get; each contraction took me deeper beneath some murky river where the surface of air seemed further and further away.

I should have called him after my baby boy, Walton, arrived. The beige phone, the same color as the bed railings, but every time I imagined picking up the clammy receiver and talking through the smell of my own blood, still as new in my nostrils as in my baby's nostrils, I smelled Lamont's new sweat that tipped my stomach with the smell of illness. I saw him answer, saw him laugh and yell in his scratchy voice high-pitched with excitement, so loud that the murky plastic over his window billowed with vibration.

Just weeks before Walton arrived, I had written to him, ignoring his illness, ignoring my pregnancy, and instead telling him about how Ms. Olatunde was harassing me to register for classes at Norfolk State. I told him Ms. Olatunde probably just wanted me to go all the way to Virginia to make more room for her and Ella Mae, but he did not entertain my denial.

Odessa,
Handle your business. Okay?
I'm still working at Express Credit Cards. I started AZT. I'm
flying to Paris one day. I always wanted to go there and sing in a
cabaret. I'm finally handling my business, you handle yours.
Love,
Lamont

I had missed an opportunity to apologize for my part in the space between us, to let him know that I was not really treating him like a leper; I was just afraid of losing him.

I should have called him, but I did not allow myself the thought that floated up in the afterbirth: that he might die one day. I lay there in the quiet of the cinder-block room, watching Walton's chest rise and fall where he was wrapped light like a Sunday ham, and I saw Lamont's smooth skin, shaved legs, a light-skinned, handsome man with big smile. I leaned over to the wheel-away nursery cart and lifted Walton into my arms, unwrapped him from the blanket and fell asleep, his raw skin against my raw chest.

When we awoke, Ella Mae and Ms. Olatunde stood over me. "Does he have all his fingers and toes?" Ella Mae, asked grinning.

"Yes," I said in a whispered smile. I had counted his toes like little BB pellets beneath rabbit skin, between my fingers. The bones of his skinny, curled digits between mine. With Ella Mae looking at me and me looking at him, I understood love for the second time in my life.

HE IS THE CERTAINTY of blood and skin and life. I wrote in my diary, *He is curled up in my mind right next to my image of you praying in Deddy's t-shirt that is weighted and floppy off your shoulders. You and Roscoe's bedside each night praying because you were told to pray; some ritual to assure waking.*

Now I lay me down to sleep
I pray the Lord my soul to keep
If I should die before I wake
I pray the Lord my soul to take
God bless Mama and Deddy
All my sisters and brothers
All my family and friends
Amen

I held Walton to my cheeks; his smell like new puppy. He and I the same, with separate hearts. His hair soft like the cotton inside of my Nakie doll, and I ached in that moment for Ella Mae on the day she lost me. My tears fell into Walton's angelic black wool naps.

The first week seemed like all the blinds were drawn and Walton wasn't out here in the world. Seemed like me and Ella Mae and Ms. Olatunde were inside the dark, small space of my womb with warm bottles and runny green diapers, washing yellow back to white, smell of vomit. The image of the beige phone disappeared, and Walton smiled his first smile. The blinds came up, and there was sun in the house again. Walton could be tickled, and tickles made smiles, and November turned to December, bringing the smell of cold, crisp sun on bleached white diapers. I dressed him in white t-shirts and little baby blue jean overalls that Ella Mae made. I was swept into the joy of new-life-reward for having endured. With the image of the beige phone someplace deep in the recesses of my mind, I went along with Ella Mae and Ms. Olatunde's illusion of me as a college student with a tiny baby. Christmas and New Year's, we were consumed with new life and the chores of preparing me for school, while Lamont was unintentionally ignored.

The four of us set out for Virginia; midyear enrollment at Norfolk State, with all of my belongings that fit into two suitcases and a box placed in the back of the truck. We slid out of January crisp sun of Mississippi and headed northeast to southern cities with sophisticated waterfront shops and clean, new cars. I found myself playing the theme song of the *Beverly Hillbillies* in my head, and I felt my foot pressing on the floorboards as if I could step on the gas to accelerate the red rusty truck. We expelled exhaust through the clean streets of downtown Birmingham and Knoxville, and finally a sign read Virginia. Water opened up on all sides as we rode in rhythm to the bounce of sea gulls over a bridge that sent the red truck out into open sea.

We were silent. Ella Mae gripped the steering wheel, and Ms. Olatunde smiled with her head out the window like a puppy. In the middle I held Walton's six-week-old body tight against mine, the same way I used to grip my Nakie doll. I slipped into a horror fantasy of the two of us sinking to the bottom of the ocean, little baby buoying up as my body sank away. *What was I doing?* I asked myself. I wanted to go home. My breath was quick, my eyes watery. "You all right?" Ms. Olatunde asked.

We had been watching the water, not the signs, and unexpectedly the red truck was swallowed into a tunnel beneath the Chesapeake Bay. We all screamed in fright and then nervous laughter, like we were on a roller coaster. We emerged with ocean all around again, and with Ms. Olatunde holding my hand, while Ella Mae steered us toward the land. Ms. Olatunde admitted, "I don't think I've ever done anything like that before." I relaxed, and noticed the sun, brilliant on the water, the sea gulls soaring on each side of the truck. This, I decided was the manifestation of freedom, and I let go my fierce grip on Walton—rusted red truck extended into the sparkle of sun on ocean, nothing but the thin pencil of a bridge beneath us—salt in the air merging with salt in tears, saliva, and blood. If the car went off the bridge and we drowned, that would be all right.

Part 3

Chapter 16

MY FIRST LONELY WINTER at Norfolk State; cold rain and leaves littered the black, shiny asphalt. Roaches and mice found their way into my half of the historic house turned duplex on the working-class side of the Elizabeth River. Portsmouth, the port city; the midtown tunnel separated me from the renovated historic houses in Norfolk. The direction of the wind—smell of diesel, sulfur from smokestacks, shipyard stench—held us to our side of the river.

Each day I drove the white Volkswagen that Ella Mae had bought, carried me and Walton to the Norfolk side of the river while my cracked muffler sent up fumes to announce my approach. When there was no traffic, school was ten minutes away, but if there was an accident in the tunnel, it was as much as an hour away. The worst was if traffic stopped while I was in the tunnel and the fumes outside the car and inside the car were so bad that I covered Walton's face with his blanket.

When I arrived on campus, I took Walton to the daycare run by the students in the Department of Child Development, and then I went to my work-study job in the Learning Center, and then to my classes. My major was English, which I always said under my breath, figuring no one would believe I had entered the age of computers wanting to be a professional poet, or professional diary writer.

At three o'clock, back to the Learning Center to help students with sentence structures that I also struggled with. Five o'clock, I picked up Walton, and on the way home I calculated the logic of dinner based on the amount of milk we had, the amount of food stamps I possessed, and what was in the refrigerator. I arrived home with Walton hoisted on my shoulder, somehow asleep in the cold damp air.

I kept up this routine through the winter and spring, straight through the sweltering heat of the summer as I played academic catch-up. Walton grew round and playful, and his crawl graduated to a wobbly stance. Summer passed, and fall and cold rain returned.

Ella Mae and Ms. Olatunde caught the train up for Thanksgiving and Walton's birthday. We sat around the little table made from one of the cable spools at the shipyard eating animal crackers, cheese crackers, and raisins, little dollar-store birthday hats perched on our heads. They giggled at Walton's persistent drooling and attempts at singing, and they complained of body aches. They swore they'd never ride the train again. They ignored the stillness on my face that awaited a conversation about Lamont, and I pretended not to notice the self-conscious glances each time there was the mention of the missing collard greens or chocolate cupcakes. And they protested too much in making their excuse for staying away from New York.

"Woo, we too old for train rides now, the body won't do what it used to. Where we gonna sleep tonight?" My eyes trailed away to the sofa fetched from trash day and the futon that lay on the living room floor. They got a hotel in Norfolk that night, and Walton and I came along for the TV and the companionship.

ONE DAY I opened the mailbox to find an envelope with my address handwritten on it. A letter from Lamont, and I saved it. I made dinner cooked slow to soften, because even with food stamps, baby food was not affordable. The letter sat on the counter in our dingy kitchen, waiting until Walton was bathed and my strange attempt at a lullaby was sung and forgiven. Walton slept and sweated, and I watched him, knowing that my peace of mind might be shifted after reading the letter. I touched the perfect wisp of hair on his neck, held his whole hand in the palm of my hand where it rested on his pillow. The second kiss goodnight was always for the little me, who I figured was once as precious, as perfect, as deserving of love.

I huddled in the tiny office I'd made for myself under the eaves of the stairs that led to the neighbor's upstairs apartment, turned on the pull-string single bulb, and read Lamont's words.

Today at work Odessa, things got boring while we waited for the next call log to print out. I made a paper airplane for you, like the ones from when we were kids. Remember, I was the airplane maker, the kite maker, the dried apple head doll maker? Later in the day I had a clinic appointment and made an airplane out of one of the chart pages the nurse had left next to the exam table. I flew it across the room, and I swear I saw you sitting in the chair across from me, and it landed at your feet and you were wearing that little blue calico jumper you hated. You bent down and all I could think is that I didn't want you touching the germy clinic floor, and you picked up the sheet of paper with my diagnosis.

I turned the letter over, but that was all. I looked back in the envelope and felt cheated. I read his words again and studied the image for metaphor: Did he not know that I already knew his diagnosis? What did he look like now? Why didn't he ask about Walton? Should I write him back? This was an opportunity. I was afraid.

The next morning I struggled to wake up, but the weight in the middle of my chest pressed me down to the bed. The remains of the night's rainfall dripped off a single pine branch outside the living-room window, where I slept on the floor. The train wailed a lonesome call in the dawn and past the smell of dampness in the walls of the turn-of-the-century duplex. The mourning dove cooed. Without permission from my waking mind, the missing Lamont bobbed to the surface through the underground passages of my sleep, the missing along with the wondering if he was okay.

I wrote him back. I concentrated over each thing said, erased the pencil marks and started over until it felt right, without apologies or reference to illness or fear:

Hey Lamont,

It's real busy for me having a baby and going to school. I miss you, I miss Ella Mae and Ms. Olatunde, and Jamella. I don't have any friends because they all talk about going to football games, going to the club, meeting up for one thing and another, and I don't have time for all that, and I hate weekends the most. Just like when I was still in Mississippi. I hate weekends, because there's just homework, and I usually take a walk with Walton on my hip. I haven't found a good stroller at the thrift store yet. I'm lucky to have a car even though I have to roll down the window to keep the fumes from killing us (ha, ha). I think Walton's cutting a tooth finally. He turned one the day after Thanksgiving and is just now cutting a tooth, but he's real good, whines some about it at night, but doesn't fuss. He must know that I need my sleep. I just put my arm around him and he goes back to sleep. Remember how Jessie was like that too, never cried unless we pinched him or something? Can you come visit?

I erased that last question, and the image of him miraculously standing in my doorway faded, but I couldn't get the depth of the pencil mark impression to lift out of the paper. Like the imprint of an insistent ghost, the words stayed, so I traced over my erased marks, breathing life back into the question.

The next Tuesday was the last day of finals, a doozie at school. I struggled to finish a final paper that I had to stay after class to turn in, and I got reamed by the director of the child-care center for picking Walton up fifteen minutes late. "One more time, and we'll call Social Services," she said. *Fine,* I thought, *as long as Social Services agrees to take us both in, feed us, and keep us warm.* I had not paid the gas bill or the electric bill, and I had to figure out how five dollars in food stamps would get me through the winter break. I walked into the foyer of the duplex and tried to put the key in my door, but it slipped out of the lock, defeating me. Walton slid off my hip, and my book bag pulled me off balance, and I held tears at bay. On the other side of the door the phone was ringing, and I wanted Ella Mae, but knew she wasn't going to stay up past her bedtime to call me later if I missed her.

I got me and Walton and my book bag in the door just in time to pick up the phone and pant, "Hello?"

Lamont replied in the raspy voice he used when he was happy. "I'm one bus stop away from downtown Norfolk. We're pulling in thirty minutes from now. Come get me, girl." I screamed like only his surprises could make me scream, and we both laughed from the gut.

The evening was unseasonably mild as we stood in our matching hooded mama and baby sweatshirts. Walton stood on his shaky new walking legs and stared up at me, uncertain if he should cry or laugh. The ride to the bus station was unfortunately cursed with the evening traffic of Christmas shoppers. The sun slowly lowered its brightness over the shipyard, drawing the color of rust out of the hues of battleship grey. My jubilance turned to nerves that caused every fourth beat of my heart to stumble. *What if Lamont is skinny and bald?* I hadn't seen anyone with AIDS, but I had looked in the school library under "terminally ill" and turned away from the "before" and "after" photos of people with various cancers; then I looked back to force myself to become anesthetized to the sight.

I held Walton's hand and pointed at the things that looked like moving houses with squeaky brakes. "Bus. See the bus?"

"Car," he insisted, and quacked excitedly.

"No, bus, Walton. B-U-S."

A film of neon radiator fluid covered my white tennis shoes where I'd stepped off the curb to keep him from leaping toward the bus-cars. I looked down at our feet, at his high-top leather walking shoes. Something about the preciousness of our feet, big and small, brought a twist of emotion for Benson, Daryl, and Jessie, a feeling that had become rare and distant now. But occasionally there was the sight of Walton's brown-fuzz hair, the feel of his bite-sized hand in mine, and suddenly I was inside some distant memory, like being lost looking through the contents of an old suitcase. Walton's little grip distracted me from the bus that had pulled in at the end of the line of diagonal-parked Greyhounds.

"Hey girl!" Lamont shouted in laughter. He wore his favorite Israeli black and white plaid scarf around his neck, even though the coolness of night had not yet descended. The orange lights above us flickered on as the sun dipped below the horizon, making his orange muscle shirt, white jogging shorts, and light brown skin look like the sepia tones of an old photograph. Face smooth, muscle over bone, he looked okay, he looked good, safe, and I swung Walton to my hip and ran to him. Our bodies pressed out the space, time and fear between us. He coughed a cry that righted itself, and we laughed again and stepped back to look at each other.

"Boy, you look fine. Richard don't know what he missing." My thoughts hovered over us: *He must be beating the disease. Maybe his diagnosis was a mix-up.*

He laughed again. "Girl, you look fine. Where are your glasses?" Then looked at Walton and whispered, "Hey," slow like air from a bicycle tire, and he reached for Walton, who went willingly. "Hey man. Oh my God," and I crossed my arms to stop the impulse of pulling Walton away from AIDS. I stood back to watched Lamont light up. He chatted with Walton, and Walton responded to the attention that I didn't realize he was so hungry for.

Lamont and I made a stir-fry, his with chicken, mine with tofu. The duplex filled with the smells of life. He said, "Girl, you need to get out."

I stirred in the pan. "I was thinking of going on a winter hike on Ocracoke Island with the school, but I can't afford it, and I don't think any babies are coming."

"Girl, I'm not talking about get out of the shelter of the house to walk around in the sticks, I'm talking about getting out on the town. Every city has evening child care. Break out of your shell. We're going dancing."

"What? You're crazy!" I responded, glad to have a reason to make noise in the house, glad for the life and light three people made.

We drove all the way to Virginia Beach for the evening drop-in center. The time away from each other dissipated, and we were in our old interactions of big brother instructing and little sister rebelling, insisting on having her opinions valued. I drove us down the highway, aware of his critical foot slamming on the imaginary brake pedal every time there was a slowdown of cars. I complained that I shouldn't take Walton to a new child care just for a one-shot night out, that I couldn't afford to pay the twenty-five cent tolls every time we got on or off the 44 expressway, but Lamont turned up the radio and said, "You gotta learn how to party!" Walton smacked the arm rest of his car seat to Salt-n-Pepa's "Push It," and Lamont laughed and egged on Walton's gurgles of laughter. The three of us shook the car with seat dancing as the bass propelled us down 44 east under the spy of streetlights to the drop-in child care.

I let myself be twenty going on twenty-one. Our first stop was Della's Street Bar, a gay club in the industrial neighborhood, where our lungs were young enough to endure the cigarette smoke clouds colored by lights that flashed like the color wheel on our aluminum Christmas tree of childhood. For hours we danced in circles to the bass that rattled the painted-black windows, until the spinning shifted equilibrium. People on the sidelines marveled at how our sibling movements synchronized, one encouraging the other, until the floor was cleared by the kicks and spins of sister-brother dances—and then on to the next club, and like the old folks used to say, "They gonna play that hard 'til somebody gets hurt," and we still did not heed that wisdom, but broke down like tired toddlers.

Lamont announced at 2 am, "I want to go to just one more club."

"Nah, I'm tired." I was spent and could only think of curling up on my futon on the living-room floor, the comfort of him on the sofa snoring in the dining room, and Walton safe where he belonged in his room. "Besides, the child care closes at 2:30." I was unlocking the car, already contemplating the danger of my driving under the influence of exhaustion. We had yet to traverse the night highways to Norfolk. Neither of us had had a beer, just the adrenaline high of too much dancing and too many uncommunicated emotions. An argument ensued. To win, Lamont threatened to stay out and just catch a cab back to the bus station. To win, I threatened to drop him at the club and let him find out that in this town there are no cabs at 2 a.m.

His strong, squat body stormed through the silver of street-lights then into the blue light of the open club door, to greet the thump of the bass and the fog of dry ice. There was a moment of doubt, of guilt, then confusion over his childishness. A question circled the rim of my consciousness for a second before I shut the passenger door and pulled away from the curb. Part of me insisted that I slow down and feel what was mismatched beneath that moment, but instead I indulged the sibling argument in my head: *He thinks I won't leave his butt here?* I insisted on the sameness of the sibling dynamic, when in fact the reality of us as children had been the first cell to die.

THERE MUST HAVE BEEN CABS that crossed the Tidewater city lines or men under strobe lights who would give rides to other men under the same lights. In my dream I saw him falling out of his mother's womb, a round, solid mass blackened with blood, and when he hit the floor I heard the sound of him slamming the door of the duplex. The familiarity of my key, copied onto his key ring, clanked in a pile on the cable spool table.

The next day, like rested children, we ate pancakes. Over breakfast we used Walton's kiddie tape player to record a deep conversation about dating, where my participation was completely theoretical. We played jacks and watched Walton attempt to run after the ball when it got loose, and I took Lamont back to the bus station.

Chapter 17

THE RHYTHM OF VISITS became regular in our lives again, that comforting certainty that is always danger-ous to take for granted.

On the next visit we celebrated my twenty-first birthday a month early with breakfast at IHOP. Then we dropped Walton off at the school day care and headed to one of the music rooms on campus. Lamont was determined to hear my voice solo, not muffled in the hidden voices of cousins in the choir stand or humming beneath the tones of the radio. As we walked, I sang the first bar of a Luther Vandross song. He said, "Girl, you can sing," but I could not convince myself to hear above the false flat notes that aunts and cousins had lied into my ear.

"You can't hear yourself?" he said, humming to repeat the notes I'd sung. "Odessa, I think all you've been through has opened something up. You used to sing flat 'cause you were holding on to the note. But you cain't let what other people think keep you from singing, from living your life the way it ought to be lived."

In the soundproof room, he played piano and demanded that I sing from my gut, to bring the sound up from my solar plexus, and I belted out "Killing Me Softly" in the safety of our encap-sulated space. We sang a medley of Donny Hathaway and Roberta Flack songs, and I could hear myself through his ears in a room where sound could not enter or escape. Sibling voices blended, reached a pitch in resonance in that harmony that is unmatched by any other sound from crows, or jays, or hawks, unmatched by jazz horns, unmatched; and we did not want to stop, but there were two minutes to cross the campus in the late spring drizzle and get me to the final exams of my sophomore year.

Lamont stuffed the sheet music in his leather satchel-like purse and slammed the piano cover down. "Girl, get to your class, 'cause I'm gonna be the one cheering you on when you finally graduate." Before he slipped on his jacket, I noticed, beneath the gentle arched brown hairs on his forearm, a shadow in the shape of his beloved New York.

That night I invited two classmates from the language lab to my birthday dinner. Lamont dressed us all up in feathers and big glasses, including Walton, and we laughed and sang into the night. When he was in town, he brought light and life to my otherwise monotonous existence.

Chapter 18

THREE YEARS into the college education that seemed impossible with a child and odd jobs of working on campus, cleaning houses, and landscaping The occasional Piggly Wiggly money orders from Ella Mae helped keep me afloat. After two summers of summer school, I'd caught up, and I had one more year before it would all be behind me. Lamont said that I would be the first of the estranged siblings to graduate college.

I spent the better part of summer taking an independent study course and perfecting the art of avoiding my landlord, who allowed me to rent the apartment for a mere $200 for another year as it was. The two women who moved in upstairs brought two dogs, a cat, and one parakeet, all in the small space of a one-bedroom duplex, but I was determined to stay put until graduation. I kept myself grounded by taking Walton to the park and studying in the library children's room, my long legs folded awkwardly where I sat across from Walton in the bright red chairs. On weekends I worried about money and wrote poems about everything that had brought me to that moment; journals like maps from my cradle to the hard futon mattress where I slept without air conditioning.

Fall came, despite my worries. Portsmouth, Virginia, in October was akin to July in St. Louis: hot and humid and bearable if I sat with my arms open, not moving. It had been six months since Lamont and I had last visited, and I was busy enough to keep myself focused, but I wondered if he was okay. I left him messages, and he called back when he knew I was not home. Somewhere deep inside, I still felt guilty for those two missed years of the pregnancy and Walton's birth.

I found myself thinking about Jamella sometimes, and I asked Ella Mae and Ms. Olatunde about her, but they reminded me that she had moved to Jackson, and no one had heard from her. Things kept moving me further from childhood and closer to an amorphous adulthood. I felt like I was nowhere, and I couldn't imagine my life in a year when school was done. What would I do with my degree in English. Where would I live? Where would I work? Each morning I went off to day care, to class, to work in the language lab, to day care for Walton, to the park, good jovial Mommy, dinner, bath, bedtime for Walton, and into the closet fashioned into an office, where I wrote in my journal, letters to Lamont that I never mailed.

I mopped every morning because the women upstairs and their organic pet farm had created a flea infestation that migrated downstairs for my flesh. The flea bites riddled my body each night where I lay on the living room floor, wondering what would happen first. Would I be eaten alive by fleas? Would the shift of Virginia's weather from hot to cold finally kill them off, or would my own poverty distract me so much from my studies that I would never finish school? I wanted to break down and beg Ella Mae and Ms. Olatunde for money to move, but the lowest rental price for a one-bedroom was next to the train, closer to downtown Portsmouth, and a whopping $450 per month.

On Saturday, I sat on the front porch of the dilapidated duplex, because the front porch was an easier place to be than the apartment, where I was convinced that the fleas were birthed between the gaps in the wooden floorboards where my mop water could not reach. Walton stooped low to the ground with his little shovel. He dug rocks and treasured each one. "Don't put that in your mouth," I said, over and over.

"Okay, Mommy," he said, and I was distracted from his two-year-old cuteness by thoughts of paying the rent, the electric bill, groceries; almost three months into the semester, and still no financial aid check. I fantasized about dramatically announcing to Ella Mae and Ms. Olatunde that I could not possibly schlep through another year of this; fantasized that I would work at the strip club near the naval base—the fantasy ended with me trying to imagine my long legs wrapped around a pole in a pornographic way.

"Good morning," the mailman said as he came into the yard, and I crossed my legs and folded my arms as if he'd been sitting in the strip-club audience. He handed me the mail and tousled Walton's head on his way down the walk.

No financial aid check, but I exhaled at the sight of one of Ella Mae's envelopes, with the return address written in chicken scratch and my address in straight and deliberate penmanship. I opened to the usual paper bag wrapper around a Piggly Wiggly money order and a small note on a Post-it in Ms. Olatunde's writing, a Post-it the two of them had obviously taken from the customer service desk, the place where the racist white store manager had once watched Ella Mae and Ms. Olatunde in his store: the young activist and the local whom Starkville had long since labeled as heathen.

We'll be there on Sunday. The white Post-it was stuck to something, and under it the flat blue and white round-trip plane tickets: dots and letters ORF and JFK, and another Post-it: *We'll stay with Walton. You should go be with Lamont.* The sun crept up the stairs in the heat of the late morning. I wept, confused about the source of my tears, embarrassed with the sun on me like a spotlight. I dried my eyes and watched Walton, his body in t-shirt and shorts, so miniature, his hands open to the gifts of things so precious to him, like machine-tumbled decorative yard rocks. He opened his hands to toss them over his shoulder after fully examining them, his lips pursed with intent. Then he glanced up at me with a little dirty hand as his visor from the sun. He saw my tears and said, "Hi Mommy?" I did not want to leave my baby, my familiar. But I would.

THE FANTASY of my first airplane ride turned into a nightmare. As the plane rolled down the tarmac, my heart beat faster and faster to match the speed of the yellow stripes passing until they were one yellow line. Water filled my bladder, and my womb and my breasts hurt, and I wanted Walton and wanted off the plane, and like an elevator lifting, we were off the ground. The earth was pulled away beneath me. My breath caught and waited and then let go at the sight of green trees like the naps of Walton's head. Golf courses like smooth green icing, blue water, ships like model toys in bathwater, clouds, sun above clouds. Heaven. My breathing steadied with the beauty of things.

I STOOD IN THE DARK grays and blues of John F. Kennedy Airport's furnishings and tight-knit carpet. People rushed around me. The sound of the overhead intercom and the line at an airport McDonald's distracted me from the thought of what Lamont would look like. Then there was his hoarse voice yelling, "Odessa!"

He came toward me, laughing, with an embarrassingly bright yellow balloon. He wore short pants in autumn; his legs hairy, his face not smoothly shaved, broken out in zits, but whole. He had dyed his hair red, and he looked like a little fox running toward me. I did not want the space and distance between us, I wanted to touch him like I wanted to touch the ground when the plane landed, wanted to close the space of the six months that should not have been left open, risking the entry of death.

We hugged, and there was an unfamiliar scent that my nostrils shut out, and our chests held us in a mold of one until he let go and said, "Girl, I'm telling you, without those glasses you look gorgeous."

I pushed him on the shoulders. "No, *you* look gorgeous." Then I pushed him harder, relieved that the horrors of him as an invalid were all in my imagination, that some miracle of AZT and sheer will had kept him Lamont. If there had been any changes, my brain registered them and dismissed them. I shoved him again, "Asshole, why didn't you call me when you knew I'd be home?"

And I could not have imagined what he said next. "Because . . . I was in Paris, and who the hell can figure out when you're home with a six-hour time difference?"

That night we caught the train to the Village, which took much longer than I had the patience for. Every now and then we looked at each other and smiled, and burst into a long exchange of stories. I told him again the story of Walton's birth and apologized at the end the way I always did.

"Don't worry about it," he said. He told me about the coffee shops, the Village Voice bookstore, and "the rue Princesse"; new words rolled out of his mouth, and I nodded, pretending to be as sophisticated as an American returned from Paris. He talked about the singing group he'd put together upon returning, called "All 4 Fun," about these months of fulfilled lifelong dreams.

"Whoo, and Odessa, the boogie-woogie boys over there in Paris!" He hollered over and over, looking as if he were eating a particularly good piece of pie, and I laughed as I followed him up the subway stairs to the street, nodding as if I knew what a boggie-woogie boy was. He fiddled with the zipper on his suit bag, which acted like a sail as we made our way down Hudson Street. "I can't wait for you to see what I have in store for you," he said, and we smiled at each other in the peach dusk against red brick. I figured the suit bag meant I was going to hear his new singing group.

It was dark when we arrived, just blocks from NYU in the night air of New York, and I remembered, despite fusion jazz chaos, how much the city made me feel alive. Lamont's step was light, and the two of us bopped along. I was his little sister again, not measuring my words and questions to accommodate his feelings. "So, Lamont, it doesn't bother you to walk around Richard's old campus?"

As soon as I asked, I felt his hand in mine loosen. Lamont let go to hoist the suit bag onto his other shoulder again, and I kept stepping quickly to apologize, because Walton had taught me well, to apologize for things that came out of my young mouth, that needed to be re-said with a mature voice. "Hey, sorry."

"Girl," he said, his face relieved beneath the orange street light. Lamont was out of breath, but his mood was still elevated by the stench of garbage combined with the sound of laughter and music from three directions. Latino brass, jazz guitar, some voice belting a show tune from a basement club. "Girl, Richard is history, I'm living in the moment. Doing what I'm obliged to do for me, living while I'm alive. *Toujours gai!*"

The evening air touched my bare face. A chilly breeze mocked my long-sleeved black dress and sandals. There had been an amorphous energy floating just above Lamont's head in the fluorescent light on the train, just above his head in the streetlights of Greenwich Village; the thing of disease, with its smells covered by cologne, its sours covered by makeup; but for the moment it was just an amorphous light.

Lamont opened his hand to the door of the basement club in front of us. "This is it," he said. We entered as if we were going down into the St. Louis basement to do laundry or skate on the cement floor or steal popsicles from the locked freezer.

We walked in and saw three men and someone whom I believed was a woman, dressed in lovely evening reds and blacks, smooth brown faces, beautiful people. Lamont introduced me to them and got us both drinks. They were Lamont's friends, and I wanted to move hand to glass with the same grace and freedom from self-consciousness that he and they possessed. It wasn't long before Lamont took one more sip of his drink and disappeared into the smoky dark toward the bathrooms, and I watched him in his waist-length jacket, like John Travolta in his handsome swagger that showed he believed in the movement of all the muscles inside his tight jeans.

Lamont's friends called behind him, "Give it to 'em baby," "We love you song bird," kisses blown to where he vanished behind a curtain. Glasses clinked above laughter and cigarette smoke inside the warm belly of this club. I crossed my legs, uncomfortable without Lamont there, the sudden awareness of stale air around me. I sipped the Shirley Temple and answered a sophisticated "Absolutely" to almost every question.

The emcee came out in a white suit, a tall Italian man dressed with Liberace flair.

"Ladies and wannabe ladies . . ." Voices erupted in laughter, and so did I, to stay in sync with the crowd.

"Have I got a treat for you. All the way from Harlem," they erupted into laughter again, "Josephine's favorite performer, just back from Paris, Miss Sara'n Dippity!" The applause expanded and then contracted to silence as the room went black. The lights came up onstage, and there was a shapely white-sequined strapless dress, white gloves, a plumage of peacock feathers that fanned and revealed eyes like Mata Hari. The light above *her* head, the same luminescence of the fluorescent light above *your* head the day we stood in the moldy air conditioning of the library trailer, and you scolded me with your eyes to get me to fill out the library card application. The light above *her* head the same as the orange streetlight where *you* stood just beyond the chain-link fence on the night when *Saturday Night Live* had gone off, and Deddy came home drunk and lifted your teenage body up with one hand and yelled, "Get out of my fucking house, faggot," and you stood, a silent protest-statue on the sidewalk, unmoving just beyond Deddy's property, visible all night to the west St. Louis neighbors. The light above *her* head unafraid to die, like the light above *your* head in the stained-glass light from your Harlem AME church. Mata Hari eyes, yours. I saw for the first time past the place where rules try to make sense out of how you are my brother. You are white sequins and feathers and black leather waist-length jacket, and I love you.

LAMONT LOWERED THE FEATHER FAN and stepped to the mic, the familiar call of my brother's voice unashamed, the sound rising up from the place where the navel chord was once clipped:

And I am telling you, I'm not going . . .

The chill like embalming fluid through my veins, and I am with him inside the dark, cavernous wombs of our separate mothers, picking up the perfectly rounded pebbles that we place in our mouths and tumble before showing them to each other, the silk of saliva still there; the soprano of song from his throat showing me who he is in the way I had not allowed myself to see him. We are the children wanting to be loved, wanting to belong so much that no number of slappings could make us change course. His voice, like the first cry for breath after birth.

Darlin', there's no way . . .

Lamont's white-gloved fingers fanned out to the audience, but I knew he was gesturing to our invisible siblings who had abandoned us.

There's no, no no no way I'm livin' without you . . .

That night in the basement cabaret in Greenwich Village, I watched Lamont let go of the root of all fear, costumed beneath lights that caught a sparkle for every subtle movement of his unexpected curves. For an instant, I felt the inevitability of his death, but turned my eyes quickly from the stage to the comfort of the Shirley Temple, to the dark audience like one quiet mind all watching one dream. There were tears in the dark on faces lit by him.

Chapter 19

S PRING NIGHTS, Lamont called me from New York to complain that the other siblings were shutting him out, but I was distracted by the impossibility of finals and the plausibility of graduating, so I did not allow myself to feel his words.

"Lamont, fuck them if they can't pull their prefrontal body parts out of their posterior body parts." He giggled and coughed, the only one who ever laughed at my linguistics jokes. And then he asked the question that caused me to wonder about his state of mind. "Can you call Mama and talk past her insistence that if I get good rest I'll beat that 'cancer'? I need to see her. Call her and talk past her homophobia and all that unnecessary laughing she does and tell her to come see me."

I shook my head no, but told him I would try, in order to get off the phone and get back to my studies.

Each night, I imagined the conversation with her and then abandoned the idea, and all I could offer him without risking my own hurt was the nightly calls where I got to be with him, without smells or visuals to remind me of the truth. On the phone he said the AZT was helping, and I resigned myself to believing him.

He insisted on not missing the event of all events, and he arrived a week early for my graduation so he could watch Walton while I wrote my final papers. At the bus station, Walton and I stood on the black asphalt saturated with motor oil and radiator fluid, the smell of diesel fumes trapped under the overhang with us. When the bus pulled up, "Norfolk" on the scroll above the bus windshield, I stood with one hand holding Walton's and the other using the camera as goggles through which to view the moment.

It was with the shock of seeing him that my finger depressed the button, the flash startled. The man I saw was thirty years older than the brother I had visited just six months before. The man I had seen transformed into a swan on stage was now withered like a crumpled paper crane. Lamont wore a tam hat and a sweater that hung open over his reduced shoulders and a white t-shirt that did not look quite clean. A pain emanated from my left ovary, and I wished I had not had the coffee that stirred in my belly, wished I had not worn the red t-shirt.

He stepped down slow, and I bent to whisper to Walton, pretending to wipe something from his face, "Your uncle isn't feeling well today, so he looks a little different." Walton's eyes on mine, open wide like in the first moments of life when he breathed; purple-skinned baby with eyes and fists clenched until I said his name and his eyes opened, permanent, here, in this world, our tears meeting in the air of the delivery room.

I smiled and hugged Lamont, inhaled then held my breath against the intake of the smell of some infection, alcohol rubbed over pus. My nose burned. *Don't cry—no.* I looked out at lush, green spring leaves on distant trees. The sun caught there on the parking lot like stage lighting for the happiness of other people receiving New York relatives from the bus, their lives in order. For those people, this day would be a normal weekend, a trip to the mall or the park with the kids, some light housekeeping, perhaps an evening ride to the Waterside, and I tried to imagine our weekend that way. *Yes, we'd play, then settle in for a week of serious study and prep for graduation.*

I told Lamont the list: "First shopping, then nachos, and your favorite movie, *Hair Spray*. My friends from the language lab who we partied with before are going to join us at the apartment." I heard my voice, like Mama's, making small talk over pain. We talked about getting the place ready for Ella Mae and Ms. Olatunde, how he would make curtains for the window in the living room while I worked on my paper, and the two of us ignored the fact that he seemed to grow exhausted with the excitement, the heat inside an air-conditioned car, our spines stiffened against my acknowledgement of emotion and his acknowledgement of fatigue.

We stopped and picked up a paper, and while I drove, he went through it and job-hunted and apartment-hunted for me, but in the back of my mind I was thinking I would ask him to stay in Virginia, where I could take care of him. I chattered about our weather, the ugly cap and gown, anything to keep the smells and sights from reaching the part of my brain that translates pain.

In his first surrender to fatigue, Lamont demanded that we go to the thrift store in Chesapeake where we had once gone. I reminded him of the forty-minute drive, but he insisted in a reprimanding voice, "Girl, I said that's where I want to go." I did not want one of our usual fights, did not want the slamming of doors and sibling ultimatums when he was not well; and stress would not help him get better. I glanced at Walton in the back seat, dirty lollipop grin of a two-year-old not aware of anything but the possible fun of the moment, and I turned the white VW around to hop on the interstate.

At the thrift store we went up and down aisles trailing behind Lamont, who seemed intent on finding something he held in secret. He stopped on an argyle sweater. "This is it. I want you to wear this to the graduation."

"Boy, it's like ninety degrees. I don't want to wear that ugly thing." But he threw it over his arm and picked up shoes for Walton that were too large. *Just follow along*, I thought, hoping his odd behavior would stop soon. The day turned surreal as I watched us through the heat waves of the day, the light sifting toward an odd depression, but I fought the gentle tug into a Dali painting where Lamont's mind distorted and melted in the heat.

At the counter, he couldn't find his wallet, forgot that he was speaking above the volume of conversation when he called me across the store. I rushed over, paid for the items, laughing uncomfortably with the clerk the way Mama would, and rushed out of the store singing the *Sesame Street* song to convince Walton that everything was normal.

Lamont limped, grimacing, behind us, and Walton switched the song to an old KC and the Sunshine Band's tune, popping his fingers to make me laugh. *We are having fun*, I force-fed myself.

In the parking lot, Lamont stopped three times, blaming me for Virginia heat. "You should rest," I said, but he spit words over the car hood where he and Walton stood holding hands, waiting for me to unlock the door. "Girl, open the damn door. I didn't say I wanted to rest. Open the damn door." He sounded like Deddy, and my hand trembled to get the key in the lock. Where had Lamont gone?

He demanded we go next to the Montgomery Ward. That was a bit closer to home, and I was glad, because I didn't want to be disrespectful and demand he rest. There he insisted on buying Walton a small TV just like the one from Mama's press-and-curl perch, just like the one in the Harlem apartment. "Odessa, I was going to bring him the TV and my keyboard, but I couldn't take all that to Port Authority." He raised his voice. "I said I want to buy it. This is between me and him." The little girl in me screamed, *He's scaring me*, and she curled up in a corner, but I smirked and said, "Have it your way, Burger King." I resisted the heaviness that began to seep into the corner of my eyes as I watched my brother limp away to the checkout, where he purchased the TV, despite my disapproval.

I looked at the clock over his head, which didn't seem to affect him, as the red second hand clicked. I quietly reminded him that Nicole and Christopher would be at the apartment soon. A year ago on my birthday, Nicole and Christopher had made Lamont laugh, dressed as Sonny and Cher. We had sprawled out on the duplex floor that night, ignoring fleas with laughter and too many beers.

He insisted on carrying the TV to the car, limping and

grimacing all the way. The sun had reached its highest place in the sky, making enduring the moment much more difficult. All of my energy seemed to go to my sweat glands, the energy to stay cool diverted from the energy to stay sane. Walton walked behind Lamont, and I walked behind Walton, keeping myself from the smell that I was sure was coming from Lamont's legs.

In the car, the tension ebbed as Lamont turned back into himself to tell me the story about his and Richard's Oriental rug. "Remember I found that rug on the street? I can't believe somebody threw away an Oriental rug." He talked with laughter in his throat. "And I took it to that Chinese laundromat down from my place on Lenox, and you know I had to fold it to get it in the washing machine, then I had to fold it to get it into the dryer, and that thing started bucking, and I had to push against the door to keep the dryer from flying open." His deep voice got more scratchy and filled with laughter as he got to the part that always made the two of us laugh. "That little Chinese woman came in screaming. 'Get it out! Get it out!' and I held that dryer door as long as I could before she started pulling on me. 'Get it out!'"

This time I was off inside my head and did not laugh until, from the back seat, Walton started laughing like he was being tickled, his voice like a waterfall bubbling over, and in his little toddler voice he started screaming, "Get it out! Get it out!" The three of us were careening down 64 now with the heat of April stuck inside the car. Smells of sickness made laughter welcomed; laughter, spewed up from the same place in my belly where sorrow is formed like hard little marbles.

Lamont's laughter encouraged Walton's, which resulted in his squealing screams over and over, until Walton fell asleep and the two of us could not ride the distraction of that joke any longer. With the rhythm of the road came the request that made it evident that Lamont, my protector, my teacher, my big brother had been possessed by virus. "I want to go to the Church's Chicken near the thrift store."

"You wanna go back? Forty minutes east of here? I'd rather not. There's a Church's Chicken on the way home. You don't need that anyway. I bought some healthy food." I was trapped going through the Midtown tunnel, a quarter mile beneath the Elizabeth River. The darkness despite daytime above the tunnel mirrored Lamont's sudden shift.

"Fucking take me to the fucking Church's Chicken. The one I wanna go to."

I was suddenly afraid that traffic would stop in the tunnel and he would leap out of the car. I heard my own voice soothing but firm, the voice I used with Walton. "No, that's too far from here." I told myself not to get angry with him, not to escalate to rage. I could hear Walton whispering something in the backseat. He was waking up, and I did not want him trapped inside of a car with a man's voice cussing and accusing in a way that would signal to him that something was not right. In the rearview mirror, I saw Walton's large eyes, just like my own in the back of our childhood station wagon, confused at Mama and Deddy's shift from happy at the fishing creek to angry behind the steering wheel; adults in the front seat of a car that the kids could not control. I exhaled as we exited the tunnel; the sun engulfed us as the darkness fell away.

I turned the car at the first right toward home, and I endured the angry rant that exhausted itself without fists.

Nicole and Christopher waited for us on the porch, the two of them huddled in the one bit of remaining shade.

"Sorry, guys," I said cheerfully, and Lamont limped with Walton and the TV past their uncomfortable glances into the apartment and then the bedroom. He came back out in a pair of shorts. The sores on his legs were yellow, the smell of pus a faint aura around him.

"Will you work on my legs? They hurt," he whined, like Walton would when he was angry with me but still wanted to be tucked in at night by my hands. My eyes were fixed on the TV, numb, staring. I answered him from that numb place, "Shh, the movie is about to start." My two friends pretended not to notice the smell or the sight, but the bowls of popcorn remained untouched for the remainder of the movie.

I knew what he wanted. He wanted touch, but I didn't know how to give him that. Touch, for me, had so often meant violation, touch had been like collision in my life, the impact beginning where skin touches skin but ending where organs collide against the cage of bones. I could not touch him without feeling the twist in my belly of the oncoming impact.

The next day he did not talk to me when he got on the bus, did not mention the graduation that he had come so far to witness, did not wave to me and Walton from the bus window. I took Walton to the park and out for a popsicle, and I did not cry until Walton was asleep and I could shut the door of my closet-turned-office beneath the eaves of the stairs, sobbing for the loss of the brother who took me to the Dairy Queen and library; the brother who stood wearing black mascara, turning man into spirit on a black-velour-curtained stage, singing. Lamont was no longer my brother with AIDS. He had become the disease itself.

I WAS GRATEFUL for the need to spend the week focusing on my last finals, my last papers, but superficial focus could not still the chaos beneath the surface. That week I confused the day for my geometry final with the day for my world history final. I forgot to take my linguistics exam altogether. On the last day to submit work, I could not find my final lit paper. With the sun and humidity suffocating me, I sat in my white Rabbit outside the humanities building, afraid to face my advisor, the pain in my head making it difficult to see.

"That's a migraine," my advisor said, disappointed that, like a runner who had sprinted too hard at the beginning of the race, I had petered out at the finish line. She opened the grating metal desk drawer, handed me Excedrin, and filled out the forms for the six incompletes. All I could say before the tears was, "My brother's sick."

"It's okay. You can do your finals next semester, which is when you were supposed to graduate anyway. Just take your time." She left me in her office to compose myself.

THE NEXT SATURDAY, I lay on the sofa wishing the sun would shine, wishing I didn't need to be cheerful for Walton each time he came running from his room, cute and scruffy. "Look, Mommy, look." I wished I could not feel the oncoming wave of emotion that I vowed to build an abutment against. The tears came faster than my sandbags of denial. On the stove, Walton's quick oats smelled like warm, wet cardboard, the aroma seeping through the faulty structure of my dammed emotions. I remembered the weekend I visited Lamont for spring break only to find out that Richard had left him. How long was the incubation period? Had Richard given Lamont the virus? That fucker.

Later in the day, I didn't remember getting up and putting the oatmeal and molasses in Walton's bowl, didn't remember if I'd kissed his forehead, but with the ringing of the phone, there was the clank of his frog spoon in his green bowl. "I'm done, Mommy." He ran back to his room to sing the Ninja Turtle song and make race-car sounds as he stomped and tumbled with sticky breakfast fingers.

I answered the phone, and Lamont was sobbing before I could ask who it was, and like the sibling voices that rose and fell in harmonic pitch, the feet that danced and kicked synchronized without a choreographer, my body lurched forward on the sofa, and I wept with him, the dam broken. I searched my head for something to make Lamont feel better, just as I searched for the right toy or a piece of candy under the car seat to keep Walton from crying. I thought maybe I should call Mama, or go get her. Just show up at her door, or at Towanda's door, and cattle-prod them into a car, onto a train, and through the streets of Harlem to his apartment.

"Lamont," I said, "why don't you come here and stay? Let me help take care of you. You can have fresh air, and I can grow

some veggies for us . . .." I stopped midsentence, the sound of
my own voice like reading a fairy tale to Walton at night; healing tomatoes full of antioxidants, like magic beans. "Lamont," I
continued, "at the library I read that if you keep up with your
antioxidants and leafy greens and take the AZT, you can live
on out the rest of your days fairly normal, except the need to
medicate." But I hadn't found any such case study of medi-
cal-miracle survivors in the library's microfiche of newspaper
articles. I was Mama, believing her own lies. I made it up, made
up the research that proved that the right combination of meds
and herbs could save him, and I blotted out my memory crying in the library basement, where the microfiche newspaper
articles on AIDS were kept morgue-style, the roll of young
black men's names like the rolls of the returning war dead, all
the names of Lamont's friends, from the men in the cabaret to
the names I'd only heard him mention, microfiche obituaries
of brothers, uncles and sons taken by the lie of cancer, none of
them memorialized under the gay stigma of AIDS.

Lamont was now silent, but I could hear him breathing, and
I sank back onto the sofa to be in that momentary relief with
him.

"Odessa . . ." His voice was a defeated whisper. "This is my
city. I know I don't have but a few friends still here, but I'm not
getting better. I'm dying." Over the image of Lamont sitting in
a southern sun eating a red ripe tomato came the slow lighting
of the basement club, and he began to sing "Killing Me Softly"
into the tunnel of my ear.

"Stop it!" I demanded, but he hummed the whole tune,
though I had already gotten up and cleaned the table, washed
Walton's bowl, and began clipping coupons, all with the cord of
the phone trailing behind me like a leash.

"You still there?" he whispered after the end of his song.

With his next words, I wished I'd known to close my ears,
close them before I heard his cry for a cavalry to hold him up
and do his bidding. "Odessa, can you call Mama and our siblings

and ask them to come see me? I called the house a couple of times, but Mama just laughs and talks about sending me aspirin and Tang, how the two mixed everyday for breakfast will keep my blood thin and help me beat the 'cancer.' I asked her for Towanda's number, but she said she didn't have it, and Benson picked up the other line and I said hi, but he hung up." His voice shifted from a whisper to the tenor cracking of a thirteen-year-old boy. "I'm so tired," he said. "I'm so tired." I distracted myself and looked at the back of Walton's little head, in silhouette to the TV, cartoons in black and white. His little ears moved up and down as his baby-corn-kernel-shaped teeth chewed on a hard granola bar that I had not told him he could have.

"Odesssa," Lamont said, his voice tenor again. "Don't ever wait to do the stuff you want to do with your life, 'cause all the excuses I had, like Richard needs to come with me or I don't have enough money, all the excuses, and I could have been to Paris a long time ago before getting sick."

I could hear the wind of sleep blowing through his voice. He was quiet and sniffed again, and I told myself not to cry. I needed to be the mother I could not fetch for him. "Lamont," I whispered, "go to sleep. You need to rest, then we'll talk again later."

"But, you can call Towanda and Roscoe and LaVern and them, right?" I agreed, the muscles of my chest squeezed around my heart to get him to hang up. My ability to hold my breath any longer faltering.

He exhaled, and I could hear him gently weeping. "Shhh," I whispered, and hung up.

That afternoon I went to the laundromat, grocery shopping, anything to keep the rain on the outside of my body from becoming the rain on the inside. I never considered the call to Mama or our siblings, and the more I cleaned the house, played with Walton, and studied, the further away his request lay in the back of some closet of my mind.

As day turned to, night I traded those distractions for ones of making Richard or somebody pay. Maybe the universe was like the scales of justice. Maybe somebody else could die and Lamont could live.

Two times a day, I mopped the wooden floors with Murphy's Oil Soap. The smell of the secret ingredient, a peppery oil of citronella, filled the duplex. My two neighbors with the two flea-infested dogs said their apartment was flea-free and maybe I just needed to clean my house. Then they ascended the stairs in safari shorts, black hairy legs next to pale white, flea-bite-riddled legs. These two women took everything about being free and wholesome to a sickening level. They did not believe in bathing dogs, these women who found it necessary to tell that they did not use pads or tampons, which might fill the landfills, but they used two sponge cups that they excavated from their vaginas with dirty fingernails that they did not believe should be scrubbed, which would only wash away healthy bacteria. I needed someone to hate, and they made it easy.

I told Ella Mae about them using the word "lesbian" each time I described their behavior. Ms. Olatunde reminded me that Lisa and Theresa were a disgrace to lesbians, to white people, to dog owners, even to flea-bitten folk, but that I shouldn't focus on the fact that they were lesbian. "Internalized homophobia," she said, and I was glad they had a phone in the house now; but I didn't like that my conversations with Ella Mae were now my conversations with both of them.

"Okay," I said, surrendering to her philosophy. "Can I talk to Ella Mae now?"

"Focus on finishing those incompletes," Ms. Olatunde advised in the background, "or quit talking about what you don't like and take action; write a letter to the county health department."

Ella Mae shushed her in the background, and it was good to be fussed over. "She don't need to write a letter," Ella Mae said, her voice echoing in the room; "what she need is citronella."

For two weeks Ella Mae and I continued a distracting conversation about miracle herbs. I told her about sorrel, that I thought it was something that grew in Mississippi, and for the next two weeks she tried to send little plants in a bubble-wrapped box, but when it arrived I had a moldy cardboard box, wet bubble wrap, and a tiny pot that contained dirt and the rotting remains of a dead little plant.

I asked Ella Mae if she believed that God made bargains; maybe he could take someone bad from the planet and leave Lamont. She counseled me with words I wouldn't understand for a long time. "Odessa, death is no more a punishment than birth. It's just part of the whole cycle." I got off the phone thinking she'd avoided my question.

That weekend, I sat on the front porch trying to write that lit paper while Walton rode his Big Wheel up and down the sidewalk, the power of hard black plastic and grinding concrete beneath him. He added a roar with his red lips in a perfect *o* and turned my way for my manufactured smile of congratulations. I heard brakes squeaking at each stop sign on our street, starting at the far end and slowly coming this way, eventually getting loud enough to drown out the sound of the Big Wheel. That should have clued me in to her arrival, but I looked up only when Walton's wheels stopped grinding and Ella Mae's boot entered my vision of book, highlighter, and front steps.

"Mae, Mae"—the closest thing to *Mama* I'd ever called her—barked from my throat. Relief stood out on my face in beads of sweat where I held onto her, one step up to have my arms around her neck, which lacked the thickness and bulk it had once had. I prayed that the flea-harvesting upstairs neighbors would peer from their windows or come walking down the street. I didn't know if they were home, because they did not believe in releasing carbon monoxide poisons and there was no car to indicate their presence; but I wanted them to see what a real woman who lived off the land looked like, how different the real thing was from two women in an apartment proclaiming their undying loyalty to Mother Earth by burning sage and beating on a drum.

Several potted plants sweated in black plastic rounds, wilting beneath the tarp in the truck bed. "Finally," she said, "you got some herbs." It was true, but I suspected her words were mere substitutes for some other reason why she had driven all that way.

We embraced on the stairs again, and Walton's wheels slipped over concrete in the background. From down the street he yelled, "Look, Mae, watch this." Not even a hello to her before pedaling in reverse, hitting the brake, and doing a three-sixty skid. Ella Mae whooped and hollered, and I looked longingly at the front door, wanting to usher us in before drawing any more attention from my neighbors, a mix of young professionals, shipyard workers, and starving, flea-bitten artists.

My dining room sported a dark blue sofa in a large gardenia pattern. I noticed my own apartment with the eyes of someone new, catalogued and assessed my possessions, and quickly realized that "junking," as Ella Mae put it, was a habit formed in her care. It was the sofa where Walton's rescued albino feral cat had ripped open an armrest, leaving fluffy sofa guts exposed; the act that got that cat sent to a farm to live. It was the sofa where I dozed half awake while Lamont talked into the receiver at night, working through the pain that gripped his legs as Kaposi's sarcoma ate him alive.

Ella Mae walked out of my living room/bedroom, not commenting on the fact that my décor had not improved over the years. I barreled past where we stood next to the sofa and the table made from a giant cable spool. I showed her the cloth fetched from the thrift store. "Makes a nice tablecloth, don't you think?"

"Mm-hm," she said, and I wrapped my arms around the solid square of her midsection.

"Sit," I said, motioning her to one of my two mismatched chairs and reminding myself to straighten my back against the embarrassment.

"Gladly," she said. She stepped gently and pulled the chair

out as if she would surely break it. "The place looks good, looks real good."

"I can't believe you drove up here. Can I get you some lemonade? I made it yesterday, and it has mint in it. What did Ms. Olatunde say when you left?"

Ella Mae laughed. "You know Olatunde's all about business. She gave me a box of the business cards, ran to get the photo book of the rugs, said she'd make a list of home stores up this way." She acted out Ms. Olatunde reaching and looking deliberate, and we both giggled. I walked off to get the lemonade and a sigh escaped my chest. I could not wait much longer before asking her again why she'd driven so far.

"Okay, Odessa," she sang after me, "get the lemonade, then come sit down." I was already in the kitchen and thinking about what she'd make of how wild Walton had gotten. He made the sound of airplanes crashing and ran in and out of his room like the kids we used to see in town and tisk at. I heard her say again, serious, practiced and deliberate, "Come sit down."

I came and sat down, and Ella Mae's voice sounded like it was made of swamps and juniper trees, peach and persimmon. Despite Ms. Olatunde's attempts to establish proper English, Ella Mae still spoke in the guttural speech that the amalgam of Mississippi grief and passion brings. She rolled the vowels around on the back of her tongue, and I listened intently but did not understand her at first. The more she spoke, her lips purple and grey from the hemp cigarettes she and Ms. Olatunde now smoked, the more I listened and saw the creeks in Starkville on hot summer days; tall, green, weeping trees that were beautiful in their gracefulness; grass gone hard and golden in the heat where it clenched and held itself to the hard orange clay the way naps of hair hold to the scalp.

"Lonindongon," she said, over and over. "Lonindongon."

It was only after I took the first sip of the lemonade that I understood and translated: *Loni done gone*. Loni, my father, Deddy. Done gone.

The spirit of my father blew away like the smoke of a cigarette after it has lingered in the air in rings, playing idly until it is ready to evaporate. Before the luxury of my thought could photograph the shape of the moment and respond accordingly, involuntary tears came from the five-year-old side of my heart, and I saw the image of him where I looked up from under the coffee table, his cigarette dangling, and suddenly my twenty-two-year-old mind tricked me and plotted to blow out the match and save him, like when I was five years old, before his madness became the pain in my life. I remembered being six, seven, eight and wanting to go to the racetrack with my father, wanting to go fishing with him, because I could not remember then his sins against my five-year-old body. I saw him standing on the porch, wild uncombable hairs shining in the yellow glow of the porch light, Grandeddy's rifle in my grip, the sin of worms of his sex crawling between my legs, bruises on my thighs crying out for me to shoot; but he was my father.

In balance with birth there is death; the way it rips through life like a vein being pulled out through an eyelid, unraveling every other vein attached right down through the toes. And in the end, mother or father, even if you didn't like them, even if you didn't know them, you want the possibility of them when you realize they are gone.

"What you thinkin about?" Ella Mae said over and over, bewildered by my tears. Then she rose to turn on the little black and white TV in Walton's room. She shut Walton's door, and as she went to the kitchen to fetch me a glass of water, she said, "What you thinkin about?" Her voice mixed with the clicking open and slapping shut of the cabinets, and then, a last time, when she brought me the glass, "What you thinkin about?"

I could not verbalize the layers of thought: guilt over asking God to take the bad one; hope that the absence of bad would leave energy in the universe for the miracle of Lamont's survival; contorted pain at the death of blood kin, blood rapist; the strange diminished feeling, as if some cells from my own body had died off; the death of an unspoken hope that Deddy might some day redeem himself and be like a father.

"What you thinkin?" she asked again.

My first words turned the attention away from me. "How am I gonna tell Lamont?"

She put the phone on the table between us. "I'll do it if you need that. It don't hurt me like it hurts you and Lamont."

I saw Lamont and me in silhouette beneath the mimosa tree on the front of that book, the only two siblings on the outside. I said, "I'll do it." I blew my nose with the roll of tissue Ella Mae had put in my grip, and I dialed the number.

At first he didn't say anything. Then I sat through sobs that were embarrassing to hear, coming from the child who had endured Deddy's punches, sobs that pulled the same salt waters out of my body and helped right my own confusion. I could not cry again for the death of my abuser. Ella Mae touched my hand, reminding me that I had her, and he had no one. The death of our father had brought the breath of mortality close to Lamont's ear, and he sobbed to push away the evocative sound of that voice.

I could see myself there at the table in the round blackness of Ella Mae's compassionate stare, and the sweetness of belonging in Walton's voice behind the bedroom door, and I wanted to regurgitate the guilt and make it make sense that Lamont cried for his father. I wanted to comfort him.

We got off the phone, and I sat there thinking, not thinking, staring, not seeing. Ella Mae talked above the sound of my musing. "You did not pray away your father. You cannot bring him back for Lamont."

We were silent. The heat of the day took hold on the apartment. I dried my eyes and said, "But his mother and sisters and brothers are still here. I wanted to do for him what he tried to do for me those Thanksgivings in New York when he handed me the phone, but I refused."

Ella Mae said for me not to go, that I wasn't going to be

able to go to a funeral and get my sisters and brothers to go see Lamont. "Odessa, trust me, I done tried the very thing you trying now. Thought goin to my mama's funeral was gonna make things different between me and her and them, but things don't change unless everybody in the situation is ready to change."

I looked her in the eyes. "Remember when you said I needed more family? Lamont needs his sisters and brothers. I can't give him anything right now, can't make him feel comfortable . . ." I walked in Walton's room and started rolling his clothes up and stuffing them into his little backpack. He got the message and ran around grabbing Hot Wheels cars, glad to be going somewhere.

"Ella Mae, I can stand up for Lamont the way he would stand up for me. I can go tell them face to face that he needs them."

I took my books out of my back pack and rolled up my black polyester dress, a pair of black jeans for Walton, underwear and socks for the two of us. Ella Mae pleaded once more. "Odessa, get on the road following me until I get to my turn-off. If you change your mind, just turn off too and come on down home with me." But I was already lost in the fantasy of talking to Towanda; the image of her in the picture with the fluffy collar. I was already holding her newest baby on my hip and trading stories with her and Roscoe and LaVern about how mean Deddy was, about how we had to stick together because we were still kin. In the end of my fantasy they were shocked and upset to find out Lamont was sick, and they packed their bags, called for flights and bus tickets.

In front of me where the heat waves made wavy lines between the white Volkswagen and the red truck, Ella Mae signaled for 64 east, and there was the sound of her horn blowing a long warning as I turned to get on 64 west.

I drove the eighteen hours with thoughts of how to tell them about Lamont, and the time evaporated like water beneath my tires on asphalt, and I was there, back in the streets of a city where sidewalks were smaller and cracked and the brick structures of row houses, alleys, and gangways slanted and tilted slightly above the fault line of time and depression.

AT THE CHURCH of my baptism, relatives walked inside in hats that made shadows of their faces. My car windows were just dusty enough to deny them an answer to the tilted-head question, *Who's in that car?*

Reverend Richards was the same, except now his hair was entirely grey. How was he still alive? Life and death made jokes and riddles in the lines of the faces all around me and Walton. They did not speak, but they greeted us with questioning faces that were parallel to the Mississippi faces in Granmama's church. I remembered how Ella Mae and I had held our heads up as we walked past our kin that morning, and I followed that cue.

I walked to the empty row behind the heads of siblings that were shaped the same, just all adult now; Mama slumped, now shorter in the pew in front of me, grinning and wiping tears, grinning and wiping tears, laughter in odd places, as if wires in her circuitry had gotten crossed; laughter at the impulse for pain or fear. My heart pounded with the reality that I was strangely still connected to this clan. Their mother's eventual tears brought sibling tears, the siblings tears brought mine, and Walton whimpered, not knowing what motivated him. All their heads strung together on a cord with their mother's. But I was Ella Mae's child, stern and silent.

Added to the row of heads were the heads of spouses, the heterosexual counterparts of my siblings, who blended well into the fabric. And there were the heads of three teenaged boys: Benson, Daryl, and Jessie. I wanted to catch their eye and have them see me, but each time one of them turned in profile to catch me in his peripheral vision, one or the other of them elbowed the curious one.

I thought about Lamont: unsought, uninvited, but wanting them the way Ella Mae wanted Grandeddy Bo with all of his faults, and me a fool for letting my thoughts trail along behind his in the fantasy of reconnecting with them. None of them even looked at me or my child, let alone inquired about Lamont's illness. It was as if he and I were dead.

Reverend Richards looked down on us from the pulpit. He counted heads and scanned, wondering about the faces he didn't know, confused about which ones didn't fit, before he began speaking. "Loni wouldn't have wanted all of this mourning. He was a happy man, and an alive man." I thought, *A dangerous man, a man who rarely set foot in this place.* Reverend Richards added, "A ladies' man," and the silence turned to a chuckle that included Mama. Reverend Richards looked down again at the faces he counted like fingers and toes and saw me, the unflinching one; the still look on my face, teeth gritted behind lips as I interpreted "ladies' man" and remembered Deddy's jokes about killing female deer. Reverend Richards's gaze was stuck on mine, having identified the face that had reportedly run away from home, had become part of myth; juvenile detention, drugs, child out of wedlock, and a list of other fabricated sins that made me as unapproachable as the son to whom Reverend Richard paid homage: "Sometimes there are mourners who are so sinful, they are not welcomed the long way home to grieve, but we bless them too in their sinful ways."

"Amen," the voices hummed like a hive of drones, and I imagined my arm extending like a giant axe, sweeping across the pews and executing them all.

They stood up to go view the body, and when the time came for my row to go, barely remembered cousins, now adult, stood; and I held on to my three-year-old child, moved the balls of my knees aside to let them by. On her way back around, Mama stared me down, her skin loose from her face, the gold tooth replaced by white when she parted her lips to say, "Give me that boy."

I held on to Walton and stood up. With the corpse at my back, I fixed my eyes on the crimson of the stained glass, apologized to Lamont, and ran to get Walton and me away from there. My breath panicked for air as I drove as far east in my white hatchback as possible before dusk.

THE LANDSCAPE CHANGED from flat repetition of oak tree, prairie grass, lonely fields of natural gas pumps, cackling starlings, to hills where trees stood up and endured the rise of the land. I breathed steady again. I felt safe again. I rolled down the windows and let the thundering wind take the caught breath. The unsafe feeling had been familiar for the first thirteen years of my life, and I didn't know how I had ever survived. The purple sunset over mountains turned to mountains with moonlight. The steady chug of the white Rabbit and the fleet of trucks that were forced to crawl steadily upward calmed me. We skirted the panoramic moonlit valley while gravity warned, *Don't look sideways.* Walton slept in a heap of warm little kid, his dreams encapsulated in puckered lips, the fluttering long lashes.

Don't look sideways, I heard inside my mind, and I steadied my gaze for the overnight ride, where I did battle with the confusion of emerging thoughts: the salty smell of Vienna sausages frying in a pan; smell of wet leather on hunting boots. Under the solace of moonlight, solid yellow line on black asphalt, I let myself cry with the surfacing of new memories, but felt comforted in my white car, over black highway and moonlight, all others sleeping except me and the truck drivers, all of us ghosts, down through where the landscape flattened again, over bridges, until dawn lifted and turned spirits to flesh, the sea salt air of the Atlantic Ocean, cleansing.

I TOLD LAMONT that I had tried, and he sank away for good after that day. Sometimes he called me to cuss me out about having stolen his candy money for the school fundraiser when he was in eighth grade, or to cuss me out for eating all of the chocolate out of his Halloween candy, and I listened while doing the dishes or running Walton's bath, or setting my books up in my office-fashioned-from-a-closet.

I need to live. I'm strong. This was the mantra that helped me ignore any onslaught of emotions. But when he called and told me to come to him as if I was his mother, I packed up my heart and put it in a little box high in my Portsmouth, Virginia, cupboard, got a sitter for Walton, and drove the eight hours without any weariness for the passing of time or millions of rotations of tires on asphalt. I went to him and stayed until he slept. It was my goal never to sleep in those hospital rooms under the insult of fluorescent lights and the constant hum and beep of death in the halls. I left my heart and my child safe in my apartment.

I waited until the pain was gone and Lamont slept, his eyelashes long and fluttering like Walton's, lips puckered in dream. Each time I took his hand in mine for just a second to feel the warmth there, then got in my car, still without the faultiness of emotion, and drove the dark overnight trip of turnpikes that took me home to the salt water of Virginia shores, to the saltwater sweat of my little boy-child who held the pattern of Lamont's DNA and held the code to my survival in his smile.

One morning Lamont called, and when I arrived, I parked my car behind his apartment. I breathed rain as I ran up Lenox Avenue to the hospital-like monolith that loomed in the distance, impossible to reach the corner of Lenox and 135th Street despite the pace that defied my heartbeat. "Come, Odessa," he had said on the phone, and this time the sound of the air between us signified that it was the last time. The rain sprayed on my face despite the light in the sky, the sun behind the hospital not yet set as the rain subsided. *Rainbow*, I thought, the way I had as a child when the combination of sun and rain presented itself over the city of St. Louis. But I wanted the sun to wait.

"Hey," Lamont said, with his light brown eyes certain on mine, and I did not yet know not to take for granted the soul's presence in the eyes.

"I want to see the sunrise in the morning . . . one more time." Another breath of oxygen; the removal of the mask. "I'm really hurting, but I want to go to sleep first, then I want to see the sun one more time." Another dose of pain medicine in the I.V.

That night, emotions entered through my accidental sleep and dreaming. I was a bird this time. The scene: Lamont and I were in Chinatown at a restaurant that opened to the street and I, the dream-bird, was flying shakily toward where he and I sat. I had never noticed the way we held our legs the same beneath a table: crossed uncomfortably at the ankle and tucked under the chair to stay out of the way of so many siblings' feet. Chinatown; I had surely ordered something with tofu and broccoli, and he had surely ordered something with pork. I could hear him breathe a steady, comforting stream in and out and I had never noticed how audible breath was.

There were crumbs on the damp cement floor that tempted me, so I swooped down to them. Above the ceiling of the table, there was laughter, and he told me how to sing: "Bring it up from the gut, open the passage straight to the solar plexus." But he did not know that I still had not cleared the airway from the regurgitated seeds on the day Jamella found the crumpled paper from the New York health department, the POSITIVE box checked next to HIV/AIDS. I had not found the way to breathe up the truth from inside my body and clear the way for song or words, for fear that my call would alert the death-call of so many other birds. Even beneath a table, small and mited, with filthy feathers, he recognized me, and I flitted from beneath to see him, the sun rising over the building where he sat, and there was still the recognizable breathing, like the recognizable heartbeat or footfall of siblings, louder now, and he and I both flew from where we sat in the open warm broth-air of Chinatown.

I woke to the sound of only one stammered breath, my own, in the sticky plastic arm chair at Harlem Medical. The sunrise over the city whirred outside the hospital window, and I felt in it Lamont's spirit flying faster and farther, and I ran to the bed to hold him.

Chapter 20

L AMONT, the sun mocked me as I felt you fly so quickly away from where I stood alone, holding what was no longer your hand.

I left the hospital. Walked down the hill to your apartment. Only retained snapshots of packing your most precious things into boxes and loading them into my car. Numb, I drove my white hatchback through city streets, and there must have been stoplights but I don't remember any; glass-black asphalt the reflection of red and white and green lights, the pummel of rain on the roof of my car.

You wanted Mama, and I did not bring her to you. Images of coffins and cradles crossed before my eyes in the red tail-lights. You wanted Mama, and I crossed onto the iron and steel suspension of the George Washington Bridge. And grief like a demon ripped the roof off my skull, removing the barrier separating me from sky, wind, rain. The dirge came up from my soul in long sobs. I cried my first word, "Mama," and that cry meant the prayer, *Hold me, hold me. Close the space around my body and hold my spirit inside my skin.*

I could not attend your funeral in the St. Louis church of our childhood.

AT NIGHT MY DREAMS came to your grave and dug desperately because you were still breathing, and it was a mistake, and I was in time to save you, to hear and feel your breath on my neck where we hugged, exhausted and relieved. In my dreams, you sat somewhere on top of a hill and called me, and I tried to stay in the St. Louis living room with the other children, but

I could not resist your call, and I flew recklessly to the top of the hill. In my dreams I saved you or went with you; but then I awoke, shivering in the reality of your death. I tried to walk with Walton to the park, but the light burned my eyes. Grieving was slow, and you were everywhere, your light floating out and through the wall, and Ella Mae said you were living with me because you and I had unfinished business, but I thought you were afraid that I would not survive the solitude of your death.

One day I dropped Walton at school and did not tell anyone where I was going, but I drove from Virginia all the way to the North Carolina outer banks, and I stood there in the pool of the ocean's eye. I stood at the life-death line of the shore, and I felt you like the feeling of a missing limb moving without the flesh.

"I am afraid to be here half living, half ghost," I said into the salt breeze. "How will I raise my child?" You did not answer. I drove back in time to take Walton in my arms as the preschool teacher released him. I parented him like an artificial life form, waiting for color and emotion above the dark surface to return.

I built an altar one night, with seeds that I took from the vines behind your Harlem apartment, the green Coke bottle from our Thanksgivings. You were there with me where I burned the sage and asked you and grief to leave me, but when Walton woke me in the morning, and his smile was still the texture of lips and teeth without the automatic response of my returned smile, I knew; but I walked to the window, and there was sun, and green and flowers, but within me no response to that list of objects and colors, and it was affirmed that I was still half dead. At my back I felt you breathing.

That night I gave in, decided I would live with you. That I would not grieve but live with your ghost and with Walton inside the dark space of this inability to perceive color. I decided to surrender, to bring you with me, and I pulled the box of your things from under my desk. I inhaled the last scent of you in those boxes as I went through the papers that Ella Mae and I had given up on sorting. On one piece of paper was your writing: *My mouth is in his mouth, flesh of the rosy flesh of my heart. I feel the warmth in my dreams.*

I fingered another piece of note paper for the lines of ink that your living hand had made in your slanted, left-handed writing. The date was a month after Richard had left you. The note: *You said you loved me!* written over and over until there was no more paper. I smelled the paper and picked up the scent of rodents.

Focus, I heard you say, and I began to make discriminate piles of save/discard. I put all music books in a pile of discard, all photos in a pile of keep that I would someday view, but for now they were piled without laying my eyes on what dwelt within the plastic portfolios. Videocassettes, audio cassettes, your voice above my shuffling: *Save.*

Inside the box, the folded-edge photo of Mama and you and Towanda in the late 1950s. A dial phone on a decorative metal telephone table, Mama's hair in a twist, floral print dress tight with cleavage, newborn baby Towanda, and you in white suspenders, no shirt, but white socks and new white walking shoes.

I took the picture of you and Bernice and Towanda from the package and walked the apartment for a place to hang it; first the refrigerator, then I considered the dining room; then I heard you breathing in boredom, and I went back beneath the eaves, took a thumbtack, and pushed past the grit of plaster to stick the photo into the wall; but regardless of the pain in my thumb, the photo would not stay. I reached back into the box to open another envelope. It was a Xerox copy of a poem that ran right off the page, and I promised myself I would get to the library to find the rest:

When my brother fell
for Joseph Beam
by Essex Hemphill

When my brother fell
I picked up his weapons
And never once questioned
Whether I could carry
The weight and grief,
The responsibility
He shouldered.
I never questioned
Whether I could aim
Or be as precise as he.
I only knew he had fallen
And the passing ceremonies
Marking his death
Did not stop the war.

I groped inside the bottom of the box for something that felt flat and was difficult to lift, a card, and I opened it to find, in your writing:

Happy Twenty-third Birthday Odessa!
Love, Lamont
P.S. Don't wait to do the stuff you want to do.

Inside the card were two purple tickets to something called a "Women's Wilderness Retreat."

And I was a little girl again, your hand in mine when the other siblings made fun of me for crying too much. I saw your fierce eyes on Deddy when he came for me, and you were there to divert his attention, the paper airplane maker, the feel of your knees on my shoulders where you held me in place to press my hair. And there was no amount of water, no number of tears that could wash away my wanting you with me.

Your spirit was silent in the room while I cried for a chance to turn back time.

Chapter 21

YOUR SPIRIT WAS SILENT as I traveled under the gaze of the Virginia sun to the retreat; Walton in the back seat, happy, but wondering if his mother is feeling at all. He smiled and sang to the radio to draw me out.

The Women's Retreat was on fifty acres where I was either in my little pup tent writing or walking the wooded paths with Walton, who always preferred to be at the child circle playing.

The sun was hot, and like the other women, I stripped off my t-shirt and wore overalls with nothing beneath, like the day when Ella Mae took me to the creek. There were birds high in the trees that made quiet shadows when they flew where I lay in the hammocks that littered the woods like human-made spider webs. The other women did not try to draw me out but left me in my silence, walking unconscious around fire circles and outdoor workshops in yurts. I sat by the creek, walked back to where Walton was playing, walked back to the creek. Exhausted from trying to feel, I lay in a hammock again beneath the light and shadow of leaves, between the children's circle and the main overhang.

Behind me music played under the overhang, where Persian blankets and the "no shoes allowed" sign created sanctuary. My mind replayed your story of the Oriental rug cleaned at the laundrymat: *Get it out, get it out!* I could almost hear your laughter.

Walton came up, hands and feet covered in mud, out of breath with play. He climbed into the hammock with me, and I did not care about the gray space between clean and dirty as long as he let me hold him in the woven cradle.

Evening fell as we swung in the hammock; stars replaced sun and trees and shadows. Polaris flitted on the end of the ladle of black paper pinholes. Behind us the overhang swelled with the sounds of guitar, violin, and spontaneous singing. There was a smell of hickory at the campfire; Walton's sweaty naps, sleep, hands and small feet, like when his hands and feet swam inside me. I inhaled, surrounded by the serenade of good memories of you; the little boy running through the Mississippi field, coaxing all of us to chase the bull who would soon turn on us; the little boy rolling his eyes and neck and telling Deddy if he wants to whup everything outside breathing, he'd have to whup the flies too. Colorful ribbons of DNA strands wrapped around you and me and Walton, and for the first time in months, I spotted color in darkness, the green fluorescent glow of a firefly, the orange and yellow sparks from the fire circle that traveled up until they were imperceptible against the stars, and I slept without dreaming.

The next morning I stood in the circle and held hands with Walton and someone I did not know. Then we all turned to the North, the South, the East, the West, and when we called out the names of ancestors, your voice in Walton's mouth:

"Lamont Blackburn."

Chapter 22

THERE WAS AN OPEN ROAD BEFORE ME, and I did not go east on 64 to head back to Virginia, but west for the interchange to go south toward my Mississippi home.

The floor of my stomach dropped to the sound of Tracy Chapman's low alto. The mountains of the Appalachian chain rose up on each side of me, green hands praying where my little white hatchback slipped through the middle on roads as dark as the stretch marks on my belly. Walton slept in the back seat, small sweaty face and stinky hands. I wanted to wake him and show him how the mist lifted like pink breath over the mountains, how the sunset kissed us in the car, but if I turned away from the road, we would end up taking a first and last flight.

Gravity took me and Walton and the white hatchback down, and it was quiet as the hills of Tennessee descended into Nashville, where there was no reverence for the beauty that loomed in the nappy green hills. Slowly down highway 51. I crawled, hot sun questioning my journey.

I pulled into a K-Mart parking lot, only the light post for shade, and fed Walton from the cooler, gave him the cool icy rag to wipe the sweat. I saw us there in the car that smelled like peanut butter sandwiches and dirty socks, Walton in the same red and blue striped t-shirt he had worn the day before, me in a t-shirt cut off at the sleeves for tank top, jeans cut off for shorts, and I felt embarrassed for a moment in the light of my spontaneous resolve, felt lost and refugeed until Walton giggled.

"What?" I asked him.

On the car radio the B-52s song "Love Shack" played quietly. He pointed at the speaker and said, "Love Shack," and cracked up again before he could finish the words, and then "Get it out! Get it out!" He yelled and I laughed until I cried at the joke that only made sense inside his mind.

Walton's little head rested back on the car seat, drunk with the simplicity of things, and we ate our sandwiches. *Walton trusts me*, I thought, and without first thinking, I put my whole hand around his bare, dangling foot and left my touch there, looked him in the eyes, and held the gaze, the impulse of touch tamed and gentle.

And with that touch, you were back, in the car with us, laughing, above the smell of old french fries and sandwiches. There was the faint smell of your cologne, and I inhaled and almost felt your breath on my ear, whispering, *Go home.*

WHEN WE CROSSED the Mississippi state line, I raced toward home, away from the temptation to steer off the mountain pass to join you, toward Ella Mae, who waited body and soul. I passed through the swamp land, smell of sulfur, home, Mississippi. My mind settled toward the reality without the troubled, grieving thoughts. Six white egrets caught my attention; the six siblings you asked me to fetch in hands that seemed too small. I turned back to the two-lane bridge and first refused to feel again your whisper, refused emotion the way the levy holds back the flood waters without regard for shifting tides. I was determined to go home, but on the radio, first the beautiful instrumental refrain so well-choreographed to the sway of swamp grass on hot air, and the sway of moss dripping gray from green Mississippi oaks, lemon-sweet smell of magnolia, and Jennifer Holliday's voice, *And I am telling you . . .*

The six white egrets took off over the marsh grass, and your voice: *Go home.*

ON THE STEPS, waiting for the evening to break into the slumbering promise of relief from heat, Ella Mae began the conversation the way she used to begin conversations long ago, and I followed the old refrains. "You cain't own a person or a thing in this world, so quit tryin."

"You own this house."

"Naw. Grandeddy Bo say he own this house, but even he don't own it."

"What! Who own it then?" I smiled playfully.

"It own itself, just like you own yoself, and I own myself, and that mimosa weed you put rocks around that decided to grow into the biggest tree in the yard own itself."

I had the same old comebacks to stomp her. "Who own the slaves and the Indians?"

"Same people who say they own that tree out there, and same people who hung somebody in it one time."

"I'm your daughter. Do you own me?"

She did not hesitate this time. "No I don't!" We laughed and looked at each other sideways. I leaned back into her. "You got me that time."

"Odessa, you ever heard anybody say you got to go backward before you can go forward?" She spoke in that way that a mother does when she dispels the pretending of child's play. I heard in her voice Lamont's voice. *Go home.*

I leaned into where she let me lean, my body as long as hers. Out in the yard, the robins hopped, stood vigil over the possibility of food, pulled up worms with precision.

"Now," Ella Mae said, "you gonna have to hurry up and go, so you can hurry up and come back." The warm drop of her frightened tear fell into my short afro.

I squeezed her hand, looking down past her lap at our feet. Me in leather sandals, her in leather sandals.

"Can you come with me?" My own quiet tears were flowing now.

"Odessa, not all my spirit is in my body anymore. It done spread itself out around here, and I cain't take half of me away and leave the other half here. When I die, all of me will collect itself from here." She put her hand on her chest. "And from here." She pointed the stick she was holding in her left hand over her shoulder and from left to right, missing me by less than an inch.

"If I could cart my body and the five acres Bo give me to St. Louis with you, I would." She laughed, and from inside the open screen door Ms. Olatunde's laugh came, like an echo of Ella Mae's. Ms. Olatunde came onto the porch. Her frame without any fat, tall and weather-worn but sturdy like the posts of the house Ella Mae built. She leaned there in the grey and brown trousers and tucked shirt, and then slid down next to where Ella Mae sat. They looked at each other, sunset orange and peach light holding gold skin and shiny cherry wood skin in time. They touched lips, and I looked away.

Was all of my spirit in my body, or in Starkville and its history, or back in St. Louis, where the souls of my siblings scurried? Maybe behind the bricks of the house on Kennedy Avenue, the house I could never imagine entering again for fear of flashbacks that I would never escape.

Ella Mae patted my back. "Roads don't get there by themselves; people who need to go someplace build them. Then when they get everything they need, and they get old, they don't need roads, 'cause they ain't going nowhere." They did the harmonic giggle again, and I giggled at them giggling.

"Listen to y'all," I said, and Walton giggled, not even looking at us where he drew the circles in the peach-dusk dirt in front of where Ella Mae and Ms. Olatunde and I sat. I had to leave and find for myself whatever it was Ella Mae said she had found for herself. *Got to own yoself, Odessa.*

THERE WERE SIX SIBLINGS who I did not believe liked me or wanted to see the likes of me. They were scattered across Midwest cities with knees that beneath a table were the same as mine. Holding myself still in that truth, I remembered for the first time a whole day of good memories: the time we found the hill at Creve Coeur Park; Mama and Deddy fishing, content that the offspring were off playing, but we had found the hill, me and my kin, ranked from you, big brother, as ringleader, to the innocent small ones dragged along unconsciously. I was still the fifth, the baby gal who cried like a goat half the time.

The hill was green grass, the most beautifully manufactured green, and at the bottom was a chain link fence that held garbage and falling bodies away from the highway below. You went first, Lamont, and like baby turtles pulled out by the tide we were tugged in the motion of your flight. We each dove, feet leaving the ground, our laughter raining around us, and death was not a thought above the texture of grass blades on skin and the crushed cut-grass odor of bleeding green beneath our bodies. We were suspended there beneath the sky and above the highway, just above the possibility of death, until we smashed into the fence: metal, bone, and pain bringing us home to the reality of a passel of rowdy siblings. I was still the fifth born of my father's children.

I ROLLED UP pairs of shorts and a skirt for me, stacked Walton's shorts and t-shirts, stuffed my socks and underwear in one pocket of the bag, his in the other, and set out with a map to make the pilgrimage that ended childhood summers, to make the pilgrimage to let them see me and decide if the myths of women like me and Ella Mae were true enough to keep them afraid or foolish enough to bring even one of them up to the surface for air.

Come what may, I left Mississippi for my own weightless tumble where gravity would carry me and Walton toward whatever barriers might stop or save us.

Chapter 23

TOWANDA INVITED ME and Walton to come with her and my nieces to church.

Three cousins were in their grown-up bodies, off-white robes with golden trim. They had shed something of the evil in their childhood smiles, and they stood like doves, swaying to the organ's music.

Our oldest cousin said it was a song you loved, "Change." They began the chorus, and their voices blended, weaving different notes into one DNA strand of kinship, one call through the bloodline, and my pores opened again; this time, the solar plexus and the underground river where the tears flowed without light for so long opened like geyser.

Their voices like yours, and mine, and those of the siblings whom we could not seem to hold in our grasp. You and I sat, body and spirit, the lost children listening like flightless small birds, and your soul whispered, *They are so beautiful. Their song so holy. Can you hear them?*

And you stepped to the edge of the pew, and I lost my place in the listening, in the internal singing, and you took flight without me, somewhere blended in that note high above me in the stained-glass sunlight above where I sat with coccyx on wood.

You sang solo, lead among the other voices, and I stood this time and opened my mouth to sing goodbye.

About The Author

ZELDA LOCKHART is author of the award-winning novel *Fifth Born*, which was a 2002 Barnes & Noble Discovery selection and won a finalist award for debut fiction from the Zora Neale Hurston/Richard Wright Legacy Foundation. She holds a Bachelor's Degree from Norfolk State University, a Master's in English from Old Dominion University, and a certificate in writing, directing, and editing film from the New York Film Academy. Her second novel, *Cold Running Creek*, won a 2008 Honor Fiction Award from the Black Caucus of the American Library Association. Ms. Lockhart holds the honor of the 2010 Piedmont Laureate for Literature in North Carolina. Her other works of fiction, poetry, and essays can be found in a variety of anthologies, journals, and magazines. Ms. Lockhart lives in North Carolina and continues to lecture and facilitate a variety of workshops that empower adults and children to self-define through writing. She is currently compiling an anthology of short stories from the lives of elders. She welcomes visits to her website: www.zeldalockhart.com.